THE DESOLATE REIGN

AMORY CANNON

The Desolate Reign
Copyright © 2017 by Amory Cannon

Cover design ©Jennifer Zemanek/Seedlings Design Studio 2017

Printed in the United States of America

Library of Congress Cataloging-in-Publication data
Cannon, Amory.
The desolate reign /Amory Cannon.
p. cm.

Summary:.

ISBN 978-0-9973903-1-5
1. Kings, queens, rulers, etc. —Fiction. 2. Christianity —Fiction. 3. Love —Fiction. 4. War —Fiction. I. Title.

First Edition, 2020

www.AmoryCannon.com

To Crystal, Amanda, and Haylee who reminded me real queens
adjust each other's crowns

Your country is desolate, your cities are burned with fire: your land, strangers devour it in your presence, and it is desolate, as overthrown by strangers.

From the lost Aletheia

1

We've been wandering in the mountains outside Aurora for almost a week when I first hear the voice.

Not so much a voice as a low hum and then a gentle whisper. It comes to me most in the twilight between waking and dreams, but the further we wind our way into the frost covered mountains, the louder the voice becomes.

It's not something I've shared with anyone. Not Hannah and especially not Felix. My two dearest friends and closest confidants they may be, but hearing voices might be enough to send them over the edge. Especially since I'm supposed to be leading this merry band of fugitives, and I clearly have no idea what I'm doing or where we're going. Felix, for his part, has covered for me with the band of soldiers that followed him—because they are definitely here for him and not me—out of Aurora where Emperor Cyrus had condemned me to death.

I wonder how many of them wish they had let me die rather than follow blindly a girl who has no idea what to do next. Just a silly princess who struggles to make decisions and has a soft spot for the empire's religious rebels—the Insurgos—but somehow managed to win the favor of the Commander of the Imperial Guard. Add to that hearing voices, and that pretty much sums up the insanity of my last few months.

Just as I have the past few mornings, I wake chasing the ghost of that whisper. All in all it's been a welcome distraction from everything else that's swirling around me, though I sense there's something important there I just can't grasp. At its strongest the voice is like a tug, pulling the deepest part of me toward something, but I don't know what.

Common sense says we should be heading northwest toward Borealis as it seems the only place we might have a chance to seek sanctuary, but the tug is driving me in another direction all together. Mostly I ignore it as we inch along an unplotted course, but this morning I can't get it out of my mind.

My stomach aches both with uneasiness and hunger as I dress in a simple dress Hannah had packed for herself. She and Cecily aren't present to insist I dress in one of the nicer dresses they brought for me. I'd wear pants if I could find any to fit me, but both of my ladies would be scandalized at the thought. If either of them could have seen me before Felix found me, scrounging around military camps and living as a common soldier, they would have been appalled.

The quality of light through the gaps in my tent flaps tells me it's still early morning. Perhaps Hannah and Cecily expected me to still be asleep and that's why they're not here to attend me. More likely, they know I can fend for myself and are out there scrounging together what food we have to make breakfast for nearly fifty people.

If I had been more decisive, more sure of myself, we would be in Borealis by now. That might have meant a prison cell—because I'm completely unsure of what we'll find there—but it would have at least meant meals for all of my guard. When Felix planned my dramatic escape from Aurora he packed as much food as possible, but I know he didn't count on me leading our party in circles, wasting precious days of rations while I try to decide if returning to my home country is the best course of action.

As if I really have a choice.

"Good morning, Highness." Antony, Felix's second in command, greets me as soon as I exit my tent into the cool morning air. It's been this way since the day after we left Aurora, but even now I realize I still hold out hope it will be the Commander who waits to give me a morning report rather than the young man who has been just as loyal to me as Felix himself.

"Good morning," I reply as I straighten my plain dress and let my eyes survey the bustle of our camp. "Anything new to report?"

Antony walks beside me as we stroll through the maze of tents towards the trees where the horses are tied. It's become our morning routine.

"The scouts found no trace of the Emperor's men within five miles of here. No signs that they've gone ahead of us or are lagging behind." There's a bit of wariness in his voice, and I know he's just as confused by the lack of pursuit as I am.

The whole point in taking a circuitous route around the mountains was to give us time to ascertain what Emperor Cyrus's plan was. It seems we're no closer to knowing it now than we were a week ago. I expected a pursuit. That's generally the consequence when you're sentenced to death but somehow make a daring escape. The lack of it makes me more nervous. Why isn't he coming after me?

We've reached the horses now, and I find my mount immediately. The black filly was untamed and wild when I first met her in Aurora. Even now she only lets a few people near her and only Felix, Antony, or I can saddle her. Athena sees me and lets out a soft nicker. I hold out my hand, and she trots over and nudges me with her velvety nose.

"How is our food situation?" I don't look at Antony as I stroke Athena's black coat, now shiny since I've taken so much care with it. I'd much rather focus on that than the answer to my question.

He hesitates. "It's manageable," he finally says. "The scouting party brought down a large stag this morning and several rabbits. I believe Hannah was going to gather some berries and mushrooms as well."

My head whips toward him. "Why aren't you with her? She can't go out alone. I've told her."

"Commander Fidelis is with her," Antony assures me.

And while that should make me feel better that Hannah is in the best hands, it only makes the weight on my chest feel heavier. Not because I think there's anything more than an innocent friendship between her and Felix, but because I've barely seen him since that night we left Aurora. Since that night he kissed me as we fled and then again in a feverish haze, and everything changed. Of course, Antony wouldn't know that.

"And how is the Commander? Is his injury healing well?" My attempt at nonchalance falls flat, and Antony's keen eyes search my face. To his credit, he lets the questions I see forming in his mind go unasked.

"He's doing well. Some pain, I think, but of course he won't admit to that."

"Of course not," I say absently. Felix took a blade in his side in the melee that followed my escape, and though the healer that accompanies us said it was a shallow wound and should heal with time and rest, I still worry about him. He will give himself neither time or rest, and though he is the strongest man I know, it's not hard to imagine this will catch up to him one day.

After a moment's silence, Antony speaks up with hesitation in his voice. "Highness, if I could speak freely…"

"Of course you may, and I've told you that you can call me Emilia. There's no need for such formality here." I've been very selective with whom I've allowed this concession, but next to Felix, Antony is my most trusted soldier.

"Yes…Emilia." He tries it out as if it feels strange on his tongue. Then he shakes his head and continues. "I'm worried about him."

I don't need to clarify the "him", and I hope I manage to keep my face neutral when I respond. "And why is that? His injury?"

"No. He just seems…lost. I'm not even sure if that's the right word, but he's different now."

I must choose my next words very carefully. "I imagine it must be an adjustment for him—for everyone really—to go from the palace to the wilderness. For the Commander specifically, he is now an enemy of the man he swore to protect. He must have had great favor with the Emperor at some point to be promoted to his position at such a young age. Desertion is not in Felix's nature." But he did it for me. I wonder how much he regrets it.

Antony shifts his weight between his feet and studies the ground for a moment before he looks up at me again. "I don't think it's the Emperor that has disturbed him. I think it's the Prince."

The word hangs in the air as I do my best to subdue the visceral reaction I have to any mention of Prince Ronan—my would-be betrothed who sat silently upon his throne as his father sentenced me to die. The same man who had the nerve to write me a letter and send it by way of Felix when he wouldn't come after me himself. This is the price of royalty. One I know all too well even if I've spent little time in a palace since I was a small child.

"I imagine Felix lost much in this fiasco as did all of you who chose to follow. I won't forget that. You will be rewarded for your loyalty."

"Serving you is reward enough." Antony inclines his head in a semblance of a bow. I'm relieved he has acquiesced to my change of subject. "You are truly a queen worth serving."

"Not a queen yet," I remind him.

"You are in all the ways that matter."

It sounds like something Felix would say to me, and I wouldn't be at all surprised to learn that Antony is simply repeating his commander's words.

Our conversation is interrupted as Cecily begins banging on a metal pot, signaling mealtime. Soldiers who will be taking over the morning watch gather at the front of the line to collect their rations before they go on duty.

I wait until all the soldiers have received a meal before I approach Cecily for my own portion. To her credit, she has adapted well to our wilderness lifestyle. Her talent for cooking has been beyond valuable as our prepared rations ran out. And she's managed to keep a smile on her face despite being pulled from a life of comfort in the palace to this.

"Make sure you eat well," I instruct her as she hands me a piece of roasted meat and a handful of berries.

"Yes, ma'am." She curtsies and I smile. It's taken much to convince her she doesn't need to call me Highness, but I'm not sure the curtsying is a habit I'll be able to break her from.

Because of the lack of evidence we're being followed, we've allowed ourselves a campfire most nights. I was hesitant to agree at first, thinking the smoke might give away our position, but as Antony pointed out, we are hardly an inconspicuous group. With nearly fifty men and all the accompanying gear and horses, stealth is not our strong suit. So we've built a fire for everyone to warm themselves. Most mornings it's where we all gather to eat. Today is no different.

Felix and I steal glances at each other across the campfire. Every time I chance a look in his direction I can tell he's just looked away from me. Some part of me knows we're acting like ridiculous children, but the stakes are so much higher. Even if there was opportunity for the sort of conversation we need to have, I'm not sure what I would say. That he should forget about any loyalty he feels to Ronan? That I could give up my throne for him? Neither of those options appeal to me, and I know they wouldn't be palatable to him.

But we can't go on pretending to ignore each other and communicating through Antony and Hannah. So with a confidence I don't feel I stand and make my way around the campfire to the empty patch of dirt beside him.

"May I join you?"

My words startle him, and he nearly chokes on the bite he just took as he does a double take up at me. Given that I've spent the time since we left Aurora trying not to look at him, I'm surprised to see he's grown his full beard back and looks much as he did the first time I saw him. Even the tenderness in his eyes has diminished.

Still coughing, he jumps to his feet with a little less agility than I've seen from him in the past. I wonder how much he's still suffering from his side wound.

"Em—Highness." He corrects himself as he dusts himself off and inclines his head.

I sigh. So we're back to this. Like Cecily, it took a while to break down the barriers of royal protocol with him. Now it seems he's struggling to rebuild them as if they confer some sort of protection. "I don't want to do this anymore."

His dark brows lift, then he glances back over his shoulder to the crowded camp. "Perhaps we should walk?"

Stepping aside I allow him to lead the way, noting that he doesn't offer his arm but remains a respectful distance from me.

There's a stiffness in his posture and mannerisms that tells me he's working hard to present an entirely professional aura. Strangely, his struggle to do so is what gives me hope.

Once we're outside of earshot of the camp, just inside a copse of evergreen trees, I take a deep breath and reach for his arm to slow his forward motion. His reaction is immediate, the muscles of his forearm tensing under my fingers. Still I maintain the contact until he looks at me.

Felix's face so rarely displays his emotions, but I can see them now, leaking out behind the cracks of the façade he's trying to present. Such pain and such heartache that I've only begun to plumb the depths of.

"Felix, I need your counsel." It seems the safest thing to ask of him. After speaking with Antony this morning and with my own paranoia incessantly whispering in my ear, I know it's time I took charge. And if anyone can help me do that it's Felix. No matter what's between us or not, I need his support and guidance. He believed in me when no one else did.

"You have it always." His words seem chosen carefully, but there's a bit more openness in his face now. Certainly he expected me to bring up the Incident. And I still might, but we have more pressing issues. As the former Commander of Cyrus's Imperial guard, Felix may have more idea what the Emperor's plan is than anyone else here.

"It's been a week now, and we haven't seen the first sign of Cyrus's men. We're hardly difficult to track with the number of our party and the amount of horses, but there's no indication that they're following us. Why is that?"

He inclines his head slightly and purses his lips in thought. "I can't say for certain. It would be the obvious choice to follow us and drag us back, but the Emperor is rarely inclined to obvious choices."

"Perhaps he's afraid of you," I offer. I've considered it many times over the last few days. Felix's defection—along with the soldiers who followed him—would be a harsh blow against Cyrus. Even the Emperor can't underestimate Felix's skill and the loyalty he commands.

He responds with a throaty chuckle that warms me despite the mountain chill. How I've missed that sound.

"He's not afraid of me. He's afraid of you."

I let the words hang there in the silence for a moment because I'm not sure what to do with them. They sound preposterous, but something in me won't let me discount them. "Who exactly does he think I am?"

Felix tilts his head at this question and motions for me to walk a little deeper with him into the trees. I follow until the foliage is so thick around us that the morning sun barely peaks through. The sounds of the camp have given way to the occasional bird song and not much else.

"There are so many rumors surrounding the Gate of Life." Even in our solitude his voice is hushed. Whether out of caution or reverence I can't tell.

The Gate of Life. The Narrow Gate. A place of power that offers immortality if Insurgo legends are to be believed. Purely metaphorical based on the little information I have. So I'm not sure what any of it has to do with Cyrus being afraid of me.

"You said it wasn't real." My tone is more accusatory than I meant for it to be, but I can still remember the conversation we had about the Aletheia and the Gate when Felix explained to me all he knew about them. Or at least I thought he did. For not the first time, I think the Commander may be hiding something very important from me.

"Well of course it isn't real, but you and I both know Cyrus can never be convinced of that. At the very least he's concerned about this potential secret gathering of Insurgos, and he's determined to find them and cancel out that threat to his throne."

"That still doesn't explain why you think he's afraid of me."

"There are rumors," he says again, "that are believed in certain groups of Insurgos. Rumors of a leader who will receive power from the Ancient One who guards the Gate and be able to reunite them all and reinstate them to their place in society and end the persecution."

Felix pauses and even in the dim light I can tell he's looking at me meaningfully.

"And you think that's me?" I laugh because the idea is laughable…isn't it? Felix says nothing and I can feel the blood drain from my face. "You think it's me."

It's what he's been trying to tell me all along but I never heard it or understood it like this. The weight I suddenly feel makes my knees buckle, and I grab the nearest tree to steady me. Felix reaches out, but I push his hand away. After a moment I stand and look him in the eyes. "You think it's me."

"It doesn't matter what I think."

"It matters to me."

"You are many things, Emilia. So many...I don't know if I believe those rumors. There's nothing... Look, without the complete Aletheia we may never know what's written in the scriptures and what is purely conjecture or wishful thinking. But," he pauses to rake a hand through his hair and then straightens, "if there is a ruler that was promised, I believe it could be you."

It's what my old mentor Levi said to me, isn't it? The message he gave his life to bring me? But it seemed different somehow when it was just his belief—even if it was true—and not the beliefs of an entire group of people who have pinned their hopes on a girl they've never seen.

"I feel like I need to know more. I don't like acting from a position of ignorance. We need to know at least as much as Cyrus about this Gate. Whether it's real or not, he's convinced it is. But he's wiped out the Insurgo settlements in Aurora and taken all their information. Where would we even start?"

Felix opens his mouth, hesitates, then speaks. "He hasn't wiped out *every* settlement. There's one I know of, one we just recently learned of and he hasn't had time to raid yet. It's north, just on the border of Borealis and Aurora."

My mouth gapes open at the possibilities. Could they have a copy of the Aletheia? Perhaps they could tell me what they know of the Gate of Life and the Ancient. I need something to go in my favor. And the voice I've been hearing for the last week has been more insistently whispering "north". I just didn't realize why until now.

But am I honestly going to do this? Lead a contingent of nearly fifty soldiers into an Insurgo village and then expect them to welcome us warmly. And what if they know nothing? Worse, what if they look at me the way Felix is looking at me—like I'm this promised queen that is going to fix everything. I don't think I can take the weight of more expectations.

"So what does this mean for our next direction?" It's one of the more pressing questions I wanted to ask him. "We're low on food, everyone is restless, and it doesn't appear that Cyrus is pursuing us—for whatever his reasons may be. We can't just keep wandering around, but where should we go?"

"Only you can answer that."

"I'm not omniscient," I snap, harsher than I meant to. "I asked for your counsel for a reason."

Ironically my brusque-ness seems to have jarred him from his submissive stupor. He stands a little straighter and looks directly at me as if there had been nothing more between us than a general and a soldier discussing battle strategy. "Borealis is the obvious choice. The country is mourning the loss of their king, you stand to inherit the throne, and you are likely to find at least some who are loyal to you. It would give you a position of power from which to act. However, the fact that you're asking my opinion at all means you are hesitant to make the obvious choice. So you need to ask yourself if your hesitation is due to your personal reluctance or something else."

"I just...I feel this pull away from the city. I can't explain it exactly. It's bothered me for a few days, and I know it makes no sense..."

"Have you prayed about it?"

Such a simple question. I wish it had a simple answer.

"Sometimes I feel like it's still not safe to be so open…about prayer, I mean."

"You're safe with me."

"I know you. And I know Hannah. But Cecily is always in and out of my tent to attend to me, and I can't go anywhere without one of your men following me—"

"For your protection," he interrupts.

"All the same, I can't get a moment of privacy."

"Then take a moment now. I'll stand watch while you pray."

I want to ask him to pray with me like he did the morning after we left Aurora. The warmth I felt then, the certainty, has been elusive ever since. And of course I equate that warmth and certainty with him, but maybe I shouldn't.

"Thank you," I say. It makes much more sense for him to stand watch and keep others away from me rather than hold my hand while I speak silently to a God I hope listens. Practical. I have to be practical. This is not about what I want anymore.

Maybe it never has been at all.

I'm not sure if it's minutes or hours later when I push through the tree branches and nearly collide with Felix's back. He spins to face me with questions in his eyes. I nod once and feel the understanding pass between us.

"Where to, Highness?"

"Due north," I say, though we both know this road will not lead us to Borealis. I'm not sure what I hope to find there, only that I must go. I've made my decision though it took me longer than it should have. The Gate over the Crown. "Further up and further in."

2

At the first sign of smoke, my gut tells me there are no survivors. The emptiness that has been slowly expanding in my soul for the last few days opens into a cavernous hole.

Two weeks but not nearly enough distance from Aurora, and destruction has followed me. No, preceded me like a ghastly herald. Maybe I should have anticipated it, but days of uneventful, albeit slow, travel have given me a false sense of security. As if Cyrus will not care that I have made a daring escape with the commander of his guards despite the death sentence he handed me. As if the Emperor himself will not worry about a rogue queen when he has just ordered the execution of all of the subservient kings of Aurora's daughter countries.

I am the fool.

The tendrils of smoke dissipating into the clear blue sky remind me I was foolish to ever dream that was true. My horse Athena prances nervously beneath me. Her wildness feeds off my apprehension. Enough that I remember until a few weeks ago she was a wild beast herself, and my taming of her is not really that at all. I am at her mercy just as I am at the mercy of so many others. A queen with nothing to command.

"Emilia? What's wrong?"

Constant as ever, Felix appears at my side. I don't look at him. My eyes remain fixed at the tendril of smoke behind the treetops in the valley below us.

"Smoke," I say, my voice thick. "They got here before we did."

I can feel the heat of his stare. "You don't know that."

But I do.

I know it as sure as I've known anything in my seventeen years. The Insurgo camp, the only one we knew of, is gone and along with it my hope of learning more about the Gate Cyrus is so desperate to find. Days of cautiously winding our way from the mountains near Aurora to this settlement have cost us the lives of those Insurgos in the camp. I don't need to see it to feel the truth of it in my heart. This is the first part of Emperor Cyrus's intended punishment for me.

"What do you want to do?" Felix nudges his horse slightly in front of mine, and I'm forced to look at him.

"I want see it." I *need* to. "There may be survivors, and we owe it to them to do what we can."

"I'll round up a search party." He cinches the reigns of his horse tighter in his fist. "I don't suppose you'd consider staying here."

"Not a chance."

My heart warms at the twitch of his lips. It's as close to our old banter as we've had in too long.

"Didn't think so."

I remain at my vigilant post as he rides off, hoping for signs of life in the valley below. A prayer rises in my heart, but even here in the freedom of the wilderness I don't let it pass my lips. God knows my heart, but I'm afraid it's too late. I should have been more decisive, less fearful. Instead of leading my caravan through the mountains as I tried to decide what direction would cause me the least trouble, I should have listened to the voice—God's voice?—telling me to go north. Once again, my fear has cost innocent lives. Just like with Davina...and my father.

"Princess?"

Felix calls me, and I nudge Athena back toward camp with my knees and a tug on the reigns. Her transformation at least has been nothing short of miraculous. It should have taken weeks to train her under controlled circumstances, but instead she has allowed herself to be ridden through these snowy mountains with barely a protest. There is something unusual in the way she senses my moods and what I need from her. We understand each other. And since there is precious little I understand right now. I cling to my horse.

Our camp is a flutter of the usual activity. Men erect tents, corral horses, and gather into hunting parties. I'd given the order to set up camp here for the night before I saw the smoke in the valley, and I now regret it. From the tension that knots the back of Felix's shoulders atop his horse, I guess he does, too. Maybe there's still danger down there, and he senses it, but that's not why I don't want to stay here. There is sorrow, heartache, and tragedy below us, and the scent stings my nostrils. I'm not sure I'll ever be able to put enough distance between myself and all the death I'm responsible for.

"It's not too late to change your mind," Felix mutters as I bring Athena alongside his horse Ares. The two animals nip affectionately at each other.

"About what?" Because there are so many things I wish I could change, but he is wrong. It's much too late for all of them.

"Camping here tonight. We could keep going. There are a few hours of daylight left, and it would it put us that much closer to Borealis proper."

As if that's an enticing thought for me. But the longer we've spent in these mountains the more antsy Felix has become. He's clearly eager to cross the boundary into Borealis as if that will offer me some sort of protection. As if it isn't the very place where my mother was executed for believing in our God and I was exiled for fear I would grow up to be exactly who I am now.

"We're staying here tonight. Everyone's tired and camp is more than half set up now. I'm not telling them to take it all down just because I have a bad feeling."

"It's more than a bad feeling. And it's justified. These men will follow you anywhere no matter how tired they are. Just say the word."

"No, they would follow *you* anywhere." I don't mean for my tone to be so harsh, but that bitter truth has been roiling inside me since we left Aurora.

Felix opens his mouth as if to argue with me, pauses, then closes it again. This irks me more than being right about the situation. He's been so very cautious with me since the incident just outside Aurora.

The Incident.

That's what I've taken to calling it in my head. Because it doesn't feel as much like rejection when I think of it that way. I don't allow myself to break it down into its pieces—the kisses, the refusal, and the letter. Ronan's letter. Except now that I'm thinking about it, it stings all over again, and despite the cold wind, heat rises to my face from embarrassment and anger.

"Just gather your search party and meet me at my tent," I snap as I dismount my horse. "And don't even think about sneaking off without me."

He wouldn't. It's something I would do, but Felix has more honor than I do. Protecting me has always been a high priority for him but not at the expense of losing my trust.

I'm only a few paces away from Felix when Hannah is at my side, taking Athena's reins from me with a gentle hand. Only a nod passes between us, and I'm grateful for the lack of words. Hannah is such a gentle girl despite the horrors of her past, and she seems to know what I need even before I do. And right now what I need is a moment alone.

While she sees to feeding and brushing Athena, I retreat to my recently erected tent. Thankfully Cecily is nowhere inside. With a deep inhale, I catch the faint scent of the sweet oils Hannah and Cecily use to try and make this place smell less like the musty tent it is. It brings half a smile to my lips. They try so hard, and they at least, do it for me and not Felix.

It's difficult to believe that a few short weeks ago I didn't know them. My life was so much simpler then even if it wasn't as full. As much as I cherish the friendships my time in Aurora gave me, my heart aches for the simplicity of my exile. When I could live out my days in anonymity as Nox the soldier rather than Princess Emilia Aurelius, daughter of a traitorous queen and a puppet king. When I could secretly meet with Levi, my Insurgo mentor, before I was forced to slit his throat.

"Princess?"

It's Antony and not Felix who calls from outside my tent. Perhaps I should read something into it that Felix sent his second in command to fetch me rather than come himself, but I'm too emotionally exhausted to give it much thought. Given the gravity of the duty he's summoning me for, most everything else seems pettily small by comparison.

With a steadying breath, I throw my shoulders back and exit the tent. "Are we ready?"

"Yes, Highness." Antony gives me an exaggerated nod that's somewhere between a bow and a simple shake of affirmation. It's been difficult to break him of the habit of bowing to me even all these miles away from the palace, so I don't laugh at this attempt even though it's quite comical.

Antony leads me through the bustle of camp to a clearing where Felix and two other soldiers, Marco and Hugo I believe their names are, wait with horses saddled and ready to go. Since Hannah has taken Athena to groom and feed, another horse has been chosen for me, and I mount the animal with a nod toward my companions.

Five of us make the precarious trip down the mountain into the valley. Though we've left the bulk of the snow and cold weather behind us, traces of spring are still mostly buried under icy crystals that hang from branches and line our winding pathway.

After several slips and slides and near collapses, we all dismount and leave the horses with two men. Felix, Antony, and I continue ahead. This time Felix doesn't bother asking me to remain behind.

As we descend the mountain, a hush falls over the forest. I don't even notice until the exposed skin of my neck and face prickle with the silence. I look up and realize there are no birds in the treetops, and the sky which was so brilliant blue from my perch on the ridge is nearly obscured with a heavy cloud of smoke.

"I hate saying you were right, but this isn't good." Felix's words in my ear are a roar against the silence of our surroundings. But I know what he means. Part of me hoped to be proven wrong.

"Do you smell that?" Antony tips his chin up and inhales deeply.

Felix and I exchange looks and follow suit.

It's faint, barely noticeable under the heavy muskiness of smoke and damp leaves, but it's there all the same.

Burning flesh.

Acrid bits of charcoal and coppery scents assault my nostrils, and I must swallow the bile and the memories that rise up in me.

When Felix's hand rests on my waist for support, I know he's recognized the smell as well.

"We're too late," Antony echoes my earlier thoughts with a bow of his head.

"No." Felix's fingers dig into my side before he pulls his hand away roughly and charges forward. "We didn't come this far to give up."

His sword whistles against the metal sheath as he draws it and begins cutting a path through the vegetation to expedite our journey to the village.

My body follows him instinctively. At this moment, I am not a princess but a soldier following my commanding officer. I feel Antony on my heels.

Leaves, thick and heavy with moisture, smack my face despite Felix's best efforts. The wetness the vegetation leaves behind masks the tears welling up in my eyes so I'm grateful for that much.

I know we're nearing the village when I lift my eyes from my path to notice the coat of gray ash clinging to Felix's damp skin. When beads of sweat or dew drip down his neck, they leave a clean trail against brown skin. It's such a mundane detail to notice in a moment like this, but it's the way my mind copes with tragedy now. And I simply cannot imagine the tragedy I'm about to witness.

As we approach, Felix slows his movements and finally comes to a complete stop behind a thin line of trees. My impatient heart pounds in my chest, but I know he's pausing to make sure we aren't walking into a trap. Ever my protector.

"It looks clear," Antony whispers after a few moments. I have to agree. The ash falls from the sky like snow on a serene landscape…if I can ignore the smoldering embers in the collapsed structures. In the distance, the glow of a fire seems muted against the cloud of ash.

"Stay close to me," Felix mutters as he lifts the brush with his forearm and steps into the clearing.

Those first few steps feel as heavy as any I've ever taken, and I've certainly had my share of tragedy. The closer I get to the first destroyed structures, the less aware I am of anything but the people who must have perished in them. Finally, I give up trying to keep my eye on the horizon for an attack. Felix will watch. This village, these people, deserve my full attention.

It's something worse than even my nightmares have conjured up. I've seen my mother executed, relived my father's death in my dreams, and seen my share of battles and war. I have never seen anything like this.

The remains are so blackened I can scarcely make out who or what they used to be. I don't want to look closely, but a hint of color in the black and gray catches my eye. A soft blue almost hidden beneath a pile of burned rags.

I approach cautiously, as if my heart knows what this is long before my mind can process it. Upon closer inspection, I can make out the shape of a woman, her long light hair darkened with soot. What I thought was a pile of rags is her charred body, wrapped tightly around something as if she were protecting it with her very life. I nudge the scrap of blue with my toe and pull it toward me. It's just a swatch of fabric really, but I finally put the pieces together.

My stomach lurches and I turn my head just in time to empty the contents of my meager breakfast onto the ground. I fall to the ground as I choke on tears and bile, and I clamp my eyes shut because I can't bear to look any more.

"Emilia? Are you all right?" Felix gives me ample space, but I'm aware, though I don't open my eyes, that he's joined me in the dirt.

"They were innocent." The woman, the baby she tried to shield with her own body. Even the worst crimes could not have made them deserving of this death. "It's my fault."

"It's not. You can't keep doing that."

I know what he means. But I must keep doing this. My crown, my decisions, my consequences.

"What are the chances this raid has nothing to do with us?" I ask coldly. "You did this sort of thing for the Emperor. Why would he wait until now to attack this village?"

Felix recoils as if I've somehow channeled the embers surrounding us directly at him. A deep pain darkens his eyes before all vulnerability disappears and he transforms back to the hardened soldier he's been since the night he told me we could not be together.

"I never did *this*." His words, low and quick, send a chill through me despite the residual heat from the fire.

"You told me you carried out raids…"

"What sort of monster do you take me for, Emilia?" He pushes himself to his feet with a disgusted shake of his head. Felix leaves me kneeling in the ashes without a second glance.

I'm not sure what hurts more. That I've insulted him or that I secretly hoped he hid the same dark shame I did. But of course Felix didn't kill innocent people. He probably did everything he could to avoid actual loss of life. But Levi's death still hangs over me. A man I actually killed with my own hands. Then there are the others who died because of me though I never dealt the death blow.

I don't move for some time. These people in this village also died because of me. Felix may have said Cyrus only learned the whereabouts of this village recently, but I know I was the impetus to act for him. They were deliberately targeted because Cyrus knew I'd be searching for any Insurgo camps I could find. And he knew, though the people likely knew little of the Narrow Gate, that decimating them would weaken me.

My thoughts are fractured as they have been since my frantic escape from the imperial palace. What am I even doing? I'm pulled in so many directions—desperate to know more of the Insurgos yet on an inevitable collision course with my father's crown. A father I haven't even had time to mourn…not that I'm really sure how.

At this moment, the only thing I know is to move forward. I trail my fingers through the ashes, scraping the remnant of fragile blue cloth into my palm. With shaking fingers, I fold it and slip it into my dress. Then I rise to my feet.

It should kill me. All of it. Watching my mother die, losing my father without any sort of reconciliation. Giving the first small piece of my heart to a prince who, whatever his plan, watched as his father sentenced me to death. Tasting the first sip of something that could be real only to find Felix is too loyal to love me. And now this.

It *should* kill me. I stand amidst these ashes in a ghostly impenetrable stillness. Lives ended because of me. Laughter and smiles and tender touches between lovers have ceased. There is nothing but death and embers now. And tears. I'm the one crying them. Pain mingles with the tears that fall as the old wounds in my soul I've tried so hard to bandage up break open. I don't even remember what it feels like to be whole.

I put a hand to my chest, hoping to ease the ache there and feel the light pulse of my heart under the layers of clothes.

It should kill me, but it doesn't.

I am wounded. Lost. Broken.

But I am alive. I have survived this long, and this will not change that. Loss, not only this one but all that I have known in my life, has not killed me. It has made me stronger. And this will be no exception.

I am alive. And more than that, so is my God. His presence thrums in my veins and is more real to me now than He has been before.

Cyrus does not know who he's dealing with. I will be the least of his worries.

3

Hannah meets me as we ride back into our small camp with hope shining as usual in her young face. The sight of it nearly doubles me over. After all the suffering she's known in her short life she still clings to the audacity of hope.

I keep my head up as I dismount my horse and thrust my reins toward Felix. He takes them without a word and leads her away where I know he'll work out his anger brushing her coat.

"Did you find anyone?" Hannah busies herself straightening my cloak as we walk toward the tents, and it's all I can do not to brush her away. I'm filthy—covered in ash and face streaked with tears, but she doesn't comment on that.

"No," I say with little emotion, though tears sting at the back of my eyes again as I think of the blue cloth tucked in my dress. "They were gone."

Let her infer what she will from that, because I hope my tone conveys how little I want to discuss it. In fact, all I want is to be alone. Except that all these people are here for me, waiting for me to decide what to do next. Sometimes I think it would have been better if I'd run away on my own instead of with a contingent of guards and servants Felix managed to gather for me.

I don't want to be in charge. I don't want to answer questions. And I most certainly do not want to be responsible for what happened in that valley.

"Then we keep moving forward." Hannah smiles as she takes my hand in one of hers and raises the flap of the tent we share with Cecily with the other. We both duck inside, and I'm grateful Cecily isn't there. "Perhaps to your home? To Borealis?"

If only it were that simple. "I don't know what state the city is in. I haven't been there since my mother…since I was a child."

Hannah doesn't need to ask me to finish my sentence. Everyone knows what happened to my mother. Her murder—or execution as Cyrus would call it—was publicized far and wide in the empire lest anyone forget how dangerous supporting the Insurgos was. Is still. I nearly died for the same sin. If it hadn't been for Felix…

And I feel bad all over again. Because I've just accused him of something beyond reprehensible in his eyes. He's a much better person than me, I think. Given the opportunity I will tell him so.

"If you don't wish to return to Borealis then will we continue on to look for other Insurgo camps?" Hannah gestures for me to sit down so she can braid my hair. I comply without a fuss.

"I don't know what I'm doing," I confess with tears pricking my eyes again. I don't do much to hold them back now. The questions come like a torrent. "It's just too much. My father, Cyrus, the Narrow Gate, and this Ancient One? What is my part in all of this?"

"Our God will show you." She smooths my hair, and I feel her press a kiss to the top of my head. Though she is younger than me, she has come to feel like the older sister I never had.

Waiting on God to show me anything seems tedious and even dangerous at this point. These soldiers who have followed me into these mountains may not believe such a god exists. Besides, did they follow me or Felix? I have no trouble believing their commander could inspire that kind of loyalty. Anyway, we can't sit still. We have to keep moving, and the direction is up to me.

The voice that was so insistent that we go in the direction of this Insurgo camp is now frustratingly silent.

Felix wants me to rejoin the Insurgos and lead them in some kind of glorious revolution. And if I refuse will he regret saving me? Not only saving me but committing treason against the empire. No, not treason exactly. He was acting on Ronan's orders if the prince's letter is to be believed.

The fact is I don't know who to believe or what I should do. I can't shake the thoughts of this Narrow Gate or the immortality it supposedly gives. Not because I'm interested in it for myself, but because if it is real, Cyrus is the last person who should find it. And he's already killed countless innocent people looking for information on the Gate and the Ancient One.

And none of this should even matter because I don't know where to begin looking for a gate or anything else, and what I do know is that I have a duty. To my kingdom, to my crown, and to my mother's memory.

I straighten my shoulders and take a deep, steadying breath. It's time for me to face this crown head on.

And so to Borealis we go.

No one complains when, as they pack up camp the next morning, I inform them we're heading west now. They don't need to ask what that means. They stand a little straighter and there's an urgency in their movements as they break camp and prepare for the three to four days travel that will lead us right to the heart of Borealis.

They have a destination, a purpose, again, and the striking difference in morale and demeanor makes me feel guilty all over again for leading them to wander aimlessly for so long.

Despite the size of our party travel is easier now. As we make the slow descent down the mountains the ground thaws, and there's a hint of spring in the air. We are able to travel longer and camp less as we make the push toward the capital city.

Even without a map, I know the moment we cross the border from Aurora into Borealis. The voice that's been silent since I prayed in that copse of trees while Felix stood guard returns with a low insistent hum. I can feel it in my bones.

Instead of warming or comforting me it sets me on edge. Though it feels like a sort of power coursing through me, it leaves me weak, and more than once I have to be helped down before I can fall off my horse. It's as if I am a conduit for something formidable, and as I weaken it grows stronger.

We are just a little more than a day from the city according to Felix's best estimate when I call a halt to our travel for the day. Felix frowns but says nothing, though the others look a little grateful for the chance at some extra rest.

They set about gathering firewood and setting up a perimeter guard while I slide wearily down from Athena and pat the horse's hind quarters. Hannah and Cecily are by my side almost immediately, each taking an arm while we distance ourselves from the din.

"You need rest, Highness," Cecily insists, a frown marring her pretty features. "You can't enter Borealis like this."

She's right about that. The only thing more dangerous than showing up as an exiled queen would be arriving as a weak, exiled queen. There's so much strategy that needs to be decided before we ride into the city, but I don't have the energy or the focus to dwell on that now.

"I'll have Antony pitch your tent," Hannah adds. "And I'll gather some plants to make a tonic to help you rest."

Protests die on my lips as Hannah leaves me with Cecily to find Antony in the mix of soldiers. As my eyes follow her, I catch Felix looking me over critically. His dark brows are knit together and a frown tugs his mouth down. We lock eyes for a moment, and he takes a step toward me before he's cut off by a soldier looking for his next set of orders.

The moment passes, and I direct Cecily to join me in reclining on a small grassy clearing out of the way of most of the men. There's so much I should be doing, not the least of which is deciding when and how I want to enter the city. I haven't let myself think too much about what we might find there because there are just too many unknowns.

"How do you feel, Highness?" Cecily asks as she busies herself undoing my braid and fingercombing my long tresses.

My eyes close with the gentle tugging on my scalp, and the humming in my bones eases as I slip into a relaxed warmth.

"Some better," I concede. "I just need to rest."

"Perhaps you've taken ill. I could ask the healer to see you when camp is settled."

"I think rest will be sufficient." The last thing I want is someone to examine me and say all my symptoms are in my head. Because I'm convinced there is nothing physically wrong with me.

God, what is happening? What are you trying to tell me?

But my prayer only makes the hum of power surge through me without answer. It's the last thing I recall before sleep overtakes me.

Darkness surrounds me, a heavy weight that has more to do with a feeling than sight. I don't know where I've been or how I got here, but I'm beginning to see fuzzy edges of things on my right and left as my surroundings come into focus. It's slow at first, but then I'm suddenly standing on a precipice, pungent wind whipping my loose hair all around me.

The moon hangs full and low at what feels like nearly eye level, and stars dot the velvet darkness around me. If I didn't feel the ground beneath my feet I would swear I was floating, flying even.

I look down at where the rocky terrain ends abruptly just a few feet in front of me. And then I look beyond. Stretched out below me is a beach of white sand gleaming in the moonlight and a violent sea crashing against it. At least I think it is. I've never seen the ocean except in paintings, and none of those have done justice to the terrible beauty before me. So raw, so powerful.

In the time it takes me to blink the beach is no longer empty, and the crash of waves is nearly drowned out by shouts and the clash of swords. Two armies are in the throes of a great battle that seems to have risen out of the sea itself.

"No." It's barely a whisper when the word leaves my mouth. I don't know why this is happening, but it's wrong. I can feel it in my bones. And somehow I know I can stop it.

I turn, desperate to find a way down to the beach, to stop the death and destruction that plays out before me. But when I spin around, I find I am not alone on this rocky cliff. Felix stands before me, a sword dangling in his right hand and his left pressed to a dark patch on his tunic. His brown eyes are wide and seem to blaze gold in the pale moonlight, and he stares at me without sound.

And I think I know what the dark stain on his tunic is. It's spreading rapidly, and his face is pale. But those eyes flickering like bronze flames fix me with an understanding gaze. I reach out a hand, and as if on cue Felix shuffles forward...and falls in a heap at my feet.

"No!" This time the word is ripped from me and swirls on the icy wind as I drop to my knees to cradle his head. But there is nothing but cold under my fingers.

"Emilia! Emilia! Wake up, my lady, please."

It's Hannah's terrified voice that greets me when my eyes fly open. The sea is gone as is the velvet dark sky, replaced with the dingy canvas walls of my tent. The armies are gone as well. So is Felix.

"Felix?" My own voice sounds strange to me. I try to sit up, but Hannah places gentle but firm pressure on the front of my shoulders to force me back to my mat. Someone, probably Cecily, presses a damp rag to my face. Only then do I realize I'm soaked through with sweat.

"Felix?" I ask again, my voice breaking. My throat feels like fire, and I wonder how long I have been screaming out.

"I will fetch him," Cecily says softly as she hands Hannah the rag and my ladies exchange worried looks.

I should say no, for her to leave him be, but confusion and terror still muddle my thoughts. What was that? Never has a dream been so vivid, so real to me. Not even the nightmares I've had recalling my mother's death or Levi's have left me with icy fear in my veins as this one has.

"W-what...?" It's all I can manage, but Hannah seems to understand.

"You were having a nightmare." She wipes the sweat off my face again and gently brushes aside the hair plastered to my forehead. "At first you were mumbling something, I couldn't hear what, but then you began to scream. It-it took some time to wake you."

Her fear is plain in the tremble of her voice, but I don't have it in me to reassure her. My mind is currently warring with itself to stay in the present or to revisit the terror of watching Felix die at my feet. I don't want to see it again, to even think about it, but I'm being pulled toward it just like the tides were pulled toward that shore.

I blink and there he is. Perhaps it was more than a blink, but time is a hazy concept right now. Still Felix kneels over me, dark smudges under his brown eyes accentuating his tiredness, but even that barely registers with me. Relief is accompanied with a heavy dose of exhaustion as I try to focus in on those eyes and remember how they look now rather than how they looked in my dream.

Felix looks over his shoulder and nods, and I'm only peripherally aware of Hannah and Cecily exiting the tent. It's the softening of his gaze more than anything though that lets me know we're alone. He raises a hand, crushes it into a fist, and then slowly releases his shaking fingers to touch my cheek.

Heat rushes through me, warming me despite the cool sweat dried to my skin. Just like on the cliff, he says nothing, only looks me over as if I'm a cool sip of water to a thirsty man. My eyes dart to his rumpled shirt, searching for any sign of a bloodstain as in my dream. Then, perhaps to reassure myself that *this* is real or perhaps because no boundaries exist in my vulnerable state, I reach out my hand until my fingertips brush his right side where his wound had been in my dream.

Muscles contract under my fingers, and I feel his sharp intake of breath as deeply as if he has pulled it from my own lungs. "Emilia."

But he doesn't sound angry. Just as his fiery eyes contrasted with his pale skin in my dream, so too does his relief contrast with a terrible sadness. I close my eyes for a long moment, wishing for…I'm not even sure what. And when I open them, he is gone.

It seems like hours before I'm able to drift off to sleep again. Though exhausted and fuzzy headed, I'm terrified I'll fall asleep just to find Felix's body lying at my feet. I'm not sure I can take that twice in one night. But finally the weight of drowsiness pulls my eyes shut, and I'm drifting back into another vivid dream.

This time I'm surrounded by lush green foliage. The air is thick with heat and humidity, and I can still smell a hint of briny air, which means the sea must be nearby. A quick look around confirms no one travels with me, but I don't feel alone. Quite the opposite actually. It's as if something other than me is living just under my skin with a pulse and longing all its own. And that thing, whatever it is, keeps tugging me forward.

At first it's a gentle nudge that makes me put one foot in front of the other and push my way through the jungle-like vegetation. Then, with each step, the pull becomes much stronger. Faster and faster I go, unsure of a destination, but knowing that I *must* get there or die trying. Something inside me pulls me forward as if I'm on a string. I couldn't resist even if I wanted to. And I don't want to.

And when I finally break through the clearing, I see the first glimpse of what I have been searching for and fall to my knees. A shimmering golden light illuminates a path into the mouth of a cave of some sort. Maybe cave isn't the right word. There is coastline below me in this valley, and the rock formation sits right on the water's edge. There are openings both on the sea side and the valley side as well as a large hole in the top from which the golden light seems to be emanating. Beyond that, the cave-like structure seems to disappear into the earth itself.

I have never seen anything so beautiful and dangerous, but I know I want to see more. I have to see more.

Soft streams of sunlight greet me as I wake before I can move any closer to the cave in my dream. Confusion hovers over me like a fog, and it takes several minutes before I can recall the details of last night.

What was that? Certainly I've had dreams—nightmares—before, but this is something new. I can't help but connect it to the tiny voice that's been urging me forward. After all this, am I supposed to believe that's God? If so, why would He send me such terrifying dreams?

I do what I can to avoid Felix's gaze as we break camp and prepare for our final day's journey to Borealis. Despite needing to say much to him—chiefly an apology for insinuating he was a murderer—I'm all out of words and platitudes. There's too much else to think about.

We make good time covering the remaining ground, and all too soon I'm standing at the top of a hillside overlooking a city I never thought to see again.

This must be home.

At least that's what the map and Felix tell me. I might be persuaded to doubt the outdated piece of paper, but I'll never doubt the Commander.

"How do you want to do this?" Felix joins me at the edge of the hillside looking over Borealis's capital city. We've wandered down the mountain, through the forests, close enough to the outlying settlements to replenish a few supplies but not close enough to alert anyone to our intended destination. All the while Felix and I have been doing a similar dance. Close enough to communicate when needed but never close enough to say what needs to be said.

"Any suggestions?" To be fair, I'm desperate enough to ask this of just about anyone, but I'm so grateful he's the one standing in front of me now.

"It would really help if we knew what the people of Borealis have been told. Emperor Cyrus is nothing if not strategic, and he controls the information. If news has reached your people that you were sentenced to death and escaped, we cannot enter the city."

Obviously. But there's little choice left to us. And despite it all, a tiny ember of hope still smolders inside me.

"I made him look weak. *We* made him look weak. Perhaps he'd rather let us live than show that weakness."

"Perhaps." Felix nods slightly. "Or there could be a show of strength waiting for us on the other side of that gate."

He's right, of course. Aside from Cyrus, there's also the problem of who currently occupies my father's throne. If they perceive me as a threat they are as likely to kill me as anyone else.

"We'll split up and go in small groups. Less noticeable than a small army of Imperial guards. Hannah and I can pass ourselves off as servant girls and—"

"Whoa, whoa. There's no need for you to go inside. I can take a small contingent of men and learn what we need to know."

Replying is unnecessary because he knows better than to think I'm staying behind. Or I assume he does. But another fight is not what I want right now so I let the silence rest between us, not exactly comfortable but certainly familiar.

"Does it look anything like you remember?" he asks after a moment, and I realize we've both been staring at the city below us.

"No," I say and then swallow down years of emotions. I haven't been this close to my home in ten years. From this vantage point, it's easy to see how the city has expanded, pushing against the large stone walls that offer it protection. Where I remember areas of green grass and tall trees near the edge of the walls, that space is now filled with several tiny houses stacked on top of each other. Whatever my father was doing for the economy seemed to be working.

"Do you miss them terribly?"

My face must have betrayed my thoughts of my father and, as always, Felix picks up on it. He means my parents of course. I'm still surprised he asked given the state of things between us.

"No one ever plans to be an orphan." I force myself to look away from the city and find Felix's face in the day's dying light. The sunset has cast shadows over his eyes, but I imagine what I would see there and it frustrates me. I don't want to be pitied.

Since leaving Aurora, I've come to reluctant terms with my position as a leader, avoided capture by imperial guards, and managed not to get anyone in my party killed—I won't think about the village. What I haven't managed is to figure out a way to pretend those kisses with Felix never happened. And I very much wish I could because things are complicated enough without the altered dynamic between us. It's part of why I haven't been able to address what I really meant when I insinuated he was a hired killer. What I meant was, please understand this thing in my past. Please know me and love me. But that sounds too much like a weakness I can't afford.

"You never plan to lose the ones you love." His words float softly to me on the cool mountain breeze. I expect to look over and see a sad smile on his face, but when I pull my eyes away from my city, he's walking back toward our camp.

I don't follow. He's been so cryptic lately. Is he talking about me? It seems preposterous to think so. His family then? I'm not sure he even has one. How pathetic is it that I don't know anything about him when he is one of very few I would count as a friend? But then what do I really know about any of them? Hannah, Felix...Levi... Insurgos, all of them, but otherwise a complete mystery to me.

The campsite we've set up is small tonight. So near the city, I decided to simply sleep here for the night so I could have a chance to contemplate the best way to approach. The weather is cool but pleasant, and I see most of the soldiers have elected to sleep under the stars instead of erecting their tents. I walk through their midst and give them a smile and nod of my head. These men have given me more than I could have ever asked of them.

I just hope after tonight I'm in a position to give them something in return.

Because this crazy idea entered my brain while I was overlooking the city. Sending a scouting party as Felix suggested is a sensible solution, but I have to see this for myself, and I don't want to do it as queen. I want to see the people, mix among them, and gauge the atmosphere in the city. I want to see my childhood home without the prying eyes of my company.

This is why I didn't answer Felix. Lying to him feels wrong when I knew I was going to go into the city. It will certainly be more difficult without the added shield of tents in the camp. I'll have to position myself near the perimeter and wait for the right moment to sneak away. And I can't risk taking Athena. Going on foot will be much quieter.

"Emilia!" Hannah calls to me and waves me over when I look her way. She's seated around the fire with a thin blanket wrapped around her shoulders.

I smile and join her. The crackle and pop of the flames is relaxing, and the tension I've held in my shoulders slowly seeps away into the night. I even allow myself to throw back my head and laugh at a few of the jokes Antony tells.

The young soldier barely notices me laughing. He has eyes only for Hannah, and that warms me in ways the fire can't. Somewhere in the last few weeks, amid masquerades and attacks and a narrow escape, Antony has fallen in love with the quiet servant girl I rescued from the market in Aurora.

When I look away I see Felix across the fire from me, and he's watching Antony and Hannah as well. His expression is a stoic mask, hiding whatever is going on underneath that shaggy beard and chiseled jaw. How deep does that well go? I can't imagine I'll ever know.

He catches me looking, and my breath catches in my chest before I look away. The heat on my face has little to do with my proximity to the fire. When he looks at me like that, I feel like he's seeing straight through me, to the core of who I am. I'm afraid he won't like what he sees there.

"I think I'm going to lie down," I tell Hannah as I stand and make great show of stretching my muscles. Truthfully, they are tight from the tension that has wound its way back in in anticipation of my plan. "Tomorrow is a big day. Will you tell Cecily she's at liberty when you see her?"

Hannah has adapted well to my relaxed manner and informal relationship with my ladies. Cecily still struggles with the freedom of the wilderness and the lack of social decorum here. She will not relax unless I explicitly tell her that I don't require her services.

"Of course. Goodnight, my queen." Hannah beams at me as if tomorrow holds the fulfillment of all the promises I've been seeking. She couldn't be more wrong.

I choose a spot as close to the edge of camp as I dare. Taking first watch would have been my first choice, but I don't dare ask and I would feel horrible leaving my post and therefore my company unguarded. So instead I spread a blanket several feet from the perimeter where I will only have to sneak past two rows of sleeping guards.

Slowly the noise of laughter and talking fades into a quiet stillness broken only by an occasional bird song or the rustling of the leaves through the trees. Though clouds would have aided me more in my escape, I allow myself to look up and enjoy the pinpricks of starlight and the tiny sliver of a moon. They have always held beauty for me, but they are dazzling now. Only two days ago I read a passage in the book Felix gave me—the Alethea—that said God spoke those stars into existence. The thought of it still takes my breath. But now it's all I can think of when I look at them. Did he give them each a name?

A hunger grows inside me to know more. Just when I think I'm beginning to understand this God, the one my mother and Levi gave their lives for and the one who has brought me full circle, I stumble across something that reminds me of how little I know. He makes me feel small, but I'm not entirely convinced that's a bad thing.

After the silence falls I force myself to lie still a while longer. When I'm convinced everyone around me is asleep, I pull myself to my hands and knees and begin the slow crawl past my companions. It takes longer than I'd like, and I have to stop twice and pull my blanket over me when I hear someone stir, but I finally reach the tree line and risk standing.

Heart pounding, I drop the blanket and pull the hood of my cloak over my head. If I have gauged the movements of our watchman correctly, I have only minutes to distance myself from the camp. So as quietly as I can, I gather the hem of my travelling cloak and break into a run toward the city I was born to rule.

As a child I was never allowed outside the palace without supervision. Travel into the mountains around the city was out of the question. So while I've never walked through these woods before, there's a weighty familiarity that rests on me like a warm blanket. At the same time my stomach feels as if I were racing down a flight of stairs and missed a step. I'm not the same girl who left this city.

The torches lining the city's wall flicker in the distance, almost dancing in and out of the trees' shadows like fireflies. Will I even recognize it? From a distance it seems it's grown so much.

Something cold grabs my wrist, and I fall backward into something hard and unmoving. I swallow the scream rising in my throat and throw my elbow back as hard as I can. A rush of warm breath ghosts past my ear with a soft "ugh", and I whirl on my attacker.

4

Neither of us move for what feels like several minutes as Felix and I stare each other down with heaving breaths in the slivers of moonlight that penetrate the trees.

"You followed me?" I hiss, searching for his eyes in the shadows.

"You lied to me?" he shoots back, though I don't hear any surprise in his voice. I suppose neither of us are really that surprised.

"I didn't lie." I hate that my voice sounds small, childish even. So I clear my throat and try again. "If you assumed I agreed with your plan then that's your fault."

"Yes, assuming anything about you has been a recurring mistake of late."

It stings and I can't help but recoil. The small bit of space between us gives me room to catch my breath. "I'm not going back to camp."

"I didn't ask you to. But I am coming with you."

"I don't need you."

Even in the shadows I can picture the tightening of his jaw, and I immediately wish I could take it back. He of all people doesn't deserve my wrath.

"Felix, I—"

"I'm not doing it for you." His words are quick and sharp. "Ronan asked me to watch out for you, protect you."

"I don't want to hear his name," I whisper. A cutting breeze floats through the trees so I pull my cloak tighter around me. "And I don't want to stand here when I could be inside the city by now."

"Emilia, I'm not stopping you, but it will look much less suspicious if we go together than if a woman enters the city alone at night."

He's right, of course. And there's more than a small part of me that's grateful for his insistence.

Felix falls in step beside me as if he's marched into battle beside me before. We put a fair amount of distance between ourselves and the camp before he speaks again.

"How did you get past the guard?"

The question isn't the one I expected.

"Very carefully," I say with a wry grin. In the darkness I can barely make out the one he gives me in return. "What about you?"

"I told him to move."

Laughter escapes my mouth before I can quell it and is greeted with Felix's hand clamped over my lips. I taste the dirt on his skin before I shove his hand away and take a few steps ahead of him. The simplicity of his answer is perfect. Lately I feel like I've spent so much time ordering him around that I've forgotten what a commanding presence he is to those soldiers who serve him.

The lights of the city are close enough now to illuminate the enormous open wooden gates in the thick stone wall. Shadows of guards patrolling the top of the wall grab my attention momentarily, but I'm easily distracted by the noise of music and laughter from inside the city. Someone is celebrating. I don't remember what that feels like.

"What do you think that's about?" I pause just at the edge of the tree line and study the scene before us. Rather than being heavily guarded as I imagined, the gate to the city stands wide open and people drift in and out with abandon. Even the guards atop the wall seem to be paying little attention to what's going on beneath them. What could cause this sort of laxity and cheerfulness so soon after my father's death? Do the people not know their king won't be returning for his visit to Aurora? Or, worse, do they not care?

"It's Natalis Solis." Felix's emotionless reply shocks me back to the precariousness of our present circumstances.

"Natalis Solis," I repeat. The celebration of the birth of the empire's chief god Caelus. The day Prince Ronan was supposed to announce which of the dozen girls had won the right to marry him. The day I was supposed to stand by his side in front of the Imperial Court and claim my place as future Empress of Atlas.

So much has happened since Felix showed up in my military camp weeks ago and escorted me to the heart of enemy territory. Too much pain, too many lies, and so much death. And somehow

I remain at the center of it all with the echoes of the storm swirling around me.

"I didn't realize until just now. I lost track of how long we'd been in the mountains." Felix hangs his head a roughs and hand over his face. "Apologies, Highness."

"Stop," I say with a roll of my eyes. "No one said it was your responsibility to keep a calendar while also keeping us all safe. Even you can't do anything and everything."

"But I would try...for you."

By the time I look up, desperate to search his face for meaning, he's already several steps ahead of me striding toward the city like it's his refuge. There's nothing for me to do but follow.

The gates of the city are thrown open wide, welcoming one and all into the celebration. As a soldier there wasn't much occasion to celebrate this holiday—or any others for that matter—but I can still recall the festivities from my childhood. The glittering lights, music, and pageants that once enthralled me as a young princess now seem garish, and we've only seen evidence of celebration that has spilled outside the city. It's likely to be much more over-the-top on the inside.

Despite the death of their king only a week—or is it two now—ago, the city seems relaxed and jovial. The guards at the gate laugh and chat with each other while providing little more than a symbolic warning to those who enter and exit the city. Beside me Felix mutters something under his breath and though I can't make it out, I know it's not complimentary. I have no doubt he's committed the faces of these guards to memory in case, once

I am queen, he ever has the chance to reprimand them. The thought gives me a small smile.

No one gives us much more than a casual glance as Felix and I wander into the city. It takes effort to keep my gate leisurely and relaxed rather than exude the tension coiling so deep in my muscles I'm not sure I'll ever be rid of it. Felix slows his pace to keep even with me, but his soldier's posture is as evident as ever if someone cared to look. Hopefully they won't.

For me that carriage has been something I could turn on and off. Perhaps because I was never meant to be a soldier in the first place. Felix on the other hand, seems as if he was put on this earth to do little else. For the hundredth time I wonder about the road he travelled to become Commander of the Emperor's Guard at such a young age.

I try to take in all of it—the colors, the music, the laughter—and try to make it fit with my image of childhood. It doesn't measure up in quite the same way. Then again, I was never allowed to wander the city like this. Certainly not an appropriate thing for a princess to do. Not then and not now.

As we approach what I assume is the city center, the crowd is denser here. I spot multi-colored lights hanging from booths and stave off my curiosity just enough to avoid approaching them to see what they're selling. It's probably something to commemorate this holiday anyway, and therefore isn't something I want.

I don't want to think about what this holiday means, both historically and symbolically for me. These people are celebrating a birth of a god who not only demands ridiculous sacrifices from them, but who isn't even real. The thought of Caelus and all the reverence shown him makes me sick. But for these people—my people—it is the ultimate celebration. Not only that, but I can't help but wonder what this celebration looks like in Aurora, the imperial city. Will the celebration be grand as always? Or have the murders of the kings and the preparations for war as well as my own daring escape put a damper on them?

Though I know Felix has certainly been watching me, I force myself to focus rather than letting my mind trail off over such thoughts. Especially now that those thoughts are coming dangerously close to Ronan.

"Where do you want to go?" Felix presses into my back, though in this crowd I'm not sure that is on purpose.

I'm ashamed to admit I haven't thought this through. Then again, he's probably used to my ill-thought plans by now.

"The temple," I say without stopping to think why. I feel him tense behind me, but he says nothing. "It's this way."

I point to the north, through the thick of the crowd to an area where the streets narrow and buildings crowd the small paths. It's in the heart of the city, near the palace, and from what I remember, its view on approach is nearly as grand. My heart thuds a heavy rhythm against my chest. What will it feel like to see it again? I remember attending services there as a child and finding them incredibly boring though the temple itself had a certain grandeur to it.

"Lead the way," Felix finally murmurs and nudges me forward a bit with his hand on my arm. The touch is reassuring in this overwhelming mass, and I'm grateful for that constant pressure as people swarm on all sides of us.

Carols of Caelus's greatness and celebration ring out all around us as we push through the throng. Rather than thinning out, the crowd is greater as we near the temple. I should have realized it would be. This is a religious celebration above all, and naturally people flock to the center of the empire's religion. Not only those from Borealis. Families will have made the pilgrimage from all across the empire to experience the ultimate celebration of their god.

I look at these happy faces and feel sick to my stomach. it feels the cruelest form of betrayal to know the truth—the ultimate truth—and not shout it out for all to hear. But then I would be dead before dawn.

Something seems to pull me forward as if I'm tethered to something invisible and must return to it at all costs. It's not unlike the feeling I had in my dream as I was running through the foliage toward a golden light. But this is not a dream, and I must get to the temple.

Finally the temple itself rises above the crowd before us. It is a soaring altar of white marble accented with gleaming gold and silver. I know without looking that thirty-six marble stairs lead from the concourse where we stand to the entrance of the temple. The ultimate holy number—six times six.

"I want to go in" I say to Felix, turning for the first time to look at him over my shoulder. I *must* go in, though I have no idea why. He frowns darkly at me.

"Must you? Now? This is already too much. Far too risky. If you draw attention to yourself by ascending those steps I may not be able to protect you."

I glance back at the stairs and see his point. Though many gather at the base of them, only a handful of people are actually climbing them. Why? Who is allowed inside the temple at the moment?

"There's a back way in," I say suddenly, remembering a small door on the palace side of the temple where I used to watch the priestesses come and go in their flowing gold and blue robes.

Before Felix can come up with a reason to stop me, I duck my head and cut through the crowd. I know exactly where I need to go now, though I still can't explain what is pulling me there. All I know is that I must go.

Behind me Felix's frustrated cry is barely audible above the noise of the crowd, and I know he won't dare say my name, to call after me, when outing me as the exiled princess would be about the deadliest thing he could do to me. At the very least I'd likely be killed in a stampede of onlookers. So I take advantage of his enforced silence and weave my way until I emerge in a small pocket of space to the right of the temple.

The door I remember isn't visible from here, but just past the short stone wall, it's hidden in a courtyard between the palace and the temple. As I'm remembering this, I let myself take my first glimpse of the palace, breath held as I slowly turn my head. And then I sigh. Because despite all my father has done to me, the horrible memories of my mother's death, something of home still calls to me in the monstrosity of stone before me.

Spires rise high above any other dwelling in the city, all decorated with lights of some sort and banners I can't read from here. The doors are closed but decorations of wreathes and flowers hang on them as well. And then I close my eyes and I can picture running through the high-ceilinged hallways and sliding down the banister to the kitchen. And then the nightmares come, and I look down to realize I'm standing in almost the exact spot my mother was executed.

The crowd around me seems to disappear and I'm transported back to that day ten years ago when an angry crowd filled this courtyard and cheered my father for ordering my mother's death. The scent of ash makes me nearly double over with memory until I open my eyes and realize it's just the smell of the torches lining the courtyard.

I don't have time for this. Losing myself in memory isn't an option. Not now, not any time in the foreseeable future. I have a job to do and it's time I started doing it.

I walk slower this time, finding it strange that Felix didn't manage to catch up to me during my moment of contemplation. The crowd is much thinner on this side of the temple and nearly non-existent near the stone wall. It's not the best vantage point to see whatever display the temple is planning on making, but it's exactly where I need to be.

My cloak hinders me only momentarily as I search for a foothold in between the stones of the wall. Finally finding one that suits me, I begin to climb the eight-foot wall as discreetly as I can. As I swing myself over the top of the wall, I let my eyes drift behind me, quickly scanning the crowd for any sight of Felix. My heart sinks a bit as I come up empty then let myself drop to the ground on the other side of the wall.

It's much darker here, but I feel the soft grass beneath my feet, cushioning my fall, before two sets of hands clamp over my mouth and arms and the sharp point of a knife is pressed into my back. I don't scream. I wouldn't even if I could—which I can't because the hand over my mouth is so tight that I struggle to draw a breath in my panic. It's nothing like the grip Felix had on me in the forest outside the city. This is hard and menacing, and I know I've committed a grave error.

"It's her," a gravelly voice announces to his companions. It's hard to tell since I can't actually see my captors, but I believe the voice belongs to the man holding a knife to the small of my back. With the sharp press of the blade, the strong pull toward the temple I've felt becomes a barely noticeable tug.

Just who do these men think I am? Could they possibly know? I don't see how considering I'm dressed like a peasant and it's too dark to make out much of anyone's facial features since the wall blocks most of the torchlight lighting the courtyard on the other side. But they seem to have been waiting for someone—me. I'm not merely a victim of an unfortunate coincidence, but a plot set into motion probably before I ever decided to enter the city.

So Cyrus's men then? I try to will myself to recognize something about any of them from my time in the imperial court. Are these some of the soldiers Felix commanded? If so, maybe I could use that to my advantage.

"Move," one of them growls at me, and I am roughly shoved forward, nearly losing my footing. The hands wound tightly around my arms hold me up, but it's a painful concession. Where is Felix? How could I have lost him so completely?

I am roughly ushered through this smaller courtyard to a door opposite the one I was trying to get to. This one leads not to the temple but to the palace, and my pulse pounds in my ears as I am pushed forward into the dark.

There is nothing familiar about this hallway and the uneven stone floors they push me down. I can tell by the pressure that their fingers will leave bruises on my arms, and I'm briefly reminded of a bruise I received from the Emperor himself.

As we ascend the palace through narrow staircases and slanting floors I begin to recognize bits of my childhood. It seems so much has changed, but I don't know if it's me or the palace itself. Still, there's the tapestries I hid behind when playing hide and seek and the high ceilings with their skylights I used to lie underneath in order to stare at the stars. Sometimes my mother would lie beside me and tell me the names of the stars. I wait for the pain of that memory to hit me but it doesn't. Instead comforts me.

I know we're headed for the throne room even before we reach that wing of the palace. These guards have already passed the staircase to the old north tower where the most dangerous prisoners were kept long ago, and we would not have continued climbing stairs if they meant to give me a cell in the dungeon.

As we continue to approach the throne room, I notice the decorations and the faint sound of music. I had almost forgotten there was a celebration going on. But the twinkling lights and gilded flowers are a stark reminder against the pounding of my heart.

"Are you sure we should interrupt?" one of my guards mumbles in a gravelly voice.

"He said he wanted her brought before him as soon as she was apprehended," the other insists. "I've never disobeyed an order before, and I'm not about to start now."

Before I have time to puzzle about this exchange, the guards put their hands that aren't gripping me against the tall ornately carved doors and push them open.

My head is roughly shoved down as they drag me forward and the music around us dies on a strangled note. Whatever their orders were, no one in this room seems to have expected this. And there are several people here, likely nobles and courtiers invited to the most elite celebration. I can feel their eyes on me.

Since looking up seems an invitation for my guards to force me into submission, I study the floor instead. Each jerky step forward takes me across the same deep blue and white tile I remember from childhood. A background of midnight blue with pale stars inlaid across the vast throne room.

When they've paraded me down the length of the room, one of the guards shoves me roughly forward as they relinquish their hold on me. I'm grateful to have some feeling back in my arms but I know better than to try to make a run for it. I still feel their glares and the ghost of a knife on my back.

I wait for what feels like ages for someone to break the silence, and when they do, it's not at all what I was expecting.

5

"E...Emilia?" The voice isn't familiar, but there's a hint of something in the intonation of my name. Something that brings back memories I didn't know were still buried somewhere underneath it all. "Is that really you?"

So I lift my head, slowly, and with purpose. A disconcerting stillness fills the room as if all the inhabitants have inhaled a collective breath. The cowl of the hood blocks most of the court from my peripheral vision, which is just as well. They aren't the ones I need to see.

My eyes land on a man who is frozen in a half crouch as if the sight of me has pulled him unwillingly from his throne.

His throne. A king.

But he isn't really. There's a hesitation, an uncertainty in him that the crown hasn't beaten out of him yet. How could it? He's worn it less than a month.

"Majesty." My address is deferential but I don't bow my head again as protocol would dictate. Instead I level my eyes at him, daring him to challenge me on it. Had he not recognized me, I'm not sure I would have had the courage to react this way.

"It's really you." His hushed voice carries through the silent hall, and I suddenly wish we were alone. Titus, my cousin, my childhood playmate I left behind, stands in front of me with a mixture of relief and confusion in his eyes and a prince's crown on his head. I wonder where that came from. Had my father named him a prince in the intervening years? Or is it a hastily cobbled job to offer the appearance of legitimacy so he can sit on my father's throne? Either way it suits him.

Titus was my father's brother's son and the nearest thing I had to a best friend when I was a child. Though he was three years older, we were often grouped together in lessons and in play. My father rarely let me play with children of the nobles so that left the only other child in the palace—Titus. He'd been a sure-footed boy with physical prowess who scarcely took his lessons seriously. But he'd known how to make me laugh and how to make our seemingly endless royal appearances fun.

There's no mirth on his handsome face now. He must be twenty, but he looks much older. I wonder how much of that has come in the too few days since he received word of my father's death.

"It's really me," I say. My words seemingly break the spell hanging over the court, and low murmurs replace the thick silence. These people used to shout my name. Now they whisper it. If Titus hadn't uttered it first, would they even have remembered it at all? More importantly, do they remember who the name belongs to? I don't think so, or there would have been more of a reaction. How strange to be the rightful queen to a people who have forgotten my name.

"Leave us." Titus's words boom in the grand hall as he rises completely to his feet.

At first I think he means me, but then the court nobles begin bustling about, presumably heading for the door behind me where I entered. I don't turn to look. Instead I keep my gaze steady on my cousin. How I wish Felix were here. He must be going mad with worry. What I wouldn't give to have his read on this situation.

Several long minutes pass as the sound of heels clicking on the marble floor die away. The heavy doors close with a loud clang, and Titus and I are alone.

I want to fill the silence with words but none come. The scrutiny should not feel new to me given the weeks I spent with the eyes of the imperial court on my every move, but this is different. This is my family…what's left of it. With a start I realize Titus is all the family I have left, and I don't know what he believes about who I have become.

I'm not sure what I believe either.

"Emilia," he says again. Titus crosses the distance between us in fewer strides than I thought possible. If he has adopted the royal posturing his position requires, he seems to have put it aside for this moment, and I'm grateful for it.

His arms are strong and somehow familiar as he throws them around me for a tight squeeze. My arms feebly raise to grasp his arms because, for as much as I want this to feel like a warm welcome, the past few weeks—years really—have taught me to take nothing for granted.

"I can't believe it." He shakes his head. "I thought the guards were bringing me a prisoner, but they've brought me a queen instead."

"You were expecting someone. Who?" My guards had said they were instructed to bring a prisoner straight to Titus, but if I'm not her, then who was he waiting for?

"The Insurgo leader. My spies have told me she was to lead an attack on the temple tonight to interrupt the celebration. I had all the guards on high alert. We've been trying to catch her for weeks."

My arms fall from him in total surprise. A female Insurgo leader? Leading an attack? No, that can't be right. They don't attack. They only defend.

"I-I wasn't sure I would ever see you again." He holds me at arms distance and looks me over quickly. He seems content to let the topic of my mistaken identity drop for now, but I'm not ready to let it go just yet. "Until the king sent you to Aurora for the contest I thought you were dead."

"The king...my father..." I thought to correct his word choice but I stop myself because he's right. It is a king and not a father who exiles his only child and then resurrects her only for his own gain.

"I'm so sorry, Emilia." Titus bows his head. "Your father is dead, killed by Insurgo rebels as he travelled back from Aurora."

My lack of eloquence has led him to believe I did not know of my father's death, and I don't correct him. I feel certain it's what Felix would advise at this moment. Titus is family, but that's little consolation given recent history.

"In fact," he continues, "the attack was extensive. The empire is in upheaval. The kings are dead. All of them."

It's no wonder he's able to believe Insurgos would attack his temple. Emperor Cyrus has done such a complete job convincing him the same rebels have just systematically overthrown the empire's countries. All except... "But not the Emperor or the Crown Prince."

"No, they escaped."

He doesn't seem to see anything unusual about this. And why would he? I'm certain the attack on Ronan was well publicized when news of the kings' deaths was carried to each country. Emperor Cyrus could not have appeared to be untouched in all of this. Titus has bought the lie as has most of the realm, I'm sure. Divulging my knowledge of the truth will serve no purpose right now.

"That is fortunate," I say instead.

"But what of you?" He takes my hand and hesitates before leading me to the steps of the dais. The callouses on my hands have thrown him. They are a sharp contrast to the lifestyle he has known—the one that should have been mine—and his own smooth hands. Titus finally sits on the steps and invites me to do the same.

"Have you had no news of me from the Emperor?" I'm reminded once again that being ignorant of Cyrus's game is the one thing that could ruin every plan.

"None," he breathes as he rakes a hand through a headful of dark hair. "The last we heard from the Imperial court was the summons your father received to the Council of Kings, and then of course the message that there had been an attack and the casualties."

"At the hand of the Insurgos?" I clarify with a bitter taste in my mouth. Cyrus's plan seems to have worked perfectly.

"Yes. And we were hardly surprised considering the attacks we've been under recently."

"Attacks?"

"Well, yes. The Insurgo attacks." He searches my face, though I'm unsure what he's looking for. "Surely you've seen and heard of the damage."

"I just arrived in the city," I remind him.

"And you saw the security around the gates and in the streets? It has consumed me since the news of your father's death. We haven't caught them, of course, but I'm hoping the extra guard presence will deter future attacks. The Kingsguard is stretched thin as it is."

"And this leader you hoped to catch tonight?"

"Yes, she's made extensive trouble for all of us. Yet no one has caught a glimpse of her. I would apologize the guards mistook you for her, but at least it's brought us together again. What were you doing near the temple? And where is your guard? Your ladies?"

What a naïve man to believe I would have been supplied with any of those things by either the Emperor or my father. Those that travel with me are loyal to me—or more accurately Felix—because of the things I stand for. Things that—if Titus is to be believed— are tearing my own country apart.

"I wanted to see the city for myself. No special treatment, no fanfare. I just wanted to feel what it was like to be home." Not entirely the truth but not exactly a lie. I've become much too adept at this gray area.

"It is good to have you home." He smiles with the sort of warmth that brings me back to our childhood. Who could have guessed we'd end up here? "We should hold a ball to welcome you properly. Emilia, daughter of Borealis, finally come home."

Somehow I doubt everyone will see it as the happy occasion he seems to envision. "Perhaps I could have a period of rest and reflection first. It's been a long journey, and I have much to think about."

"Of course, dear cousin. Would you prefer your old rooms or something in the guest wing? I can have them prepared for you at once."

A booming crash echoes through the hall, and Titus and I both rise to our feet. His hand is at his waist, fingers curled around a dagger, and though my actions mirror his, I'm quickly reminded I'm bereft of a weapon.

Except my weapon is now storming down the long hall, hand on his sword pommel with the palace guards stumbling over themselves behind him. Felix looks as fierce as I've ever seen him, dark eyes blazing and jaw tense with what I know to be his own mixture of worry and anger.

"Majesty, I apologize," one of the guards behind Felix pants as he struggles to catch up to my commander. "We tried to stop him but—"

"Four of you could not stop one man?" Titus's question is void of any of the pride I feel.

"He has the imperial seal," insists another guard, stumbling to a stop beside his comrade. "We dare not—"

"Silence." Titus gives the command without raising his voice, but it still rings with authority in the nearly empty hall.

My eyes finally meet Felix's, and suddenly I'm hot all over. Certainly I'm used to the anger and relief I find in his gaze as I've been the cause of it more than I'd like to admit, but there's something much more dangerous there, and I find myself drawn to it like a moth to a flame.

"Cousin," I say with as even a tone as I can manage, "this is Commander Felix Fidelis, Captain of the Imperial Guard and Champion of...my own guard."

Queensguard. It's what I meant to say, but now doesn't feel like the time to announce myself as queen when the man next to me is wearing the crown and has his hand on a dagger. But at my announcement Titus visibly relaxes, and his hand moves from the dagger to straighten his crown.

"Welcome, Commander. Any representative of the Imperial court is of course welcome here."

"My duty is to Her Highness not the Imperial court." Felix doesn't bow. Every word sounds torn from him as if it had to fight to get past his clenched teeth.

Titus glances sideways at me and raises his brows. "You must have made quite and impression in court, cousin, for the Emperor Cyrus to make you a gift of the Commander of his own guard."

I can feel the anger radiating from Felix, but to his credit he doesn't speak. It feels wrong. Why hasn't Cyrus sent riders to all corners of the realm to apprehend the traitorous princess and soldier on sight? Titus might have been willing to harbor me even if he knew I was a fugitive, but Felix? Certainly he would not take a chance on a man he doesn't know. Titus doesn't know the truth of my flight from Aurora, and that means I have underestimated Cyrus once again.

"I'm exhausted, cousin." I place my hand on his arm, hoping to diffuse the situation before it escalates. "Perhaps someone could show the Commander and I to the guest rooms?"

"Of course. Why don't you take a turn in the garden while I have the rooms readied. The same ones your mother favored when she had guests at the palace. I'll send for you when they are suitably prepared." His smile seems genuine but it doesn't give me comfort. "Guards, please escort—"

"I remember where the gardens are." I offer a sweet smile to diffuse the situation. "Commander Fidelis is more than enough escort for me."

"Very well then."

I descend the few stairs before he can change his mind and take Felix's offered arm. He's nearly vibrating with tension as we exit the room at a quicker pace than would be considered proper for a queen.

No words or glances pass between us as I navigate him toward the gardens at the center of the palace. It's easy to forget the celebration going on outside when the halls are so still and quiet. But when we step into the night air the sounds of revels float over the palace walls and high hedges that shroud us in the darkness.

The Commander walks a few paces ahead of me as he studies the hedges and flowers, occasionally poking the bushes with his sword. It takes several minutes before he seems suitably satisfied that this garden is reasonably secure. He turns back to me with an odd, distressed look on his usually stoic face.

And then Felix is pressing into me, his hands in my hair and his mouth desperately close to mine yet still not close enough to touch. I have no idea what he's doing but I want more. For a hopeful second I think he's going to kiss me again, and I'm surprised by how disappointed I am when he pulls me into his chest instead and buries his face in my unbound hair.

"Please, Emilia. I thought I had lost you this time." The hitch in his voice and the tightness of his arms around me breaks my heart. What did I do to deserve the unswerving loyalty of this man? He is too good for my mess.

"We've survived worse." I try for levity but he isn't laughing.

"Things are different now. More dangerous. Can't you feel it?" His breath somehow penetrates the thickness of my hair and tickles a spot just behind my ear. I shiver.

He's right of course. We're fugitives, a threat to the Borealis crown, and supporters of the movement that—according to Titus—is attacking the city. And yet I don't for a moment think he's speaking of those dangers. Because I'm remembering the kisses we shared as we fled the imperial city. And nothing could be more dangerous than the pounding of my heart when he's this near.

But then he's gone, unwelcome space between us as he paces in front of me and roughs a hand over his scruffy face. I don't dare move for fear that it might shatter everything. Selfishly I've dreamed of having him that close, of feeling his arms around me in a way that's less protective and more desperate for closeness. And it's still not enough.

"Please," he says again, refusing to look at me. "Don't run from me again."

"I won't." And I mean it. Not if it's within my power. I have caused this man far too much distress in too short amount of time, and more times than not he's been right about being cautious. We are on the same side, and I suppose it's time we stop working against each other.

Felix seems to have regained the composure he left at my feet and gestures for me to join him on a nearby bench. I do, careful to leave a sliver of space between us. I know that momentary lapse of self-control cost him, and I don't want to be the reason for his internal battle of honor.

"Well, what did you learn?" He's all business again with his back straight and his tone devoid of emotion. He might as well be asking me about the weather.

"Too much to say here." This garden is a maze of hedges I remember well from my childhood. No matter how much Titus may seem to trust me, I would not be surprised if there were eavesdroppers planted here. Maybe spies that are not in my cousin's employ. I don't know the state of the court here anymore.

Felix only nods in response. "I will ride out in the morning to escort the others into the city, and I'll see to it that rooms are arranged for them near the palace."

"*In* the palace. There are more than enough rooms here. Titus can't have filled them all. Besides, I want them close."

"As you wish." He stands and resumes his pacing in front of me. I don't interrupt him. There's nothing to be said here.

After what feels like ages a young maid appears at the garden entrance, bows, and escorts us both to the west wing of the palace. It's not a place I was allowed to explore much as a child as it was usually filled with visiting dignitaries and other important people my father didn't want me to bother.

We're led to a door at the end of a long hallway where the maid stops and curtsies. "This is your room, milady. I've taken the liberty of filling the bath with water. Will you be requiring anything else?"

Felix and I exchange looks. Her omission of titles tells me much. She doesn't know who I am, and I'd like to keep it that way for a while longer. I'm not sure if Titus has his own reasons for hiding me or if he seemed to sense I needed a moment before being presented as the exiled princess. Either way I'm grateful he's chosen to keep my identity quiet.

"That will be all." I nod my head.

"And your room is right next door, my lord." The maid blushes slightly as she addresses Felix and gestures to one of the doors we passed on the way to mine. "I've also drawn water for your bath as well."

"Thank you, miss." He offers her a slight bow and her face reddens further. "You've been most helpful."

Without fanfare, the maid curtsies once more and practically vanishes from our sight. Felix and I are left alone in the hallway outside my door.

"Will you come in?" My voice catches a bit on the words, and I feel the heat rising in my neck.

"Emilia," Felix sighs. "You know I can't."

And though I do know it and I know why, it still feels a bit like a punch to the gut. Because I want nothing more than for him to throw his arms around me again as I relate the things Titus told me. But his momentary indiscretion in the garden is past him now, and I'm certain his resolve not to put himself in a compromising position with me will be stronger than ever.

"Very well." I gather myself and straighten as tall as I can, hoping to present a confidence I do not feel. "Rest well, Commander. We can speak over breakfast in the morning."

"Sleep well, my queen." He takes my hand and brushes the lightest of kisses across the back of it before disappearing behind his door.

Everything feels like a blur as I enter my room and approach the steaming bath in the corner. The ache in my muscles I've ignored for days suddenly demands attention as I look at the warm water. As wonderful as sleep sounds, it would be nice to wash the filth of travelling from my body and drown the whispers in my head with relaxation.

I remove my travelling cloak and sit on a stool placed beside the bath. My fingers begin to work a few knots from my hair as I look around my room. It's much smaller than my quarters at the imperial palace, and I'm glad of it. There's a large bed with navy blue curtains and crisp white linens that calls my name. My time in the imperial court softened me a bit, and I hadn't realize how used to sleeping in a soft bed I was until these last weeks on the run.

With my hair mostly untangled I begin the work of unlacing my simple dress. Hannah's fingers are so much more adept at this, and the ache to see her fills me with a surprising suddenness. She takes such wonderful care of me even in less than ideal circumstances, and she's become the first true friend I've had in more years than I can count.

With the laces finally undone, my dress slips to the ground leaving me in my thin underdress. My fingers reach for the hem to remove it as well, but a spot of dingy blue cloth catches my eye and I pause. Amid the pool of my dark dress on the floor is a scorched, crumbling piece of fabric that takes me right back to the destroyed Insurgo village where I last wore this dress.

Tears, so hot and fast I can't breathe, pour from me. I fall to my knees beside the tub, clutching the remnant of that tiny blue blanket in my hand. How could I have so quickly forgotten? The burned village. That mother wrapped around her sweet child. How much more can I take? How much more can *they* take? And I have the nerve to ensconce myself in this palace while they struggle for food and survival. Isn't this the very sort of princess I vowed not to be? But I don't know how to be better. Everyone has an expectation of me, and I've somehow failed them all.

The dam has broken and there is no bottling back up the torrent of emotion I've released. A high keening sound fills the room, and I don't realize it's coming from my own mouth until arms wrap gently around me and pull me away from the bath.

"Shh." Felix is there, pulling me against him with a tenderness I've rarely seen from him, and I come along willingly. The heaviness on my chest feels a bit lighter this close to him. He wraps his cloak around me, covering my bare shoulders and thin chemise. If he notices my state of undress he doesn't seem to care.

"I can't do this," I sob into the front of his shirt. My hand shakes as I raise the blue fabric for him to examine. "This is what happens when I try."

His fingers curl around my wrist, his thumb sliding into my palm with a gentle caress as he looks from the fabric to me. "No. This is *why* you have to try."

My sobs finally subside to quiet sniffles, but neither of us make an effort to fill the void. Tears and exhaustion make my eyes heavy, and I pull his cloak tighter around me, eager to surround myself with his scent of leather and dirt.

"Let me carry you to bed," he finally says, voice low and soft.

"Stay just a little longer," I whisper.

And he does.

6

My night is a haze of memories that haunt me both waking and sleeping. Levi is there, pale and blood-soaked, telling me that I have been chosen. He repeats the words again and again until I shove a sword that appears in my hands into his chest. He smiles as he slides to the ground, fresh blood mingling with the dirt.

And I plead with him not to die. I scream out my apologies to the empty darkness around us. But it's no use. There is no one to hear us and no one to witness my desperate penance. I take the sword still in my hand and wonder if I have the courage to use it on myself. A life for a life.

But there's only a moment to consider it when the earth begins to shake violently and the sword is jarred from my hands.

I wake surrounded by blue curtains, white sheets, and a haze of memories that come rushing back when I try to move. My head aches from crying, and my muscles are as tense and fatigued as ever.

This isn't the first time Felix has carried me to bed while I sobbed in his arms, and while I probably should feel ashamed of that, I don't. Because he was right in what he said last night. I have to try. This isn't my fight; it's something so much bigger than me. I owe it to those who follow me, and even those who don't, to commit to the cause. Now if I only knew what that looked like.

When I pull the bed curtains aside I can just see the first light of dawn peeking through the doors to my balcony, outlining a familiar form leaning against the railing. My heart aches for a way to capture this image forever, to claim it as mine. But no matter what intimacy Felix and I share because of our beliefs, it's not something that can be acted upon in the light of day.

My travelling cloak is still lying upon the floor next to my dress, and I pull it around me before opening the balcony doors. Felix doesn't look at me as I join him leaning against the iron rail.

"You stayed."

It's not a question, but he nods anyway. "You had nightmares last night."

I suppose I was wrong to think because Hannah has never mentioned my nightmares waking her I must not cry out in my sleep. Or perhaps Felix is once again more intuitive than I've given him credit for. Because he's right. I dreamed of Levi and of blood running down a sword and through my fingers. I dreamed of his words to me and of his certainty that God had called me to save the Insurgos. It's a small blessing he isn't alive to see the devastation and ruin I've left in my wake.

To his credit Felix doesn't ask me more about the nightmare. I'm grateful for that much, because I don't think I could bear the disappointment in his eyes if I told him of my mentor's death at my own hands.

"Thank you for staying. I had hoped you would get some rest though. Did you sleep at all?"

"Some." He looks at me with faint dark circles under those brown eyes. A weariness that mirrors my own seems etched on his handsome face. "More than I would if I'd known you were alone."

As much as I needed him last night, I hope one day we can reach a point where he doesn't feel responsible for me and my happiness. "I'm sorry you heard me crying."

"I'm not. You don't need to hide that part of yourself from me." His studies me with such intensity that I have to look away.

"Most men wouldn't support a queen who shows that much weakness."

From the corner of my eye I see him hang his head. "I had hoped you knew by now that I'm not most men."

My eyes snap back to him. "You know I didn't mean—"

"The stables are on the east side of the palace, correct? I need to borrow a mount and ride to the others so they can join us. They're probably already in a panic over our absence."

"Yes," I answer simply because he's closed the door on that topic for now. "And when you return and have seen to it that everyone has food and rooms, you must get some sleep."

"Emilia, I'm fine."

"It wasn't a request." I need him sharp. There is much to discuss about our strategy. Aside from perhaps Hannah, I value his counsel more than anyone, though we have certainly disagreed on the best course of action in the past. But things were more hypothetical then. Now it's time for action.

"As you wish." The openness in his face vanishes as he bows slightly and leaves me alone on the balcony.

It's not fair to him, to anyone really, for me to continue in this uncertainty in who I want to be. The queen or the rebel? I tried to be both with Ronan and failed miserably.

The thought of the prince's blue eyes and kind smile fills me with a roiling mix of emotions. I might have loved him given time. Certainly a strong affection. But I'm not sure I can forgive his lack of action in his father's court no matter what pretense he claims.

The letter he wrote me as I fled Aurora is tucked away safely in a small box I left with Hannah. But the words are imprinted on my mind, and if I close my eyes I can see them in his tight scrawl.

My dearest, Emilia. I trust my words find you well though I'm sure you're far from me now. You must hate me for my silence, and I don't blame you for your anger. But it was only what was necessary. Had I spoken in your defense, nothing would be gained except I might die in the arms of a beautiful woman. My father certainly would not have spared either of us. While your death might have given you martyrdom, mine would have counted for nothing, and you've made me want to change that. I arranged for Felix to help you escape, and though it pains me to be parted from the man who became as dear as a brother to me, I've given him to you—to protect you, to command as you will— until such a time I can come to you and we can finish what we started.

Finish what we started.

I wish I knew what he meant by that. Our marriage? Or, dare I hope, something more?

I resign myself that I may never know what he meant by it. With so much else demanding my attention, it seems foolish to give time and energy to dissecting the words and motives of a man I will probably never see again. My energy is better spent elsewhere.

A bell near the door allows me to ring for a maid, and within an hour I've had a fresh bath drawn, scrubbed myself of dirt and tears, and dressed in borrowed clothes from the palace. The dark blue dress is simple enough that I'm able to lace myself in reasonably well, and with my hair loose and slightly damp, I exit my room to explore.

The rumbling in my stomach drives me down the main staircase and toward the informal dining room where my parents used to take breakfast. The savory smells wafting from behind the closed doors suggest Titus has kept up the practice. A guard stands at attention outside the door, and I stop in front of him.

"Is Titus in there?"

The guard raises his eyebrows, probably at my lack of formality, and nods slightly.

"Tell him Emilia would like to eat with him." My voice lacks the bravado and confidence I'm aiming for, but apparently I convey enough authority that the guard nods once and disappears into the room.

Seconds later Titus himself opens the door and welcomes me in with a wide smile and a kiss on the cheek. "Dear cousin, please join me. I had hoped perhaps you would still be resting or I would have sent someone to escort you down here."

With a guiding hand on my arm, Titus directs me to a large chair beside his own and then gestures to a maid who seems to have been waiting quietly for just such a moment. Almost instantly a plate is placed in front of me and filled with smoked meats, eggs, and delicious looking fruit-filled pastries. It's all I can do to keep from drooling on myself.

"You must be famished," he adds as he returns to his chair and takes a bite of a pastry on his own plate. "Were you even able to enjoy any food from the celebrations in the city last night? Or did the guard apprehend you before you could partake?"

"No, I didn't try anything," I answer before inhaling a raspberry and chocolate filled pastry. It may be the most exquisite thing I've ever tasted, and I don't care how undignified it makes me look as I lick the chocolate from my fingers.

"Such a shame," Titus says with a shake of his head. I notice, finally, that he's not wearing a crown today. So at least he's not as attached to it as my father was. "I had heard the celebration in the commons was particularly wonderful this year. On the heels of such tragic news, the people clearly threw themselves into this distraction. We all deserve a little happiness, don't we?"

Tragic news? Is that what he's calling it? Granted I didn't take much time to people-watch last night, but it seems no one was still observing the ritual mourning usually required after the death of a king. If I had to guess, I would say the people seemed glad of a reason to move on with their lives. I don't think my father was a particularly beloved king.

"Happiness is relative," I say, "and often fleeting."

"Yes of course. You would say that. How very callous of me to forget who I'm talking to when you've lived with so much pain in your life."

Pain is an old friend, such a familiar companion that I notice its absence more than its presence. "My life is certainly not what I used to imagine it would be. But it has shaped me, prepared me for greater things." I choose my words carefully, watching his face as I speak.

Titus breaks into a relieved half-smile. "Greater things. Yes. I had hoped you might say that. I confess I was awake most of the night thinking of your return and what that might mean for the kingdom and for me."

Despite my best intentions my eyes flick up to the absence of the crown on his brow and then back down to his green eyes. "I'm not here to stage a coup."

"But aren't you?" He tilts his head as those sharp eyes appraise me. "It won't be necessary, of course. The crown is rightfully yours. You don't have to pretend you aren't here for it. Why else would you return after all this time?"

If only it were that simple. "Titus, I haven't seen home in ten years. I can't go back to my military unit now that they know who I really am. Where else could I have possibly gone?"

"You could have stayed in Aurora. Obviously you have some favor with the Emperor if he lent you the Commander of his guard."

I bite back a bitter laugh. The concept of Felix allowing himself to be borrowed like a piece of property is almost as absurd as me being on Emperor Cyrus's good side. "All of us in the competition were sent home after news of attacks reached us. Staying wasn't an option. And Commander Fidelis is with me because I was the only girl who stood to inherit a crown in her own right. As the heir to the Borealis crown it was decided I needed extra protection."

Maybe I've laced enough of the truth through my lies because Titus relaxes back in his chair with a sigh. "I'm so sorry you've had such a difficult time, Emilia. I can't imagine what the last several years have been like for you. Or even the last several weeks for that matter. From this palace to the military camps to the imperial city to compete for the highest crown in the land. You must have whiplash."

All I can do is nod. Somehow having someone sympathize with my plight brings all my emotions dangerously close to the surface, and I feel the burn of tears in the back of my throat. Titus and I sit in silence for several moments before I can swallow emotion well enough to speak.

"The truth is I would like some time to get acclimated to Borealis again, and I'd like to do it as Emilia. Not as a princess or future queen."

"You're asking me not to announce your return to the court?" He sips the red juice in front of him and returns the glass to the table. "I'm afraid your entrance last night makes secrecy more than a little impossible."

"If you must speak of me to the courtiers or anyone else, I am simply your cousin. Your mother had several siblings, so no one needs to know I'm not part of her side of the family."

"But the crown is yours. You can't wear it while you're hiding."

He's right, of course, but nothing is that simple. "And I can't rule a people I no longer know. Please, cousin, just for a short time. And then I'll take my place."

Titus sighs and drags a hand through his chestnut brown hair. He looks so much like the boy I remember in that moment. "I can give you a week, and even then you'll have to be careful. The Council has spies in court and throughout the palace. They won't be satisfied only knowing you're my cousin. Not when the appearance of the long-lost princess could reshape this entire country."

The Council. A group of five old men who advised my father. And from the sounds of it, another pit of vipers. But I am wiser than when I stepped into Emperor Cyrus's court, and I have allies now.

"I can manage."

Titus looks at me for a long moment before offering a nod and a small smile. "I believe you can. How can I help you?"

I don't hesitate. "Commander Fidelis rode out early this morning to gather the rest of my entourage—a small contingent of guards, horses, and two of my ladies. I would like the soldiers to be given rooms in the palace barracks if possible and allowed to continue their training under Commander Fidelis once they are recovered from our journey."

"Yes of course." Titus takes another sip of his juice. "Our barracks are unfortunately not as full as we'd like them to be at the moment. Too many deserted after your father's death. The Commander of the Kingsguard resigned as soon as he returned with your father's body. There are few royal guards remaining.

General Auror had donated some of the military personnel to provide palace protection when court is in session. Your contingent of palace guards will be a welcome addition to our ranks. And your Commander, should he be given rooms with the soldiers, or do you wish him to remain adjacent to you?"

I'm grateful I chose to leave my hair loose this morning. It swings forward to hide my blush as I reach for my own glass of juice. The cool liquid does little to cool the heat rising in me. Titus's question is innocent, of course, but my thoughts are not quite so.

"Give him the choice when he returns," I say with what I hope appears as a nonchalant wave of my hand. I know where I want him, and I think I know where he wants to be, but I will let his honor make that choice rather than my selfishness.

"Very well." Titus nods. "And your ladies? There is a suite across the hall from your quarters that they could share if that would be amenable to you."

I raise my eyebrows and he laughs.

"Come now, Emilia. You have not changed so much after these years that you would have your ladies given less than the best. Even I can see that."

"Well, yes, that would be wonderful," I say, imaging the looks on Hannah and Cecily's faces when they realize they get an entire suite to themselves rather than being sent to the servants' quarters or a small closet of my own rooms.

"It's done then," he says with a single clap of his hands. "If you'll excuse me now, I'll see to it that someone begins preparations for your company's arrival and then I must attend some very dull meetings. Please stay as long as you like and finish your breakfast. Lunch will be served in the grand garden today if you and your guests would like to attend."

I don't want to attend, but I also don't feel as if I can refuse. Titus's hospitality is more than I could have hoped for, and after my entrance to court last night others will be expecting to see us together.

"That sounds lovely," I agree. "Though I'm afraid I don't have anything fine enough to wear to an open court luncheon."

"It's not a problem. I had your mother's clothes brought out of wardrobe last night. They'll be brought to your room this morning. I trust your ladies are decent seamstresses? If not just summon one of ours to tailor a dress to your needs."

He says this as if it's not a big deal. As if seeing—*wearing*—something of my mother's when she's been so off limits all these years won't evoke any sort of response in me. And so I try to conceal the jolt it gives me with a gracious smile.

"Thank you. Yes, my ladies are very capable with a needle. I'm sure I can find something to wear."

"Be ready by eleven and I'll have someone fetch you to give you a tour of the palace and grounds prior to lunch. It's a customary offer extended to visitors," he adds quickly when he sees the protest rising on my lips.

Of course. Though I spend my childhood years in this palace and should recall every crevice I explored, I need to appear as merely a visiting member of Titus's family. And since it's been years since I've been here a refresher is probably in order. Besides, Felix will likely want to tour the grounds to get an idea of what he's dealing with from a protection standpoint. So I agree without argument.

The tour of the palace is more painful than I could have imagined. As I anticipated, Felix is eager for the opportunity, and Hannah and Cecily graciously accompany us as well. Our guide is a scholarly- looking youth, someone much too young to recognize me, but with ample knowledge of the architecture and history of my childhood home. Clearly he studied well.

He takes us through the more public places—the throne room, the ballroom, the formal dining hall, the library, the salon, and so many others—before directing us up the stairs to more private areas. There he waxes on about works of art and statues that I found boring as a child and possibly even more so now. My companions are more attentive, asking questions about art, gossip, and traditions in Borealis. Our guide answers them all with a smile.

Felix engages him in conversation about the rumored hidden tunnels within the passage, and the two of them walk ahead of us while Hannah, Cecily, and I stop to admire a tapestry on the wall. The boy had little to say about it, and it certainly isn't as grand as the others we've seen so far, but it tugs on a thread of a memory inside me.

"Oh, this is lovely!" Cecily exclaims as she lets her long fingers trail over the image of fairy lights dancing over water woven into the tapestry. "So magical."

"I used to love this one as a child," I say softly. "It reminded me of the stars." Even as I say it, warmth seeps into me as I remember the night sky just outside Borealis as I looked up at the wide expanse of stars against the velvet sky, in awe of the God that brought me here.

And then I know. The memory this image has been pulling at comes rushing at me full force. I inhale sharply and close my eyes, experiencing it all again. My mother's hand in mine, the whipping of my loose hair against my face as we raced down the hall, the shouts of guards and her maids. And somehow behind this panel a secret room, a safe place. For me only. Not for her.

I want to pull the tapestry aside, to search for what I'm sure is there, but now isn't the time.

"My lady?" Our guide calls to me, and I look up to find he and Felix are waiting on us at the end of the hall.

"Coming," I say sweetly, hoping I've managed to conceal all the emotions bubbling up within me at the moment.

As we rejoin them and I take Felix's offered arm, he gives me a sidelong questioning glance, but I just shake my head slightly. This is not a memory I'm ready to share with anyone just yet. Maybe not ever. When I thought of all the ramifications of coming to Borealis, of coming home, I didn't fully account for these moments. These little pangs of remembrance—both good and bad—that would assault me without warning. Felix would have, though. He seems to account for everything.

He seemed to agree with my plan to keep my true identity under wraps for a while as I get reacquainted with my city. When I told him my plan he looked relieved. I'm sure part of him was afraid I was going to storm in and demand my crown, force him to back me up. Not because he believes I truly desire the crown, but he knows me well enough now to know my impulsiveness gets out of hand.

We spend the next week settling into the palace. Felix keeps his quarters next to mine—a decision I'm secretly pleased with—but spends most of his time falling into a routine training with the palace guard. I'm not sure how Titus has explained the presence of an Imperial Commander to the existing palace guard, but from the little I've observed in my daily walks through the palace grounds, the Borealis soldiers seem to take to Felix as well as the Aurora ones did. He is genuinely well liked and respected.

Hannah and Cecily are nearly giddy with their quarters across from mine and the beautiful but simple wardrobe they are provided. Hannah has certainly never seen anything so fine, and Cecily gushes over the fine fabrics. They have ample free time now that we are settled in and there are no official appearances for me to make. Though they help me dress each morning and ready me for bed each evening, I'm mostly left to my own devices.

This suits me just fine. I mostly stick to the palace grounds at Felix's request. There's more than enough here to keep me occupied for a while. But once or twice I venture out into the markets to walk among my people.

On those days I feel even more a stranger here than I do in the palace. The statues and images of Caelus are everywhere, and though I've tried very hard to not think about any of that for the last week, they are hard to ignore.

Harder still to ignore are the throngs of people that gather outside the temple in the evenings to sing songs of praise while the priestesses burn incense. I can see all this from my balcony, even imagine I can smell the earthy scent of the incense wafting up on the breeze.

The hair pricks on the back of my neck, and I realize there's another breeze coming from…behind me? I turn away from the balcony and reenter my room.

Everything looks as it did earlier. Cecily straightened everything up after a few servant girls brought up more racks of my mother's old dresses and stowed them in the wardrobe this morning, and I haven't been in my rooms long enough to move anything out of place. But there is a distinct draft coming from somewhere, and I've never felt it before. Something must be different.

Curiosity gets the better of me, and I move cautiously toward the wardrobe. I refused to look at the dresses earlier when they brought them in. I'm unsure I want to see them now, but they are the only thing that's changed in my room in the last several hours.

As I near the large wooden structure on the wall opposite my bed, I notice it's shifted slightly. Not enough to notice at a glance, but it's certainly no longer flush against the wall. It probably happened as the servants were struggling to fill it with all those heavy dresses.

When I reach to move it back into place, I feel the draft again. I definitely haven't imagined it. There's something behind the wardrobe. Something I must see.

Rather than returning the furniture to its usual position, I lower my shoulder and push it farther away from the wall. It's no easy feat, and even with all my strength it takes several minutes to budge it even a few inches. Finally I have made enough room that I can see an aged wooden door recessed into the stone wall.

My heart leaps at the sight, and I don't give myself time to contemplate before I shimmy behind the wardrobe and push the door open. Right away I know I'm going to need some sort of light. The area beyond the door is dark though I can make out where unlit torches hang at intervals up and down the corridor.

Sliding back in my room, I grab a long piece of kindling stacked beside my fireplace and stick it in the flames long enough for it to catch. The fire cracks and pops for just a moment before I feel it's safe enough to venture back into the passageway with it. I have to be careful not to burn myself as I squeeze behind the wardrobe and through the door again, but once I step into the drafty passage there is enough room to move freely.

I use the kindling to light the first several torches I come to, and light blazes against the stone walls. When the kindling is almost burned out, I toss it to the ground and stomp it out completely. Then I lift a torch from a bracket and set out on the path ahead.

It crosses my mind once or twice that this isn't very smart. No one knows where I am, and if I'm injured or run into trouble, it could be a long time before anyone finds me. Felix would certainly have a few things to say about that, but he isn't here and my curiosity is stronger than my fear. So I keep moving forward.

Not far ahead the passage comes to the first of many forks. I'm going to have to use all my focus to keep my whereabouts and remember my way out of here. For simplicity, I decide to keep choosing the right fork each time I come to a crossroads. This decision leads me on a downward path, and the air cools with each step.

Though I use my torch to light the others along the wall, it seems darker down here than it did when I left my room. My feet stumble upon the uneven stone path, and I wonder just how deep into the castle this trail goes. It feels like I've been descending forever.

Finally, just when I've convinced myself I'll have to turn back without reaching a destination, I can just make out another wooden door in the wall ahead. This time caution slows me. If the other door led to my bedroom, it's impossible to guess where this will come out.

I press my ear against the aged wood and listen for what feels like ages. Nothing. No voices, no moving about. I kneel before the door and place my fingers under the crack between the bottom of the door and the stone. It's small, but it's enough to feel cool air on the other side. Does it lead outside the palace then?

Carefully so I don't burn myself with my still flaming torch, I lower my head to the cold stone and try to peer through the crack at the bottom of the door. It's faint, but I think I see a flicker of light.

Well, there's nothing for it but to go through. I stand and place my torch in a bracket with one I've yet to light. My fingers curl around the doorknob and begin to turn ever so slightly. I pause after each flex of my wrist, waiting to hear something on the other side of the door. Nothing happens.

After several agonizing minutes, the door clicks and I pull it open only a fraction of an inch. It's enough to see what's on the other side though, and despite my commitment to stealth, I gasp at what I see.

A life-like statue of my father stares at me from across a small circular room. Torches are already lit in here so I have no trouble making out his features carved in the same white marble that adorns the temple.

I have found my way to the crypts. Death hangs in the air here, and there are dried flower petals scattered around the base of my father's statue. Someone, likely a priestess of the temple, has been here to complete the requisite mourning rituals. Otherwise the tomb looks desolate.

Despite the storm of emotions brewing inside me, I step through the door to face my father.

The stone mason has done an amazing job rendering my father's likeness. I stare at him now with an intensity I was never permitted while he was alive. Though I look so much like my mother, I see myself in the set of his mouth and the shape of his eyes. Of course the stone effigy also accentuates the hardness of his face that I remember so well. He was never a doting father even before he turned on me and my mother.

Tears surprise me when they prick my eyes. The anger I feel is to be expected, but the sadness isn't. I want to hate him. I want to be glad he's dead. But I can't.

We parted on neutral terms at best. When he came to Aurora for the Council of Kings he also effectively ended my exile. It wasn't the reunion most people would have dreamed of, I suppose, but he did tell me I was welcome back in Borealis if I didn't win the competition for Prince Ronan's hand in marriage. Because of my stubbornness it's as much reconciliation as we'll ever get. I was too late to say goodbye or to try to make amends.

"What would you think of me now?" I whisper to the statue and the silence. "Disappointed, I'm sure."

Of course he would be. From the man who sacrificed the woman he supposedly loved to save his crown, my indecision and general weakness would be an abomination. But on some level it's always been my goal to disappoint him. Didn't I vow never to be the type of ruler my father was?

"You were right about one thing. The choices are more difficult than I imagined. I'd like to think I'd choose differently than you, but would I? I killed Levi. The only person who sought me out to tell me the truth. And I killed him to keep from being outed myself. Maybe we're not so different after all."

I sit in silence with my father's remains. And I hear the voice again. The one I delayed in listening to when it told me to head north, which resulted in the destruction of that Insurgo village.

It's time.

Two words. That's all it takes to shatter any illusion of contentment and reawaken the restlessness in my soul. I came here for a reason even if the details of that are still blurred in my mind. Even if I feel beyond unworthy. But the next step is clear. I did not come here to hide. Whatever the consequences, it's time my people met their queen.

7.

My feet fly over the stone floor as I navigate back to my room. I'm grateful I chose to keep my route simple. There will be time for further exploring later. Right now I have to see Titus and tell him what I've decided before I lose my nerve.

It has to be nearly dinner time judging by the rumbling of my stomach. Hopefully Titus is once again taking his meal in the small dining room. As soon as I reach my room I waste no time in tidying myself up. My dress has a bit of grime from the dirty stone passageway around the hem, but it'll have to do. I don't want to wait on Hannah or Cecily to come lace me into another gown. I run a brush through my hair and take a quick look in the full-length mirror. Hardly suitable for a court appearance, but it'll do.

As I did on my first morning here, I wind my way through the palace until I arrive at the informal dining room. Sure enough, one of Titus's personal guards stands outside with a long spear in his hand. I start to breeze past him, but as I reach for the door the spear comes down, blocking my way.

"His Highness is occupied, ma'am."

It's utterly inconvenient this guard doesn't know who I am. Then again, I've tried to keep a low profile for precisely that reason. No reason to maintain that now, I suppose.

"I am Princess Emilia Aurelius, and it's very urgent I speak with him."

The guard raises a skeptical brow. "I'm sorry, my lady, but my orders are to let no one enter."

I sigh. "I'm going to get through that door. Either you can move this," I tap the spear barring my entrance, "or I can move it for you."

He blinks. Once, twice. It's all I can do to keep from smiling. He doesn't know what to make of me. If Felix were here he'd whip this man for his hesitation. Fortunately Felix is otherwise occupied.

"I'm under orders..." But he seems very unsure of himself. It takes all of two seconds to duck under the spear and push my way into the dining room.

I halt when I see Titus isn't alone, and the guard who has followed me into the room crashes into me. We narrowly avoid falling to the floor in what I'm sure would have been a comical heap. Instead Titus takes one look at me and rolls his eyes.

"Is this a common practice in the Aurora court? Barging past the guards, I mean. First your Commander and now you? Really, Emilia, they are there for a reason."

"My apologies." If it were Titus alone I might have some smart retort, but I too busy studying the man sitting across the table from him.

He's older, graying, perhaps a little older than my father would be. He's stout, and it's easy to see there's plenty of muscle under the royal blue uniform he wears. The glint of medals and the royal insignia fastened to the shoulder of his cape confirms my suspicions.

"Emilia Aurelius." The man stands and offers me a cordial bow. "Or would you prefer I call you Nox?"

I bow my head deferentially. "Whatever you prefer, General."

Titus slumps back in his seat. "Well, I see there's no need to bother with introductions. I assume you two have met before?"

"Actually no," the General says as he returns to his chair. "I never had the pleasure of meeting her, but even her father couldn't enlist a princess in my army without my knowing. I've heard stories of your battlefield prowess."

"Greatly exaggerated, I'm sure." I don't know why I'm being so modest, but as I've already made an idiot of myself upon entrance, I might as well show some humility.

"Considering what easy work you made of this guard, I doubt it." General Auror laughs, and I immediately like him. His lined face brightens, and he relaxes as he takes a sip of some red liquid.

"I-I'm sorry, sir," the guard stammers. He scrambles to stand to attention. The General waves him off.

"I think you would have been the one that was sorry if you'd tried to stand in her way."

Despite the awkwardness of the situation, I smile. It feels good to be recognized for something other than my birthright or my mother's treachery.

"I apologize again for interrupting your meeting. I'll see myself out. Titus, perhaps I could speak with you tomorrow?"

"You might as well stay. If you'll agree, General, I think she may as well be updated on the situation." Titus gestures for me to take the seat next to him. I resist the urge to stick my tongue out at the guard as I sit.

"As Alector's—Caelus rest his soul—heir, I think it prudent she be apprised of what's going on around the empire," the general agreed.

Well, that's a bit of surprise. Even I didn't know if my father would name me as his heir until I saw him in Aurora. In fact, until Felix came calling at my military camp, I had assumed exile would mean a permanent abdication of the throne. Evidently that's not an assumption everyone made.

"Did you speak to my father about the line of succession?" I really should focus on whatever situation Titus and General Auror want to discuss, but I can't help but be curious about what my father might have told him. The general was rarely seen around the palace when I was a child, but he was one of the king's most trusted advisors and friends.

Auror nods. "I witnessed his signature of the document just a week before he left for Aurora. Would I had known that would be the last time I would see him. But he was very hopeful to see you in Aurora, and perhaps hoped you'd even return with him. I'm sure he would have been proud if you had been chosen to marry Crown Prince Ronan, of course."

He knew a very different version of my father. A different version even than the one that greeted me at the Council of Kings.

There was no warmth between us when we spoke. Even now as I recall that tense conversation in my room and how Felix stood ready to strike him at the slightest provocation, I shiver. Hard as the stone statue in the crypt and just as unforgiving. He'd made no apologies for his actions in my mother's death or my exile.

But he had signed an official document naming me as his heir. It's honestly more than I could have hoped for. It may be exactly what I need to overstep Titus and claim my throne.

"Speaking of the Prince..." Titus coughs conspicuously to draw my attention back to the matter at hand. "Any news of him? The poor boy was left bride-less in this whole matter."

Boy. Titus is barely older than Ronan, but I don't know why I resent his usage of the condescending moniker so much. Aren't I furious at Ronan? Why should I care how he's doing?

"No news of the Prince, I'm afraid," the general replies. "All news out of the Imperial city is being strictly controlled. More so than usual. We hear nothing except propaganda against the Insurgo rebel they say killed the kings."

Titus raises his brow. "You don't believe it?"

"With so many rumors it's difficult to know what to believe. I know our city has suffered much recently at the hands of the Insurgos, but that doesn't line up with what I've witnessed as I've toured our military camps. The small pockets of resistance we've encountered from Insurgos have mostly been due to our own provocation. As I'm sure the princess can attest, they seem to be a largely peaceful group. I find it difficult to imagine that so many isolated groups could band together to pull off an assassination of this magnitude without any of them being caught."

"I heard two were caught." Titus frowns. "The two that were foolish enough to infiltrate the palace in search of Prince Ronan."

I swallow hard. What else has Titus heard about that incident? Certainly not my involvement with it or he would have asked me before now.

"Yes," the general agrees before taking a slow sip of his drink. "But I find that curious as well. Only two men to infiltrate the palace and kill the Crown Prince? Not very well thought out." He looks sidelong at me. "I heard your Commander was the one to foil the attack against the prince. Is that true? I thought Commander Fidelis was the one who rode out to assist your father's caravan. At least that's what was reported by your father's former commander."

My dress does nothing to absorb the sweat on my palms as I try discreetly to rub my hands dry. I didn't anticipate so much chatter between those that survived my father's attack and those that were in Aurora for the attacks. I have to tread carefully here.

"Commander Fidelis did ride after my father's caravan," I concede. "On my orders. I had missed saying farewell to my father before he left and wanted to know if he would consider returning or granting me an audience so that we could bid farewell properly."

Neither Titus or the general believe me. I can tell from the looks they exchange. But they seem gracious enough to let it drop without further probing.

"It seems I am not the only one having a difficult time believing the Insurgos are capable of such organized violence," General Auror continues. "The real reason I sought this meeting, Titus, is that I'm receiving correspondence from the other nations asking if we plan to send troops in support of this crusade of the Emperor's."

So not everyone has bought into Cyrus's ruse then. And it seems not everyone is so eager to send their men to die for the Emperor's own agenda.

"Austrina has attempted to send troops but nearly a quarter of them deserted on the march. I believe Zephyros has supplied a small amount, and Euros has yet to act."

"And what is your council, General?" Titus asks.

Auror looks at me for a long moment as if sizing me up. Perhaps he expects me to interrupt with an opinion of my own. But I hold my tongue. I am the uninvited guest to this meeting, and though my first impression of the general is a good one, I'm hardly ready to reveal my feelings on the matter to him.

"This is not our war to fight," Auror finally says. "I'm not entirely sure it's anyone's. Regardless, I think this is an ill-advised time to march off to war when there is so much turmoil at home. The monarchy is unsteady, not only here, but all over the empire. Forgive me, but you have unproven leaders at the helm of each country except Aurora."

By the skepticism in his tone, I know the general finds Cyrus's motives questionable at best. But has he guessed the extent of his culpability? Perhaps, but to voice it even here would be treason of the highest order. Still I'm encouraged to find not everyone is so blindly accepting of the news that comes out of Aurora.

"It would be difficult," I saw slowly, testing out the men's reaction to my intrusion, "to fight a war against a people so scattered across the empire. A people that are adept at hiding anyway. I don't know what could realistically be gained by gathering a large army to Aurora and then marching out against the Insurgos."

Yes, I sort of do. But accusing Cyrus of seeking a likely nonexistent gate that offers immortality would probably diminish my influence here.

"Precisely." Titus nods. I don't know how much he agrees with me and how much is just relief over not having to be the first to take a stand on such a controversial topic. I don't think he would mind my Insurgo beliefs if he knew the extent of them, but he's not exactly ready to convert himself.

"Shall I send word back to Aurora that we will not be sending troops?"

"Not at this time," Titus agrees. "Let their generals know our situation here is too precarious to risk depleting our resources of military personnel."

"Very well." General Auror stands and offers a bow, first to Titus and then to me. "I'll visit the aviary to send the message right away. Then I ask your leave to return to my soldiers along the western border."

"You have it," Titus says. "Thank you for coming, General."

"The pleasure was mine." He bows again to me. "Take care, Princess."

He exits the room, and Titus and I are left alone. We sit in silence for a few moments before I remember why I was in such a hurry to see him in the first place.

"Titus, I—"

"Can it wait?" he interrupts. "I know you have something to say to me, and I know it's important. But I have an endless evening of meetings to attend, and I want to give your words a proper audience."

While it's not exactly what I want to hear, I can't fault his reasoning. So I agree and give him leave, making sure I wink at the guard on my way out of the room. He only frowns back.

I don't have to wait long for another opportunity for an audience with Titus. It's long enough though that some of my resolve has waned. With a night to sleep on things—another night filled with nightmares and cold sweats—I don't feel nearly as sure of myself as I did when I left my father's tomb yesterday.

There are so many things that could go wrong just with this conversation with Titus. No matter what he says, it seems risky to assert I'll be taking the crown from him. I'm still an outsider here, or at least I feel like one. Spending the last week trying to learn the city has only solidified that in my mind.

For such an important conversation I expect to be invited to a meal or maybe even the throne room to discuss all the unspoken things between us. Instead Titus summons me early the next morning with a request that I accompany him on a horseback ride.

It's not as if I want to refuse the request, but I do find the nature of the offer suspicious. When I reach the stables and find there are only three horses saddled, I grow even more suspicious.

I expected Titus to ride out with a full contingent of guards, but only one stands at attention just behind my cousin. Both of them are dressed in common clothes and do a well enough job of blending in. My riding leathers are fine but simple, and I'm grateful I talked Cecily out of the dress she wanted to put me in. Still I stop at the stable door and raise an eyebrow at my cousin.

"This is…unexpected."

"I thought you'd prefer less fanfare." Titus smiles as he clasps my forearm and embraces me. "Maybe one last bit of anonymity?"

So does he know my intentions? Or does he have an agenda all his own to reveal my identity to the court?

"That seems appropriate," I agree as I release him from the embrace. "It seems we have some things to discuss."

"Indeed." He turns and nods towards the guard standing stoically behind us. "My man will be accompanying us at a discreet distance today. I thought we'd take a turn though the city and then out the northern gate for a ride through the foothills. I've packed food for a lunch."

Curiosity wells up so strong within me I barely have the wherewithal to think of Felix and what he would have to say about all this. But Titus is the king, and I can hardly refuse even if I wanted to. And I don't want to.

I size up the guard joining us. He's big and muscular, but that likely means he's slow. I could take him down if I needed to and certainly I could outrun him. And Titus, well, he was never much of a fighter when we were children. I don't have any reason to believe that's changed. I can hold my own with these two even if it's not ideal to be outnumbered. Part of me is sad I have to even consider these things.

The three of us mount our horses and exit the stables toward palace's main gate. There's so much traffic here when court is in session that no one takes much notice of three more riders exiting into the city.

True to his word, Titus's guard stays a few horse lengths behind us while Titus and I keep our mounts side by side. It's not easy through some of the more crowded streets, but we mostly ride along unabated.

"The people are thriving," Titus tells me as we ride past the colorful merchant stalls. "At least financially."

"I've noticed," I say. "Everything has grown so much since I was here last."

"Including the unrest," he says softly.

I do what I can to keep my face neutral because I sense his eyes on me. This is a test, I'm sure of it, but I don't know how he wants me to answer.

"They just lost a king. Any transfer of power, no matter how peaceful, is sure to have its share of unease. In my short time here it seems to me the people like you."

"It's not me I'm worried about."

He lets the words hang until we exit the city's northern gate and take a deep breath of mountain air. These are my mountains, the same ones I was exiled to after my mother died. They are unlike the ones I just travelled through with Felix and my company if for no other reason than I feel safe here.

We continue our ride in silence until Titus pulls his mount to a stop in a meadow at the top of a particularly steep foothill. It offers little cover but does convey a good vantage point from which to see anyone approaching. I dismount and help Titus unload the basket laden with food from the palace kitchens. Our guard takes the reigns of our horses and leads them a short distance away to graze and give us our privacy, which has been the purpose of this all along. Even for the king there is nowhere completely safe in the palace from prying ears.

"What's this all about, cousin?" I ask carefully as I join Titus on a blanket and bite into a crisp apple. He reclines back on his forearms, but he looks anything but at ease.

"I think you know."

I do. But there's something more to it. Titus is dictating every part of this meeting which means it's less about what I wanted to say to him and more about what he needs to say to me. Someone or something is pressuring him to have this conversation with me, which must mean someone has discovered who I am. "What was it that gave me away?"

"You simply look too much like her. That and you have yet to attend the temple... Well, it wasn't going to take long for people to put two and two together. I did warn you."

"You did." I can't fault him for that. Still, given all those marks against me, I'm surprised it took people a week to put it all together. "And what do they want to do with me now that they know I'm my mother's daughter?"

"No one is quite sure what to do with you," he admits. "No one knows who you really are, what you stand for. They are afraid, of course, that your presence here, once known around the city, will only fan the flames of these Insurgo attacks. I think they—all of us, really—would like your assurances that you will do your best to make sure that doesn't happen."

There's no accusation in his tone, no hint of a threat. Still his words put me on guard. He, or someone, thinks I may hold some sway over the Insurgos. "You mentioned when I arrived that the city had been under attack by Insurgos, but I haven't seen any evidence of that since I've been here."

"Yes, they do seem to have become rather quiet since your arrival. But in the past few months we've had serious injuries to two of our head priestesses, a fire that destroyed some ancient texts, and the ransacking of one of the Council member's personal apartments. And of course, it goes without saying, the assassinations of each of the kings."

"Titus..." But I stop myself. Because what am I going to tell him? That instead of the Insurgos murdering the kings of four nations, it was the Emperor who ordered their executions? That knowledge earned me a death sentence in Aurora, and I don't think it would be well received here either. "Perhaps there is more to this than we realize. The general seemed to think so when we spoke yesterday."

"I agree. I don't know the Insurgos, Emilia, not like you do. There's no use in protesting. At the very least you have your mother's knowledge of them, and I'd be a fool to think your curiosity hasn't plagued you over the years. But I do hope that curiosity and knowledge might be put to use for your people."

Well, this was unexpected. No one—not Cyrus, not Titus—is reacting how I expected them to regarding the Insurgos and my return to Borealis.

"What is it you think I can do exactly?" Now is the time to choose my words carefully. One wrong admission and it's right back to the dungeons for me.

"Lead." There's a note of imploring and longing in his single word response. And I realize, like me, he's in a position he never asked to be in. "I don't know what's going on in the rest of the empire, and frankly I don't care. I need to take care of our people here and now. If you would take the crown, sit the throne, you could bridge the gap. Find out what the Insurgos want and keep the peace with them."

I take a long moment to let his words sink in. Because this seems too good to be true. "You want me to negotiate for peace with the Insurgos in the city?"

"For a start, yes."

"But I have no leg to stand on. Any peace I offer is meaningless. I'm not a queen, and no one is going to make me one simply to barter peace with the most hated people in the empire. Neither side would trust me." As I say it I realize how true it is. I have interacted with a few Insurgos in the Borealis mountains and near Aurora proper, but this group that terrorizes my city is a different breed. Clearly they are not the same peaceful people I've come to know, which means I don't trust them, and I doubt they would trust me.

"We will make them trust you." Titus sits up and takes my hands in his. "Emilia, you are the rightful ruler, the true heir. The

Council can't ignore that. Let me speak to them on your behalf, arrange a meeting. I've looked at the records. You'll come of age in a few weeks' time. What better time than this?"

Words from Levi, my mentor, come unbidden to my mind. *You can be the one to save us all. That is why you must embrace what's coming. You are who you are, you've been placed here, for such a time as this.*

How can I argue with that?

I turn away all visitors that evening. Even Felix receives a sendoff from me. With all the thoughts and questions racing through my head, I can't possibly be expected to carry on a coherent conversation with anyone. He most of all will have expectations for me to do the right thing, and right now I'm still uncertain about what that looks like.

The ever-present voice is still very insistent that this is the next step. And while that should give me some sense of relief it doesn't. I felt certain about the voice's guidance when it directed me toward that Insurgo village, but I still arrived only in time to witness destruction. Is that what's about to happen here? More destruction and catastrophe under my watch? Not if I can help it.

I spend most of the night pondering what exactly it would mean to be queen. It's a question I wrote off long ago during my exile. I swore this life was not for me and I would be happier for it. Yet here I am.

To wear the crown means to settle here. It would mean to command an army and manage a treasury and decree laws. It would also mean to pay tribute to the Emperor, go to war when necessary, and barter over trade routes. It would also mean giving up the pursuit of the Narrow Gate.

A bitter laugh escapes into my otherwise silent room. The Gate. Once again I'm considering giving up the crown for this gate that probably doesn't even exist. Just a metaphor for eternal life that Cyrus doesn't even believe in.

But what if...

No. Even Felix doesn't think the Gate is real. Why should any of the stories around it be real either. I could do some actual good here. Rather than chasing after some story I could accept my destiny as Borealis's rightful ruler and negotiate for a peace the city hasn't known in years. Even more, the Insurgos here could be free to worship openly under my rule. It's more than they could have hoped for.

But it will not save them all.

No. But it's not fair that all that be laid on my shoulders. How can that be asked of me? And will not a queen have more power to bargain for change than a fugitive on the run?

Which reminds me once again that I have no idea what Cyrus's play is in all of this. He's let me escape with basically no consequences, and told no one in Borealis of my treason against him. To what end? Would making my bid as queen only antagonize him? Or does he expect me to do just that?

Either way, I know what I must do.

A sealed note on a silver platter greets me when I wake. Someone, probably Hannah, must have brought it in when she brought the plate of pastries and fresh fruit I see sitting on the small table near my balcony. With keen interest shaking off the last vestiges of sleep, I sit up, stretch, and take the note in my hands.

It's sealed with wax and stamped with the royal seal. It's my father's design, of course. Titus hasn't had time, nor the desire I suppose, to make his own seal. Someday soon that will fall to me.

Running a fingernail under the fold, I break the wax and open the note to read. It's in Titus's own hand and is rather less informal than the packaging would suggest. He wants me to be present in court tonight. I roll my eyes at the thought.

I've attended court once since I've been back to Borealis, and while I kept a low profile and mostly meandered among the guests to eavesdrop, I'm not eager to repeat it. It reminded me too much of my time in the Aurora court—all flattery and nonsense. And then there were the tittering girls who couldn't seem to take their eyes off Felix. They passed around enough gossip about him to make me blush even though I'm sure none of it was true.

Still, Titus's note leaves little room for argument on my part. I am to attend court without making an entrance and keep to the back of the crowd. There is an announcement to be made that he wants me there for, but for some reason he doesn't want me seen. I don't like the sound of that. It reeks of deception and even danger.

With the whole day open to me until court this evening, I call Hannah and Cecily to me to share breakfast and then to help me dress. They pull one of my mother's simpler gowns from the wardrobe, and, upon seeing the pained look on my face, assure me they're having my own gowns commissioned. My aversion to my mother's clothing must be obvious.

After breakfast, because I have nothing better to do, I decide to spend the day with my ladies as they go about their plans. It turns out they have commissioned some lovely clothing for me. The three of us visit the seamstress and approve of the fabrics and designs. I even make a few suggestions for a design of my own— a split skirt with pants underneath. The seamstress looks scandalized at the thought of me wearing pants, but Hannah and Cecily just laugh and assure her it will soon become a new trend.

They're probably right. If I become queen everything, including my clothes, is going to make a statement.

We leave the seamstress and wind our way up a back staircase to exit the palace near the stables.

"Where are we going?"

Hannah and Cecily both respond with shy laughter that reminds me of those insufferable court ladies. Coming from my friends, though, it is sweet and innocent.

"When we have a few spare minutes, we like to go down the training area to watch the guards train," Cecily explains with a slight blush on her cheeks. "But we don't have to today..."

"No, I want to," I say quickly. Too quickly in fact, because Hannah and Cecily giggle again before each take one of my hands and pull me toward the barracks. I haven't seen Felix in too many days, and the prospect of seeing him in his element excites me.

No one seems to pay us much attention as we enter the small outdoor arena set aside for military and guard training. To my annoyance there are other women present, some of which I recognize from court. They could be here for any number of reasons, but it seems their eyes linger on Felix longer than any of the other soldiers.

But who could blame them? My eyes find him immediately as Hannah, Cecily, and I take up a position leaning against the wall that hems in the training arena. He's dressed in his usual pants and shirt, but the shirt is partially untucked and dirty due, I'm sure, to repeated rounds of sparring with his guards.

He walks among the sparring pairs of men, shouting correction or encouragement to them as his eyes scan their every movements. Some pairs fight with weapons, others with their bare hands, but Felix gives them all equal attention. He is fully in charge here, and it makes my heart swell with pride.

Something seems to draw his attention away from the men he's been coaching, and he looks my direction. When he sees me, a wide grin breaks out on his bearded face. It's such a rare moment of vulnerability that I want to freeze it so it can last a little longer.

He calls Antony over to him and imparts some instruction before Antony takes his place meandering through the men. Felix walks confidently toward me without a glance over his shoulder.

"My lady," he says with a careful side eye glance at the courtiers standing near me. I know he's just trying to conceal my identity, but I would love to hear him call me by my name right now.

"The guards look impressive," I commend. And truthfully they do. Much better than that guard of Titus's that I easily bypassed yesterday.

"Thank you," he replies. His eyes take a long moment to look me up and down, during which I feel laid bare before him. "You are very overdressed for a training session. To what do I owe the pleasure?"

I straighten my dress and pray the heat I feel rushing up me isn't plainly obvious on my face. "I'm accompanying Hannah and Cecily today, and they wanted to see the guards. I can't imagine why."

It's a lame attempt at a joke, but Felix glances over his shoulder at the men, and then back at me with a smile.

"Yes, I do see them down here a lot. I thought at first they were spying on me for you, but I don't think they've even noticed I'm here."

Sure enough, I look over to see Hannah and Cecily whispering to each other, occasionally pointing to a particular guard. I'm still fairly certain there is something between Hannah and Antony, though I've never asked her about it, but there is no shortage of options among the well-muscled men.

"If I wanted to spy on you, I definitely wouldn't send someone else to do it."

"No, you wouldn't." He smiles again. I've forgotten just how much that simple act changes his looks. "So what really brings you here? Did you purposely wear that dress so I wouldn't pull you down here and ask you to demonstrate your skills to the guards?"

"I could still fight in this dress."

"Yes, but Cecily would be scandalized for you to ruin something so beautiful."

We both laugh, and I feel the stares of the courtiers on me. I'm making a few enemies by capturing Felix's attention, but I just can't bring myself to care. After several days of little to no contact, it feels good just to be in his presence again.

"I do need to speak to you...privately." I lower my voice to make sure we're not overheard. "I have news to share. Big news."

He raises dark brows and nods. "Can you give me an hour? I have to take the men on a run, and then we'll be finished for the day."

"Of course," I say, though I'm burning to tell him everything now. "I'll meet you back here when you're finished."

"I can come to you," he offers.

"No," I say too quickly. I'm afraid he'll be accosted by one of these ladies when training is over, and I don't want anything to delay our conversation further. "I'll come back."

I manage to pull Cecily and Hannah away from training by promising I'll return with them another day. They eagerly accompany me to the stables where we all dote on Athena and brush her mane while she nips at an apple Cecily feeds to her. My horse seems to be happy here so long as she can keep Felix's horse, Ares, in her sights. I don't fail to notice the irony there.

After nearly an hour I ask my ladies to return to my room to prepare a bath and a simple gown for court this evening. Both are hesitant to leave me alone, but when I tell them I'm meeting Felix they happily excuse themselves with knowing smiles.

When I return to the training arena, I'm pleased to see the court ladies are gone. Probably already at home and primping for this evening's court appearance. Whatever the reason, nothing now stands between me and Felix who waits for me while leaning against one of the short stone walls.

"Commander," I say deferentially as I approach him. There are still a few guards milling around, and I don't want to appear more familiar with Felix than would be appropriate in front of them.

He pushes off the wall and gives me a slight bow before offering his arm. I take it, but not as tightly as I normally would. Instead I just let my fingers lightly rest on his forearm as we walk away from the arena.

The silence between us is comfortable enough despite the anticipation buzzing through me. Once we are out of sight of the guards, I drop Felix's arm and we resume a more comfortable gait and posture.

"I met General Auror yesterday."

"Yes, I did hear something about you making a fool of a palace guard while interrupting a meeting between Titus and the general."

"You only find it amusing because the guard isn't one of your men," I accuse.

"True. One of my men would have never let you pass. I've warned them all how stubborn you are and taught them how to employ countermeasures."

I stop just outside of the stables and glare at him. "Is that so?"

"It is. Sometimes I think the person you most need protecting from is yourself."

I can't exactly argue with that so I change the subject. "Well, I did meet the general, and I heard some interesting news from Aurora."

At the mention of the capitol, Felix's smile fades into a hard look.

"It seems not everyone in the empire is eager to engage in Cyrus's war with the Insurgos. General Auror said that Euros has declined to send troops. Zephyros sent a small amount, and several of the ones ordered from Austrina deserted along the march."

"And where does Borealis stand officially?"

"Titus has declined to send men. The general agreed it was for the best." I look around to see if we have company. Even though we are alone, I still lower my voice. "I think he has his doubts about Cyrus's motives."

"Well, that certainly is unexpected." Felix scratches his beard as he considers the information. "Is that your big news?"

"No, actually." I nod my head toward the palace, and we begin walking again. "But I thought you'd want to know about the mood in the other countries even though I'm not sure exactly what it means for us yet."

He only nods in response as we near the palace. We pass a few men, coachmen by the look of them, loitering in the courtyard, and they each give me an appraising look. Felix rests one hand on the pommel of his sword and hurries me into the palace.

"Am I going to have to beg you to tell me this big news?" he asks after we've reentered the palace through the same door Hannah, Cecily, and I exited earlier.

"I've decided to become queen."

I drop the words casually as if I'm simply telling him I've decided to take up cross stitching…which is just about as ridiculous a proposition. To his credit, his step beside me doesn't falter, and when I chance a glance at him, I see the hint of a smile beneath his neatly trimmed beard.

"I knew you would."

"How could you possibly know when I didn't know myself?"

"Because it's who you are. And how could you be anything but you?"

I contemplate that for a moment. Is he right? Because it wasn't a decision I came to easily. Felix has always been more certain of me than I have been of myself.

"So is that what this big court announcement is about?" he asks. I raise my brows in question and he adds, "those court ladies couldn't stop speculating about it. And loudly."

I resist the urge to roll my eyes, but don't hide the annoyance on my face very well.

"They're harmless," Felix laughs. "This isn't Aurora, and they aren't those Zephyros princesses. I don't think you have anything to worry about where these ladies are concerned."

Ah, yes. Cassia and Gloriana, the Zephyros princesses who were with me in the Aurora court, were ruthless and cruel. Murderers, too, I suspect though I could never prove it. I would agree with him that these women are not dangerous on that level, but that doesn't mean they might not threaten one of the things I value most in this world. This sort of jealousy is a very new feeling.

"What were they saying about the announcement?" It feels safer to change the subject.

"Just speculation. I don't think they know anything. One of them was hoping Titus was going to announce a competition to be his bride like the one held in Aurora."

These are the women my father should have sent to compete for Ronan's hand. Not me. They would have been more than willing to represent Borealis for a chance to be queen, and I would still be somewhere in the north mountains with my military brigade.

But then there would be no Felix. No Hannah or Cecily.

"I think we can rule that possibility out." I try to laugh as if this whole thing is just a joke, but it comes out as more of a choked sound. "But no, I don't think tonight's announcement has anything to do with me being queen. Titus and I have discussed it—agreed upon it—but there are still hoops to jump through. He hasn't met with the Council yet to announce his intentions to abdicate so I doubt he'd be so foolish as to announce it to the whole court first."

"Well, he is your cousin."

"What's that supposed to mean?"

"Only that it does sound more than a bit like something you would do. A keen bit of strategy if you ask me. Announce it to a room full of the country's most powerful people as if it's already written in stone. I imagine even the Council would have a difficult time taking that back."

He's right. A bold and risky move, but a strategic one. And not one, I think, Titus would have the courage to make. No, this is something else. Still, I file Felix's idea away for future consideration.

"Whatever it is, Titus sent me a note this morning asking me to attend. But he wants me to remain inconspicuous. So I don't imagine he's planning on introducing me to the court, but don't know what to make of it."

Felix frowns as we reach the hallway that leads to our rooms. "I don't like it. If he wants you to know the information without making yourself known why not just tell you in person? Or include it in the note he sent you?"

"I don't know, but there must be a reason."

Felix stops me with a hand on my arm, and we pause just outside of his room. "Do you trust him?"

Do I? Maybe I shouldn't, but... "Yes. As much as I trust anyone but you."

"Then we'll attend court tonight. There's a servant's entrance we can use to enter after everyone has been announced."

We agree to meet at 8:00, and we both retire to our rooms. My bath Hannah drew for me has cooled slightly during my meandering walk with Felix, but it's still comfortable enough for me to undress and soak for a while.

When my skin is wrinkly from soaking and I can't sit still any longer, I dry myself off and pull a full-length satin robe around me. This was not my mother's. It's something new Cecily must have laid out for me. It makes me smile. In the midst of everything that's happened, God has surrounded me with amazing people.

I run my hands up and down the smooth fabric as I step out on my balcony to feel the cool breeze on my skin. It prickles my flesh in a pleasant way as strands of my unbound hair sweep across my face. I tuck them back as I hear a familiar voice coming from the room next to mine. Felix.

I shouldn't eavesdrop, but his balcony door is open and it's not that difficult to hear him from this close. He's inside his room somewhere, and I wonder who he's talking to. Crossing my small balcony, I lean on the railing closest to his room and close my eyes in concentration.

It takes a moment to realize what I'm hearing, but something surges through me when I do. He's praying.

"Nothing exceeds Your power. Nothing is too hard for You to do or too good for You to give. I know I ask much, but I ask great things of a great God."

Power—the kind I felt in the mountains that left me weak—rushes inside me with such force that I feel dizzy. My heart pounds in my chest as something within me reacts to Felix's prayer. It reminds me of times I heard my mother pray as a child, but this is something so much stronger.

I want to hear more, but Cecily calls my name from inside my room, and I hurry to her before Felix can step on the balcony and catch me eavesdropping.

She and Hannah dress me in another one of my mother's gowns and twist my hair into a simple but elegant style. The dress is navy and simply adorned, and we all agree that it makes me look well-born enough to belong in court, but not ostentatious enough to stand out.

When a clock tower in the distance strikes eight, I step into the hall to find Felix waiting on me. I wait for that feeling that struck me on the balcony to hit again, but it doesn't. Still, I struggle to look him in the eyes. Fortunately he takes my reaction as a sign of nerves.

"I won't let anything happen to you tonight." He doesn't offer his arm, and I'm grateful for it. Not because I don't want to be near, but because I don't want the formality of it.

"I know." And I do.

Both of us stay lost in our own thoughts as Felix leads me down a back staircase to a side entrance to the throne room. I smell the savory hint of food on the air and assume the kitchens must be close by, which makes sense if this is the way the servants enter and exit. They must all be walking around the throne room with trays of food at the moment because the hall to the entrance is deserted.

Felix raises his brows to me in a silent question, and I nod in response. I take a deep breath as he pulls the door open and we step into the crowd just beyond.

The entrance puts us near the back of the room where the crowd is thinner, but I still take Felix's arm to keep us from being separated. No one seems to notice as we make our way forward until we can stand against a column and remain out of the way.

"I have news," Titus booms. His voice rings loud and clear around the perfectly built acoustics of the main throne room. It's where he's chosen to gather court today, and the long hall is lined with finely dressed men and women who've fallen silent at his words. He stands at the front of the room on a dais, still looking like a bit of an imposter in front of my father's throne. "News from the Imperial throne."

All heat drains from my face as dread pools in my stomach. Beside me, Felix grasps my forearm so hard it hurts. But I don't pull away. He's just as terrified as I am. This is the moment we've been anticipating. Cyrus has decided that we've run free long enough.

"Our Great Emperor Cyrus, Defender of the Faith, Father of Atlas sends his greetings and blessings to the people of Borealis. He also wishes us to know he still mourns with us in the loss of our great king and his dear friend King Alector."

All around the room people bow their heads and mumble an automatic blessing at the mention of my father's name. It doesn't feel the least bit genuine, but I hardly have time to ponder what that means about the mood of the nobles concerning the monarchy because Titus continues.

"In the wake of such tragedy, Emperor Cyrus is glad to bring good tidings to us from Euros, Austrina, and Zephyros. In the interest of promoting stability and commitment to unity, each of these countries has recently held a coronation for their new king. Atlas is once again strong against our enemies. With such strong rulers we will take swift action against those who plotted to destabilize us. We will show them we are strong and united."

Titus pauses, takes a deep breath that raises his shoulders, and finds my eyes in the crowd. There's an apology in his gaze that lets me know I'm going to like what follows even less than the words that preceded it.

"The Emperor is very much looking forward to celebrating Borealis as we crown our new monarch in the coming weeks. He is being lenient with the timing because he knows there may be many details to finalize before we crown the empire's first queen."

Murmurs sweep through the hall like a wave, soft at first then building to a low din that Titus must silence with a raise of his hand. Felix pulls me closer to him, and we take a few steps back until we are nearly hidden behind thick drapes of fabric swathed between the columns. No one seems to have recognized me, but that doesn't stop me from feeling exposed.

"According to Emperor Cyrus, Her Royal Highness Princess Emilia Aurelius will be arriving in Borealis from Aurora. Having spent weeks in the Imperial court as a candidate for Prince Ronan's bride, she will now come to Borealis as a daughter of King Alector, heir to the throne. Long may she reign."

The crowd of nobles and courtiers absolutely erupts this time. No whispers or murmurs, but shouts greet Titus's words. Felix and I don't stay to hear what's being said. Even if I'd wanted to, Felix has grabbed my hand and pulled me past the drapes, out of the side door of the throne room and into an alcove where we can do nothing but stare at each other with wide eyes.

"What is he playing at?" My words come out as a gasp, my chest heaving. The panic claws at me from within, and it terrifies me more that I can see it reflected in Felix's eyes.

"What do you want to do?" he asks. "Say the word and I'll get you out of here tonight."

"We can't keep running. Maybe if it were just you and I, but it's not." What I wouldn't give for it to be. Felix and I on the run but together would be a dream come true compared to this situation. But there's a long game that must be played here. Cyrus is playing it... is Ronan? I can't help but think of the letter he wrote me. He had an agenda separate from his father's, or so he would have me believe. What are the chances he's involved in this latest development?

"Felix..." For so many reasons I'm hesitant to bring up the prince's name. It's remained unspoken between us but still a constant barrier. Giving voice to it now could make things immeasurably more difficult. "Do you think Ronan could have..."

I'm not exactly sure what I'm asking, but Felix doesn't make me finish.

"I don't know. It seems unlikely though that he'd be able to change his father's mind so drastically and so quickly."

I nod because I know he's right. He knows Ronan better than anyone, and he's been privy to the dynamic between the Prince and Emperor for more years than most. I'm not even sure Ronan would *want* to change his father's mind. There's still a huge part of me that remains skeptical about the sincerity of that letter.

"So we're left with Cyrus. What does he have to gain by putting me on the throne? It would have been just as easy—probably easier—for him to announce me as a traitor conspiring with the Insurgos and order me to be arrested on sight. Instead he practically issues an imperial decree for my coronation."

"We know he wants information on the Gate more than anything. He must think he can use you more effectively as a pawn than as an Insurgo martyr. There's something he needs from you, and only you, or we would both be dead by now."

"That's what terrifies me. I'm no closer to knowing any more about this Gate, and I'm being pulled in so many different directions. What is the goal here, Felix? Do I try to learn more about the Gate? Do I throw all my efforts into making Borealis a safe place for Insurgos? And why are the Insurgos here so violent? I have more questions than answers, and I don't even know which one to address first."

Felix grabs my wildly gesturing hands and stills them in his own. After a moment we both take slow, shaky breaths.

"First you address the crown," he says. "Go see Titus in the morning. You need to know how he feels about all this. Even if he meant to peacefully give up the crown, this may have wounded his pride. Tomorrow I'll ask around about the Insurgos with the palace guard. You and I can meet tomorrow evening and share our information."

I nod, feeling a little calmer. At least we have a plan. It's not much of one, but it's a next step.

"Let's get you back to your room. I'm going to have Antony and a few others patrol the corridors tonight just in case anyone who has worked out your identity gets any ideas after that announcement. I'd like for you to take dinner in your rooms with Hannah and Cecily. Will you agree?"

"If you'll join us. Antony, too," I insist.

"Agreed." He pauses and tilts his head slightly to look me over. "I must say you're making this easier than I thought you would. You usually fight me when I try to protect you."

"I'm scared," I admit softly as I bow my head to keep from meeting his eyes. As I do, his strong arms wrap gently around me and pull me against him for a hug. I let my arms wind around his back and hold on for dear life as he presses his face against my hair and whispers two words that chill me despite his heat.

"Me, too."

9

I don't have to seek Titus out the next morning. Almost as soon as I am dressed, before I can even ring for breakfast to be brought to me, there's a knock at my door.

"Who is it?" I call in what I hope is a brave voice. Surely if someone has come to harm me they're not going to bother to knock.

"It's me," Titus answers with annoyance. "Will you call off your guards and let me in?"

I laugh at the thought of Antony and the others barring the regent king from entering my room. No wonder Titus has an inferiority complex. My entourage has hardly treated him like royalty.

"It's all right, Antony," I call. "Let him in."

Seconds later the door opens and Titus strolls in, dusting his clothes as if Antony might have wrinkled them. The tall soldier enters the room behind the king, looking to me for direction.

"Just outside the door is fine," I tell him. "See that we are not disturbed."

"Yes, your Highness." Antony bows himself out the room and shuts the door behind him.

"Well, you've certainly got a loyal palace guard. That's a good start." Titus helps himself to one of the plush chairs near the balcony and looks up at me with a rueful childish grin. "We've gotten ourselves in a mess now, haven't we?"

"I'm not sure I'm willing to take the blame for this one," I say as I sit in the chair opposite him. Unlike him I don't relax. "What were you thinking? Reading that announcement to the entire court without any sort of warning? I mean, you could have at least warned me."

"There wasn't any time." His handsome face takes a serious turn. "The imperial messenger was instructed to remain until I had read the contents of the letter to the Borealis court. He was to report back to the Emperor that I announced everything just as it was written." He pauses as if to let those words sink in. "Emilia, what did you do?"

A retort is on my tongue before I can process it, but I bite it back just in time. This is not Felix I'm speaking to. As much as I want to trust my cousin, I have to be careful. Allegiances are fickle things when crowns are involved.

"I imagine I've pleased the Emperor in some way if he wants me to become queen." It's hard for me to even choke those words out.

"Emilia," Titus deadpans. "He had me throw you to the wolves. You heard the way the court responded. To be queen, yes, but to announce it like that? What else could have been expected? Even if they grow to love you the nobles cannot be expected to take well to surprises on the heels of a tragedy like the death of your father."

"What do you propose then?"

"I don't know yet. I'm meeting with the Council this morning, but I wanted to know how you felt about things before I did so."

And how do I feel? Cyrus has all but handed me the one thing I wanted and that terrifies me. So do I accept it with guarded thanks? Or run the other way into more questions with no sense of direction? It seems obvious what I have to choose.

"I want what is best for the people of Borealis. If I can bring peace and reconciliation between them and the Insurgos—and I believe I can—then I need to take my place as queen."

"I was hoping you'd say that. The idea of a queen may be a difficult sell to some members of the Council, but you have much to offer the people. I believe they can be convinced."

"Let us hope so."

That afternoon another sharp knock on my door jolts me from a brief rest. I don't even have time to respond before the door swings open. I'm on my feet in an instant, readying for a fight before my mind registered a frazzled Titus standing in front of me.

"Emilia," he nearly pants as if he's run here. "You have to come to the Council meeting this evening."

I take a few calming breaths and decide if he's this disconcerted, I must remain cool and level headed.

"And why would I want to do that? You seem to have everything well in hand." And that may be a lie but I don't really want anything to do with the council of men who likely advised my father to send me away in the first place. And it was so nice, for however short a period of time, to think that Titus could simply deal with them for me until everything was wrapped up nicely.

"They are insistent upon seeing you if you have any hope of sitting upon that throne. I may be a sitting monarch, but there is only so much I can do against them."

Titus was not born for the crown. His lack of confidence in his own authority makes that clear. But he may also have a point. The Council is comprised of five men who represent the people of Borealis. Each one of them commands their own loyal following. All are loyal to the crown in theory, but I imagine they only need to see a sign of weakness in order to begin to plot a new dynasty. No matter what Emperor Cyrus has suggested, Borealis is a sovereign nation and as such may choose its own monarch. I don't really see a way out of this.

"Very well then." I sigh and set my shoulders back to straighten my posture. "You may let them know I will be available this evening after Commander Fidelis returns from training the guard. He will escort me."

"He can't."

Titus grimaces as if he's afraid this will wound me. Certainly it surprises me. It's well known Felix is my near constant companion and the chief protector of my well-being. Of course I would want him with me at the Council meeting. It's not up for negotiation.

"Titus," I sigh, "we both know I'm going to tell Commander Fidelis everything that's said in that meeting. Couldn't we just save me the trouble of having to remember the nuance of it all and let him sit in on the meeting himself? I'll ask him not to speak if that's the problem."

Titus shakes his head. "That's certainly not the problem. Emilia, surely you remember that no military personnel are allowed in the council room. They are very strict on that rule."

Men and their ridiculous rules. "What do they possibly have against the military?"

"You really don't remember?" He roughs a hand over his face. "We learned about it in our tutoring as children. Our great-grandfather brought his guards to a high stakes meeting and had the entire Council slaughtered because he feared they were going to overthrow him. Because of that, no one with formal military training is allowed in that room. If one turns on the other five, they all want the odds in their favor."

I'm dumbstruck, but only for a moment. "Then what do they think I did for those years when I was exiled? I was at the military camps. I was a soldier."

"But you are a woman."

I glare at him with a wave of white-hot anger rising up inside me. Felix would tell me to be silent, to use this to my advantage. But Felix isn't here.

"I have trained with the best. I could put daggers between each of their eyes and walk out without a drop of blood on me."

Felix himself taught me daggers, and the Borealis officers saw my potential early on and trained me among the elite ranks of soldiers. I am more than capable of holding my own with a few old men who probably haven't held their own swords in years.

Titus looks as if he might be sick, but he recovers quickly. "This is why they need to see you. Our kingdom has never seen a woman as strong as you, and we've never had a queen in our recorded history. Though I would gladly give you your crown, the Council will not acquiesce so easily. They must see how strong you are and that you are more than capable of leading our people."

Ah. There's the problem.

I'm not sure I'm capable of leading these people. But I have to try, if for no other reason than the Council needs to see that a woman—this woman—can be a force to be reckoned with. Of course I do have other reasons. Ones that will become readily apparent with time.

"I will accompany you to the meeting," I finally agree. It feels like a concession on my part, and it's much too early to be conceding anything when I haven't even begun to negotiate for my crown. Not a good sign.

"Am I going to have to search you for daggers before we go in?" He's smiling, and I can't tell if he believes I'm capable of what I claim or not.

"You would be foolish not to," I say with a sweet smile of my own. Then I leave him standing in the corridor to puzzle over my words.

Felix has not returned from training by the time I am to meet Titus for the Council meeting. I had hoped to at least inform him of this new development before I left, but I settle for leaving him a short note in his room before joining Titus for the long walk to the Council's chambers.

We take the walk mostly in silence, occasionally reminiscing about a particular game we would play in a certain area of the palace when we were children. But we avoid the impending discussions at all costs. I supposed we'll get to them soon enough.

Sooner than I would like we're in an area of the palace I was never allowed to visit as a child. It housed my father's study, the headquarters of the palace guard, and of course the council chambers.

The council room is much smaller than I imagined it would be. As a child it was strictly off-limits to me. My father spent countless hours there making all sorts of decisions and deals with these men who helped rule our country. But it was no place for a lady. He told me as much once. But here I am now, the lady in the midst of the Council.

We are the last to arrive, and I think this is by design. Still all the men look at me as if I am some entity they've never encountered before. I feel that's a quite likely scenario, and they don't even know the half of it.

Nevertheless Titus escorts me into the room and gives me a seat next to his at the head of the table. Something inside me balks at this, but I have not earned a seat at the head of the table. Yet.

One of the men, about my father's age with a liberal sprinkling of silver hair at his temples, rises and offers me a bow that amounts to not much more than a nod of his head. "My lady."

"Highness," I correct before he can even return to his seat. Though I'm not one for titles with those who know me, this disrespect cannot be permitted. "I am the daughter of King Alector and therefore your princess, am I not?"

"Forgive me, but that remains to be seen, Highness."

What?

I look from Titus to the man and back again. My cousin doesn't seem surprised by this, and maybe I shouldn't be either. After all, Titus did tell me the Council had doubts about my ability to rule. I assumed that would be based on me being a woman, or that I'm suspected of being an Insurgo sympathizer. But their approach is much simpler.

The simplest way to keep that privilege from me is to just deny who I really am. I'm just not used to anyone looking at me and not being able to see I'm my mother's daughter. Usually that's a bad thing, but I was counting on it here.

"And just how would you have me prove my identity to you if that's what you require of me? Certainly the word of my cousin is enough."

"Even if you are our princess, you have been absent for court for so long. Forgive me, Highness, but no one knows you or if you're suitable for our throne. The laws of an interregnum—"

"Your throne?" Though it's something I wasn't sure I wanted ten minutes ago, I suddenly decide I will sit on that throne if only to spite this man.

"Let's get down to business, shall we?" Titus smoothly puts an end to what would have been an epic argument. Perhaps he is remembering what I said about being able to kill them all without getting a drop of blood on me. "Lord Orrin, call the meeting to order please."

"Very well. The right and noble Council of Borealis under the direction of Prince Titus, Regent of our great nation, is hereby called to order."

There's a slight echo to his words as they bounce off the high ceilings and close walls. I have to wonder who they are to benefit since no one seems to be writing down the official call to order or taking notes of any kind. Perhaps they are merely meant to assert Titus's place of authority and my lack thereof.

"Yes, thank you, Orrin," Titus says. "As my dear cousin has already mentioned, I'd like to discuss her position as queen."

The five other men around the table exchange dubious looks. Orrin clears his throat. I'm starting to wonder if the other four are even capable of speech. "You have to understand, Highness, that our country has never had a sovereign queen."

"But the law does provide for it. And His Majesty King Alector was very clear in his intention that Princess Emilia was his one true heir."

The memory of my last conversation with my father is not something I've allowed myself to think on often. It's locked away in the part of my brain where I stored Levi's death and my mother's. But it seems lately that the lock is irreparably broken and those memories keep sneaking out when my guard is down.

"That is true but—"

"We have our reservations," a short round man interrupts Orrin. "Forgive me, Princess, but you haven't spent any time in our fair city since you were a child. And the circumstances of your departure were…less than desirable."

"Less than desirable? For who exactly? Could you possibly be under some sort of delusion that I had a choice in the matter?" Anger rips through me like the slice of a knife as my words startle the Council members. Perhaps they expected me to stay silent. I will not.

"Not a choice, no, Highness. But it was Caelus's will you be sent away. If you had remained here you would have been trained in the ways of a princess, groomed to be the leader of our country. We must have the country's best interest at heart. Under no circumstances can we afford a diplomatic incident when you interact with the other nations. Forgive me, but your manners leave something to be desired."

Titus grabs my hand and squeezes so hard that a yelp comes out of my mouth instead of the sharp retort I was planning.

"If it was Caelus's will to send her away, it was also his will to bring her home," he says before I can recover. "And she has spent weeks in Aurora, being groomed by the Empress and making powerful allies with the other nations and, most importantly, the crown prince. She holds sway with him as I never could."

"Yes, well, a beautiful woman may charm a prince, but will he negotiate trade routes and taxes with her?" Orrin looks around as if daring someone to answer him.

"We need a strong leader," the round man says. "One who can anticipate what the country needs and knows how to obtain it."

"And you've already decided I'm not that person."

"No one is saying you cannot become that person with some aid from the right person."

"What exactly are you saying?"

"We would agree to your coronation if you can make an advantageous match."

"Match? You don't mean—"

"Marriage, Highness," Orrin interjects. "You need to choose a consort who will revitalize the country and the monarchy. You need someone who will help the people accept you and forget about your connection to your mother."

Forget my mother? Titus doesn't have to work to silence me now because no words come. I'm at a loss. The reminder is a sharp stab to my gut. Not the reminder of her memory, which is never far from me, but of how the Council and my people remember her. A treasonous queen.

Some of the fight leaches out of me. The more I argue the more they see my mother—or at least the image of her my father and Emperor Cyrus worked hard to create. And if they see me as her, not only do I have no hope of wearing the crown but I have little hope of leaving this city alive.

"Do you have any suitors in mind?" Titus asks. I feel his eyes on me and know he's wondering why I'm suddenly so quiet in the face of such a huge issue.

"Zephyros has a prince, a second son, who shows promise. There are also a few sons of Lords from northern Austrina and a Count from Euros. We will extend a formal invitation to each and welcome them to the palace so you can meet each of them."

"The Emperor expects my coronation soon, doesn't he?" I can't believe I'm about to use Cyrus as my bargaining chip. "Perhaps to please him we might go ahead with the coronation and deal with matrimonial matters afterward." If at all.

"Borealis is a proud nation with old traditions," Orrin insists. "The Emperor understands there are...issues to be worked out before you may sit on the throne. Besides, you are not even of age."

And not one of them seems to see the irony in holding that against me while also asking me to marry.

"She will be of age in a little more than two weeks," Titus speaks up. "We'll throw a ball then to celebrate her birth and have all the suitors attend. A masquerade ball. Then they can officially present themselves for consideration before the court the next day."

The men nod in solemn agreement, but I don't like it. It sounds very much like the charade I was thrust into in the Imperial court when I was meant to be competing for Ronan's hand. That obviously didn't end well. I don't have high hopes this will either. But of course no one cares about my opinion.

I barely listen as they set about dividing the tasks of arranging the ball, contacting the suitors, and scheduling my official presentation to the court. Because, of course, everyone will be clamoring for a glimpse of their mysterious princess after an absence of so long. Especially now that the Emperor has implied she will be their queen.

The thoughts in my head tangle like a bowl of yarn, hopelessly knotted and frayed. I don't even know where to begin to process this. I expected some opposition from the Council. Maybe even being asked to jump through some hoops. But, perhaps naively, marriage never entered my mind. And if it had I would have just pushed it away. Because with that thought comes a tidal wave of feelings that I can't do anything with. Not anything productive anyway. But they bring to mind a face, a face I'm desperately yearning to see, and suddenly I can't get out of that room fast enough.

I rise to my feet, pushing my chair back so fast it nearly topples over. The men look up, startled from their plans

"Emilia?" Titus asks, a hint of concern in his voice.

"If that's all you require of me this evening I'll be going." I somehow manage to keep my voice from shaking. "Please let me know when the arrangements are finalized." I don't wait for them to agree before I turn on my heels and exit the room, not caring if it makes me look decisive or overly emotional. Honestly, I'm sure I could do nothing to please them today.

My feet somehow find their way back to a more familiar area of the palace, though I can't remember how I got there. Thoughts of marriage and crowns and masquerade balls occupy all of my headspace at the moment, but I'm grateful that some intrinsic part of me seemed to be paying attention when Titus led me to the

Council chambers. I finally stop to take a shaky breath in front of the tapestry that Hannah, Cecily, and I admired what feels like ages ago on our tour of the palace.

The hallway is empty, though there are presumably guards stationed nearby, so I allow myself a moment to sink to the floor. With my back pressed against the tapestry, I close my eyes and rest my head back against the wall.

God, this can't be your plan.

I hadn't realized how much I'd been hoping to do this on my own since I left Ronan behind. Marriage to him would have been a means to an end—though my feelings about it were nothing short of complicated—but not precisely the resolution I'd hoped for when I started all this when Levi told me those troubling words all those months ago in my tent. Words that set all this in motion and gave me this stupid idea that I was somehow meant to be a deliverer of these people.

Somewhere along the way I'd come to believe it. Maybe because Felix and Hannah believed it, too. And here in Borealis, with my own country and my own crown, this seemed like a better way. But the Council wants to take even that away from me. I won't be allowed to rule as the sole monarch. At the very least a King Consort will sit at my side. What if they want to make him king? Then this has all been for nothing.

"Why?" I whisper, still not trusting completely in my solitude. "Why bring me all this way just to put me in the same situation?"

Trust Me.

The voice is so loud in my head that I open my eyes and look around for the owner. Of course the hallway is still empty, but the ringing of the clear tone still echoes in my ears. God wants me to trust Him.

Did He say the same thing to my mother?

Suddenly I can't stand to be near the tapestry that reminds me of her anymore. I push myself to my feet and lift my skirts to take off at a run back toward my room. But my quarters are not my destination. There's only one person I want to see, and I hope he's returned from his training by now.

The sound reverberates down the deserted hallway as I pound on Felix's door. I don't pause between knocking, and suddenly the door is pulled open, and I nearly hit Felix in the chest. He catches my fist deftly and pulls me inside after a quick glance up and down the hall. He releases me as soon as he shuts the door behind me.

The room is identical to mine in structure, but as different as can be in content. Where there are dresses and jewels and books scattered on every available surface in my room, it's difficult to tell anyone occupies Felix's room at all. Much like his quarters in Aurora, it's clean and tidy, and I'm fairly certain that's due more to his diligence than the maids' cleaning. His few clothes are all hidden away, and his even fewer possessions aren't noticeable at all. What is noticeable—or perhaps I'm just biased considering the news I've just received—is the large bed against the wall his room shares with mine.

"Would you be more comfortable on the balcony?"

I hadn't realized I was staring at the bed so intently, but Felix noticed. Do I imagine the slight flush to his cheeks? I get a good look at him for the first time and notice his freshly washed hair curling at the nape of his neck, the partially buttoned shirt, and his bare feet. He's clearly just finished his bath, and I have to fight a blush of my own.

"Yes," I reply truthfully, "but we need the privacy. I don't want anyone to overhear this."

He sobers and gestures for me to sit on the bed. I hesitate but breathe a sigh when he pulls a chair from across the room and places it opposite me. Felix sits in it as I lower myself to the plush mattress. It sinks gently below me and releases a faint scent I've come to think of as Felix's.

"What did you think of the Council?"

His question jolts me out of my comfortable warmth and back to the foreboding present. Of course he got my note and must have been anticipating a summary of the meeting, though probably not like this. I take a deep breath and gather myself.

"They are a bunch of old men who have no idea what their people want and what sort of ruler this country needs." That much is certainly true.

Felix frowns. "Did they fight Titus on his decision to step down?"

"Surprisingly no. In fact they might have been happy about it until they met me. I get the sense that Titus is too radical for their taste, but I'm so far beyond him that they look at me as if I'm something they've never seen before."

"You are something they've never seen before. A powerful woman with a brilliant mind and a fierce spirit. They won't understand you." His dark eyes shine with pride and a fierceness of his own, and I can feel my stoicism melting.

"I wish you could have been there."

"So do I."

"They might change their minds on allowing guards if they think you'll keep me in check." I smile weakly and he returns it. "They don't like having their ideas challenged."

"Well they were doomed to dislike you then."

So much passes between us without a word. How can I possibly tell him about the Council's decision? Foolishly perhaps, I had thought that now we were away from Ronan, Felix might come to care for me even if I was his queen. Now something just as large stands between us.

"Felix?"

"Yes?"

"They want me to get married."

Silence. I see the muscles in his neck tighten, but the rest of him remains just as visibly unchanged. I'm disappointed and ashamed. I selfishly hoped for more of a reaction, though to what end I'm not sure.

"To whom?" he finally asks, his tone even and giving nothing away.

"I don't know yet. They are willing to let me choose so long as they approve the choice. They don't think I can sit the throne on my own. It's ridiculous I know, but if this is the course we're taking, if I want to make a difference here, I don't see how I can get around this."

Nevermind that Titus has been allowed to sit on the throne, unmarried, for the preceding weeks without one hint of wedding bells. Maybe it has nothing to do with me being a woman. Perhaps they would have treated a formerly exiled prince the same way.

But I don't think so. Because this is about me making strong alliances and having a steady hand to help guide me in ruling. Or so they want me to think.

Felix stands suddenly, pushing his chair back with a screech much the way I did in the council room. He paces a short distance back and forth then stops in front of me. Arms crossed over his chest, he looks at me evenly.

"So you're going to marry for power, alliances?"

It breaks my heart to hear him say it. As if I've somehow disappointed him.

"We've always known I would, haven't we? It's not that much different than Ronan, really." Except it is. I cared for Ronan once even if it wasn't what I always imagined love to be.

He looks away, unwilling to answer my question.

"What will you require of me?" he asks, still looking toward the balcony rather than at me.

"Require?" I screw up my face. I don't like where this is going. "I've never required anything of you. But I would like your help in screening potential suitors. Titus wants to have a ball for my birthday and invite all the suitors. Of course I'll meet them all before then, and it's those initial meetings I'd like you to attend if you will."

Still not looking at me. "If that's what you want then I'll do it. I serve you."

"No, stop it." I stand from the bed, heat and anger and tears all threatening to overwhelm me. But I have to keep it together for just a while longer. "Drop all the pretenses. I don't want to have this conversation as queen and commander. I want to have this conversation as friends."

Felix shifts slightly, turning himself more toward the balcony so I can barely see his profile. "Is that what we are?"

"Felix... this isn't what I want either. I'm not happy about it. Just please look at me."

"I know what you look like."

My heart cracks. I don't know what I expected, but it wasn't this. How can he possibly think this is what I want? "And that's enough for you, is it?"

"You know it's not."

Now I'm grateful I can't see his face, because the emotion in those words shakes me to my core. I've never heard him so raw, so vulnerable. And maybe it would break us both if we had to look into each other's eyes while he said them.

Silence hangs like an iron curtain between us for what feels like eternity. Everything I start to say feels wrong, and I feel foolish. Because what I said was true. I've known—at the very least since Felix arrived to escort me back to into royal life—that I would marry not for love but for political advantage. Why did I let myself get my hopes up that it could be anything else, especially with a man as honorable as Felix who would not be with me because of his duty and loyalty to Ronan?

"I'm sorry," he finally says, still with his back to me. "I have no right..."

And he doesn't. Because I am to be queen and what's between us can never be. So I do my best to suppress the protests that rise to my lips. They will not help the situation.

"It's not an ideal situation," I say evenly. Somehow his uncharacteristic lack of stoicism has galvanized my own. "But I want to be strategic about this. With all that's at stake here we can't afford to be anything less than calculating."

Felix nods and turns slightly so he's more in profile than with his back facing me. He stares out onto the balcony, but I know he's listening intently to my words. And now I must ask even harder questions.

"Felix? Do you think Ronan meant it? When he said he would try to come for me, I mean." The prince has been trying to force his way front and center into my thoughts since the Council proposed a marriage alliance, but I've mostly pushed him aside until now. Emperor Cyrus is certainly playing a game, and I need to know what role, if any his son has. Is he even a factor? Or were those just nice words in a letter meant to placate me and bind Felix with a sense of loyalty?

"I don't know."

It's the first time I've heard true bitterness in his voice when it comes to Ronan. As if this is somehow all his fault.

"Very well then. It's probably for the best if I never see him again anyway." Is it, though? "We'll move forward in our plans without him then. Agreed?"

There's a long pause before Felix answers. "Agreed."

I wait a minute more for him to say something, anything, else, but he doesn't. Without words but too many emotions, I cross his room and exit, closing the door softly behind me.

My room is dark except for a dying fire when I return to it. Before attending the Council meeting I had insisted Hannah and Cecily take the night off because I anticipated spending most of my night after the meeting with Felix and didn't want them waiting up on me. How wrong I turned out to be. I wish I had their company now. In the short time I've known them they've become much more than servants. They're my friends and confidants, and I'd love to tell them all about this marriage debacle and have them commiserate with me.

But I don't want to wake them if they've chosen to turn in early, or disturb them if they're out having some fun for once. So I decide to brood alone in my room tonight instead of forcing my gloom on anyone else.

Maybe my pity party is why I don't realize that I'm not alone. Or maybe my company is just that good. Either way, I don't realize until much too late what's happening. A rough hand clamps around my mouth and nose, and seconds later everything goes black.

10

When I wake, a swift surge of panic courses through me once I realize I can't see anything. I blink my eyes rapidly, making certain I've actually opened them, and my lashes brush against something pressed close to my face. Blackness and silence muffle my senses, and I wonder for a moment if this is what it's like to be dead.

But my next breath reminds me that, though death and I have been scandalously intimate for some time now, we are not yet married. Damp mustiness fills my nose on my next inhale, and I calm myself. I can still learn much about my surroundings if I focus.

My captor likely entered my room through the passage behind the wardrobe. At least that's what makes the most sense to me. Either that or he's someone that looks so at home in the palace he was able to make his way to my room without questions being asked. That seems far less likely given the roughness of his hands. A working man. Not likely of noble birth.

Some type of scratchy fabric—the kind used to make peasant dresses, not the silks found around the palace—binds my eyes so effectively I can neither make out light or shadow. A thick rope seems to bind my hands behind my back and my ankles in an awkward position. My fingers tingle as I tug against my bindings. They don't give at all. Whoever tied this knew what they were doing. I struggle a bit more against the rope before my fingers go completely numb. Just beyond the harshness of my own breath I think I hear a breathy laugh. I freeze, eager for more clues of my would-be captor.

"Awake I see."

A woman's voice. Young, with the hint of an accent I don't recognize. Certainly not what I expected. Because just from her first three words to me, I don't think she's here to befriend me.

"So you are the celebrated princess," she continues. "The Princess Who Is To Come." She laughs bitterly. "I expected more."

The Princess Who Is To Come? I don't like the sound of that one bit. There's a weightiness to it beyond that of the usual crown even without knowing exactly what she means by it. Or maybe I do know. Is this the fabled leader Felix was telling me about? The one some Insurgos believed would reunite them? If so, why does everyone seem to think I'm the fulfillment of a prophecy I've never even heard?

Still I say nothing though my chest heaves with a wave of anger. A hot retort rises in me, but experience has taught me silence is the best tool I have to mine information. If I hope to get out of here unharmed I need to know as much about my captor and surroundings as I can.

"So many rumors and so many stories," she continues. I hear the soft tread of her feet as she circles me. "Warrior. Favorite of the Crown Prince. Daughter of a worthless king and a martyred queen."

What? I can't stop the gasp that tears from my lips. It's the last thing I would have expected her to say. She must know those words are treason, but she clearly doesn't care. She also seems to know exactly how to draw a reaction from me.

"Yes, I know your story. Probably better than you do. But rumors are so exaggerated, and I needed to see for myself. You're not what I'd hoped, but you'll do I suppose."

"For what?" I can't help but respond this time. If she wants a rise out of me she'll get it and then some. "If it's money you want, I'm not sure you've kidnapped the right person. No one missed me for years. I'm not sure they'll miss me now."

"Money? There's nothing I want that money can buy…except maybe a good assassin. But I prefer to get my own hands dirty."

I recognize the ice in her voice from my own experience getting my hands dirty, and I know she means it. The anger roiling in me is tempered with a small measure of fear.

"You are worth much more than money. We need something from you. A task only you can do."

We? So she represents a group, something bigger than herself. Not terribly surprising since it was clearly a man that kidnapped me from my room. It's obvious she's not working alone, but who is she working for?

It would be foolish to outright refuse her demand, not when I could use it for bargaining. "Not unless you tell me who you are."

"You can call me Nox."

I think maybe I've heard her wrong, but the name rings in my ears.

Nox.

That's my name, the name I gave myself when my father exiled me and sent me to the military camps. The name that kept me shrouded in secrets and mystery for years while I pretended I wasn't heir to a crown and the legacy of a treasonous mother. What are the odds this woman has randomly chosen the same name? Slim to none. Maybe the more important question: does she know of my connection to the name?

"Try again," I insist with a thread of pride in my voice. "Nox is a great warrior of the Borealis north mountains. You are not her."

She laughs, a patronizing sound that grates my nerves. "Do you actually think I'm that stupid? Or do you think that I won't kill you if you try to bring the might of the crown down on us?"

"Neither of those things, actually. But I won't blindly do the bidding of someone who thinks so little of me they steal my identity, drug me, and bind me thinking I will bend to their will. I am not that sort of princess, and I think you know that."

"What sort of princess you are remains to be seen. You seem, unfortunately, woefully ignorant which is so often the problem with royalty. You show…potential. It's just such a shame you're the one with the crown and not me."

I don't know this woman, not at all, but she would terrify me as a queen.

"I don't exactly have the crown yet either," I admit. "If you know as much about me as you say, then you know the announcement of my position as heir wasn't as well-received as it could have been."

"But you are the heir, and I am in a position to make sure you sit on that throne. I just need to make sure you're the right person."

What position could she possibly be in to influence the Council and the people of Borealis that I should be queen? I only have more questions the longer she talks.

"And if I'm not?"

"I do not think Levi would have given his life to get you the message if he had not believed you were the one to end all this."

My blood turns cold. She knew Levi? My world has become much smaller in a matter of seconds, and I'm suddenly claustrophobic. Does she know exactly how he died? If so, I may not make it out of here unscathed.

"I do want to end the persecution," I say carefully.

Silence. I think for a moment she has gone, but then I hear the quiet shuffle of feet. And when she speaks again, she is much closer to me this time.

"Then prove it," she hisses. "Prove your loyalty to the Insurgos and your mother."

"How?" My voice shakes but I don't care. The Insurgos? My mother? It's the last thing I expected. But something about it clicks. These are the Insurgos who have been terrorizing the city. The violent ones who have injured priestesses and ransacked homes in the name of a God I believe in. But I don't believe in what they're doing. Still…

"I am loyal. There was no reason to tie me up and blindfold me. I want to help. I've been trying to help."

"And failing. Miserably I might add. Did you really think you'd be of any use sitting on a plush throne in Aurora? If so you're more naïve than I thought."

She knows so much more than I've given her credit for. Where did her information come from? I think for a moment this stranger might know more about me than I know about myself and maybe it's time to play to her ego.

"I-I didn't know. I didn't even know there were so many of you—of us. The Aletheia…I want to know more."

"The answers you seek are at the top of the old north tower. There's a prisoner there, forgotten by all but the man who was charged to bring him food and water until the day he dies."

Well, that seems simple enough. "Okay, maybe I can talk to Titus and get him to pardon him, set him—"

"You think it's that easy? Titus will never agree to override your father's order and pardon him, and if he did, the man would be dead by nightfall. That's what your city does to known Insurgos. Do you want more blood on your hands?"

How does she know?

"No," I whisper while thinking of Levi and the tiny scrap of charred blue cloth tucked beneath my mattress.

"Then do exactly as I say. You must visit the temple and tour it. Visit the undercroft. There is a room there the priestesses are afraid of. Enter it alone and look under the leg of the broken altar. You'll find your next instructions there. When you have followed them, return and leave a thistle on the altar. I will come to you again after that."

"Wait, you'll come to me? No. No more of these clandestine abductions."

"You are not in charge here. You may wear the crown, Princess, but you are no queen."

"And you are?" Those words cut much deeper than I expected. Why am I letting this stranger get to me?

"We are both daughters of the High King. There is no higher calling than that. Now do you want to help the Insurgos or not?"

"Of course I do."

"Then follow my instructions."

"How do I know this isn't entrapment? How do I even know you're Insurgo?"

"Blessed be the Lord, my rock, who trains my hands for war, and my fingers for battle," she quotes as if the words are always on the tip of her tongue. "Watch the sky tomorrow at the evening sacrifice, and you'll have your proof of what we can do."

"You plan to return me to the palace then?" Or at the very least remove this blindfold.

"Of course we do. There's only so much whining I can take from royalty, and I'm afraid I've reached my limit for today."

"Untie these ropes and we'll see who's whining." I don't even know what this woman looks like, but I'm certain I could channel the anger pulsing through me to beat even Felix in combat. A self-assured fighter like her would be no problem.

"As much as I hope to take you up on that offer one day, today is not that day."

I hear the snap of fingers and moments later I'm being lifted to my feet by rough hands. A man's hands. Probably the same one I was so unexpectedly acquainted with earlier in my room.

"We will of course have to drug you for the return journey. Can't have you knowing how we get in and out of your palace. Not before you need to know anyway."

And before I can protest, the scent of poppies is in my nose. Already disoriented from the blindfold, my head spins. Then I begin to fall.

11

I wake in my bed, mouth dry and limbs heavy. When I turn my head to look around the room, my whole world spins. They certainly didn't take any chances with the amount of poppy extract they gave me this time. I peak under the sheets and am relieved to find I wear the same clothes they abducted me in.

How am I going to reconcile what I thought I knew of the Insurgos with what just happened to me? Kidnapping, assault, extortion…Those are things I expect of the Emperor, not of the people who follow my God. What would Felix say about all this?

Felix.

Should I tell him at all? We didn't exactly leave things on the best terms last night. And aside from being consumed with a rage probably beyond what I've yet seen from him, he would most certainly prevent me from visiting the north tower. Even if it meant locking me in a cell of my own. And that can't happen. I need to get to that tower. But first I must visit the temple.

And what did Nox—I hate to think of her by my chosen name—say about the evening sacrifice? That I should watch the sky. With the effects of my kidnapping still hanging on, I know I won't feel up to attending my first temple service since my return. But the view from my balcony should be sufficient for me to see whatever she wants to show me. I have my doubts that anything she could do would be enough for me to implicitly trust her. She didn't come across as the most forthcoming person with the truth.

One thing is for sure, she is not like any other Insurgo I have met thus far… if that's what she is. She claimed we were both daughters of the High King, and I know of no other way to interpret that. But her sneaking and deception feeds into exactly the sort of clandestine treacherous narrative the empire has been spinning about them for years. The same narrative I'm working hard to break. How then can I reconcile the two? Maybe she is as much my enemy as the Emperor.

A knock at my door jars me, and I struggle to a sitting position, pulling the covers up around me.

"Come in," I call, my tongue thick and stiff as the rest of my muscles. I clear my throat and prepare for my visitor.

Fortunately it's just Hannah who breezes in and shuts the door behind her. "Good morning," she trills as she throws back the curtains and lets the clear morning light stream in. I blink against it, but she doesn't notice. She's in a remarkably good mood, and I'm grateful for it. As long as she's lost in her happiness she doesn't have the care to notice my condition.

I quickly rake my hands through my hair, trying to smooth it as much as possible, and pinch my cheeks to give them a bit of color. Even without a mirror I imagine I must look like death, and it's only a matter of time before I have to answer questions about it.

"Good morning," I manage in my cheeriest voice, turning it into a stretch and yawn in hopes that will disguise the effects of the drugs on my voice.

"Did you rest well?" Hannah is now fussing with the bath tub. She twists the handles until she deems the temperature just right and pulls a small vial from the pocket of her dress to pour into the steaming water. Almost immediately the scent of lavender and honey reaches me, and my muscles involuntarily relax against the pillows.

"I slept deeply," I say honestly. Being drugged will do that to a person.

"And how was the Council meeting?" Hannah asks as she readies the towels next to the bath and then opens my wardrobe to select my dress for the day.

Ah yes. She doesn't know yet about the Council's demands, but I'm not sure I have the strength to have this conversation at the moment. "Interesting. There are several details that need to be resolved before they agree to my coronation, but they seem open to accepting a queen as their monarch."

That's putting it rather generously.

"Well, after the Emperor's announcement they would be foolish not to," she says solemnly.

Yes, someone's certainly a fool in this tangled situation, but I'm not certain who it is anymore.

"Here," Hannah says as she pulls a simple but elegant royal blue gown from my wardrobe. "What do you think of this?"

I raise an eyebrow. "For a day dress? It's too much, don't you think?" My plans for today mostly consist of bathing, lying in bed, and then stepping out on the balcony to watch the evening sacrifice. That dress looks much to constricting for any of that.

"No," she laughs. "For this evening's festivities. Your cousin sent word this morning that you were to be presented to court this evening before a procession to the temple for some sort of ceremony."

"What?" I sit straight up in bed, my head pounding with sudden movement. Presented at court already? And a ceremony? I don't like that last part at all. I can't shake the notion that it has something—maybe everything—to do with Nox's instructions to watch the sky at the evening sacrifice.

"I'm sorry. I thought you knew." Hannah dips her head slightly and clutches the blue dress tighter. "I assumed it was a result of the Council meeting yesterday."

"It-it was, but I just wasn't expecting it to be so soon." Beneath the blankets my hands are shaking. I'm not ready. I just want to scream and throw the blankets over my head until it all goes away.

"Well, there's no need to worry about that. I'll get you pampered and prepped. You look like you could use a relaxing morning. I'll ring for some breakfast to be brought up while you're taking your bath."

Hannah's soothing tones and gentle confidence calms me, and I sink back against the pillows. "Will Cecily be joining us?"

"Not this morning. She's with the jewelers trying to work out details on your tiara for tonight."

Of course. I will have to put a crown back on my head. Afterall, that was the goal in all this.

"Should I invite Commander Fidelis over for breakfast instead?" She tries to keep her question neutral, but I can tell she's fishing for something. The feelings between Felix and I haven't been much of a secret to anyone who knows either of us well.

"No, that won't be necessary." I swing my legs over the side of the bed and stand shakily. Hannah eyes my attire with raised eyebrows but says nothing. I'm grateful. At this point I'd rather let her think my sleeping in my dress from yesterday has something to do with Felix rather than being kidnapped by a rogue sect of Insurgos.

"He was certainly in a state this morning," she muses as she helps me undress and I slide beneath the deliciously hot water. "I quite literally ran into him in the hall, and he looked like he hadn't slept a wink."

"Hmmm," is all the reply I offer. Though part of me does find this interesting and maybe even a bit worrisome, I have too much else to ponder than whether Felix lost sleep over me. At some point I'll need to figure out what I want the dynamic between us to be moving forward, but with all the news of last night and this morning I hardly have space to consider where there will be space for him in my new life let alone my heart.

After failing to draw any gossip about Felix from me, Hannah leaves me alone to let me bathe. I suppose my surliness and reticence is clue enough, because after I dry off and we enjoy a late breakfast of scones and cream, she excuses herself to help Cecily with the tiara and to make some last-minute alterations to my dress for this evening.

I allow myself a bit more sulking and a nap before an itinerary for the evening is slipped under my door. I pick it up and frown at the list of events. Dinner with the Council and elite nobles in the grand hall. Processional to the throne room where Titus will present me to the court as the heir to the throne. I'll no doubt be expected to make some sort of remarks to the gathering crowd here. From there it appears we're all to make our way in a processional out of the palace to the temple where the sacrifice and blood ritual will take place.

Everything is scripted and laid out for me. Even the overall effect of my look is calculated. From the simple dress that covers most of my browned skin to the delicate tiara that sits atop my head. It is not the crown of a queen but rather of a childish princess. Maybe not childish exactly, but innocent, pure. Certainly not a warrior, a soldier, or a potential traitor. And that they've downplayed my sun darkened skin by either covering it up with fabric or makeup suggests they want to remind the people as little as possible of my mother. I've been made to look safe and delicate. I feel anything but.

Felix raises eyebrows at my appearance but doesn't comment. I'm certain he sees the point of it all, maybe even agrees with it to an extent. After all, keeping me safe is his highest priority as he keeps reminding me. But after that meeting with Nox something seems to have awoken in me that I haven't felt in weeks. I am a warrior, and I will make sure everyone knows it.

"Are you still upset with me?" I ask under my breath as Felix and I follow our herald toward the dining room.

"I owe you an apology," he whispers back. "Maybe we could speak tonight after all this is over?"

My first thought is "all this" will never be over. It's the path we're on now. But I'm so grateful we're speaking to each other and he's willing to have a conversation that I choose to be hopeful.

"Of course," I agree. "My room tonight." Which means I have just a few short hours before I have to decide if I will tell him about my impromptu exit from the palace last night or my visit with the Insurgos. Because after we see whatever Nox has in store for this evening, I'm certain the topic is going to come up between us, and I have never been a very good liar.

It's certainly not that I don't trust Felix. But I need to make sure that we're on the same page before I share everything. Certainly we both have our own agendas. They have dovetailed nicely until now, and I pray they will continue to do so. There's also a part of me that doesn't want to see the hurt on his face when he realizes he failed to protect me from a threat neither of us knew existed. I've caused him so much pain lately that I'd like to spare him this bit.

Dinner is as tedious and trite as I knew it would be. The Council members are no less condescending when removed from their official chambers. Despite Titus's best attempts to include me in the discussions, the men simply talk over me or dismiss my contributions.

This is especially infuriating when talks turn to which potential suitors will be invited to the palace. Each of the men seems to already have a favorite for their own selfish reasons—old family ties, better sea access, more precious gems... Not that I expected them to, but no one seems to have a care what I think.

Perhaps more disturbing is that no one seems to actually care if any of these men can help run a country. If I'm going to have to go through with this sham, I'm going to choose someone based on their ability to help me rule fairly and justly and not because their family has connections to a few specific resources that might make my nobles happy. After all, what will the common people benefit from an influx of precious gems?

"I personally would like to see a suitor who knows how to handle himself in battle," I say with a raised voice. It's the first time tonight I've made much of an effort to be heard, but it's time to stir the pot a bit and remind them who I am.

"Surely you jest," Orrin laughs. "A king in battle? We are not barbarians. Those days are long past."

"A King Consort, you mean," I correct coolly. I level my gaze at him. "Let's not forget who the heir to this country is. And if you think it's not necessary for royalty to be able to defend themselves then you've not been paying attention."

Silence greets my words, and I hope they're all thinking of the slaughter of my father and the other kings.

"The time has passed for relying on others to save us," I add as I take a sip of my water. I have their attention now even if the looks they give me are uncertain. "If Borealis is to survive—to thrive—then we must do what is necessary to save ourselves."

"Necessary within reason, I hope," Titus speaks up. He's not chastising me exactly, but there is a hint of a warning in his tone, and I take it as my cue to leave it there. I've planted a seed, which was more than I thought I'd have the opportunity to do.

"Of course," I answer my cousin with a sweet smile. Immediately some of the tension at the table dissipates.

"So you would prefer a fighter," one of the other Council members speaks up. I can't recall his name, but I do remember him being mostly silent during the meeting. "Do you have any other requests of your suitors, Highness?"

I search his tone for any hint of sarcasm or patronizing but find none. Perhaps he is the first to realize that my choice in this should matter.

"I- we need a leader. Someone who has experience making difficult decisions. Someone who can inspire loyalty among the subjects. Connections are well and good, but they can be lost without warning. If you have someone the people trust, someone who can make hard choices, then no matter what they face we have the best chance for the best outcome. That's who I would want by my side. Someone to advise in the areas where I am weak and know that they have my people's best interests at heart."

"Well of course we want someone who will be loyal to Borealis," Orrin says. "But loyalty can be bargained for. You'll find this is all about negotiations. But that's why we're here to guide you, Princess."

'Princess' has never sounded so condescending as it does coming from his mouth. Behind me Felix steps forward until he's directly beside me, and out of the corner of my eye I see his hand resting lightly on the pommel of his sword. Orrin visibly recoils into his chair. He's frightened, I realize, of Felix. With good reason, but I wish he had the same respect for my skills. I need to find a way to make that happen.

"Well, I look forward to seeing the fine specimens you have for me to choose from." I smile sharply. "I'm afraid I've set the bar fairly high, so make sure you bring me only the best."

I stand, this time with much more grace than when I made my sudden exit from the Council chambers. Everyone around the table mirrors my actions. "Dinner is over, I think. Titus, isn't it time for the presentation?"

Without waiting for an answer I take Felix's offered arm and leave the table. I can feel several pairs of eyes on me, so I make sure I keep my head high as I lead him from the room.

"Too much?" I whisper as we step into the hall.

"Just right," he replies, and I'm relieved to hear a smile in his voice. It brings one to my own face. It occurs to me then that the man I've just described as my ideal suitor is none other than Felix. He has all those qualities in spades.

"I'm not going to let them make this decision for me. There's a way for all of this to work out, I'm just not sure how yet."

"We will pray about it." It's not a suggestion. It's a confident statement he knows I won't disagree with. "Intentionally. And together."

"Yes. Together."

Felix and I have only shared a prayer once. On the mountainside as we stood in the snow outside Aurora with no direction and no plan beyond getting as far away from the Emperor as possible. It was brief but powerful, and I'm hungry with anticipation to feel that again.

The dining room doors open and the Council members and Titus slowly file out to join us in the hall. They are solemn but deferential as they march past us. No one speaks, but I wonder what quick conversations might have been had behind that closed door before they exited.

Once the men have disappeared around the corner, Titus approaches me and Felix with a sigh. I'm struck once again by how much he looks like the little boy I used to play with and how little he looks like a monarch.

"You really have a flair for the dramatic, don't you?" His smile is weak, and I'm reminded he's probably dealing with most of the backlash of my actions for now. He will be as glad for this to end as I will. "Maybe tone it down a bit for this next part? We don't want a riot on our hands."

If only he knew. I can't stop thinking about Nox and what sort of chaos she has planned for this evening. Am I doing the right thing by keeping that bit of knowledge to myself? The last thing I want is for any harm to befall the citizens of Borealis, but I also need answers from her. Because if she knows as much as I think she does then that could change everything for me.

"So I will enter the throne room first," Titus is saying when I manage to focus back on him. "And I'll introduce you. You'll enter with Commander Fidelis and take your place next to me. I'll announce you as the true heir to the throne, and you can say a few words if you wish... but, Emilia, please don't antagonize them. Keep it simple."

"I will." Because it isn't the pompous group of Councilmen I'll be addressing, but rather the court of Borealis as a whole. Yes, it will mostly be nobles, but they represent a much larger cross-section of my people than the Council. I don't want to alienate them.

"Good. And then after you've spoken, we'll adjourn in processional to the temple. As I'm sure you recall, the sacrifice is performed on the portico, so we'll climb the stairs to participate while everyone else will remain below. Unfortunately, Commander, that includes you."

I remember how crowded this area was the night Felix and I entered the city. Something in me then had pulled me toward those stairs, and now I will be climbing them. I don't like the idea of doing it without Felix, but it's important I assert my ability to stand on my own.

"It would be better if I'd had a chance to assess the risks in this maneuver," Felix says. His tone is respectful, but it's hard to miss that he addresses Titus much more like an equal than a superior. "To put the princess on display with so little security measures in place and a potentially uneasy crowd is not advisable."

"Nevertheless, it is necessary. This sacrifice only happens twice a year, and it will be a strong show of her commitment to Borealis to have her participate. And I'm afraid the priestesses are quite insistent that only myself and Emilia be on the portico with them. It is part of the ritual."

Perhaps I should have asked a few questions about this ritual. Despite Titus's assumptions, I don't remember anything about this biannual sacrifice from our childhood. Probably another thing I wasn't allowed to attend. Given who my mother was, I didn't exactly take great interest in the temple and its rituals. They were a sham to me even then.

"I'll be fine," I assure Felix, if only to alleviate any tension building between him and Titus. "You know I can handle myself."

"That's what I'm afraid of," Titus groans. "Could you just try not to 'handle' anything until tonight is over? Let's just get through this, Emilia, and then we'll face whatever's next."

Of course. Much easier said than done.

12

The nervous energy from the crowd gathered in the throne room is palpable even as I stand in an alcove off to the side. Felix at least got his way about that. Rather than march down the center of the crowd to join Titus on the dais, I will enter from a side room directly onto the dais. It isn't the grand entrance the Council wanted, but they've made it clear they have little regard for my best interests.

The herald announces Titus, and the murmuring in the throne room stops. I clench my hands into fists to keep them from shaking. Almost immediately a large, calloused hand covers them. I look up into Felix's dark eyes.

"You can do this."

There's nothing overly sentimental in his tone, but it harbors the same quiet confidence he's had in me since the beginning. "You were born for this."

I think of Nox. Of her calling me The Princess Who Is To Come. And I'm so very close to spilling all of it to Felix when the door to the alcove opens, and I hear Titus speak my name. And so I pull my hands from Felix's and step forward into the throne room and into my birthright as queen.

The room is utterly silent except for the click of my heels on the marble floor. It's unnerving, but I keep my head high and my eyes on Titus until I reach him. He clasps my hands, kisses each of my cheeks, and then turns me to face the gathered crowd of nobles.

"It is my pleasure to present to you my cousin, the true heir to the Borealis throne, Her Royal Highness Emilia Aurelius, Princess of Borealis."

Before us the people kneel like a wave. Still they say nothing. I look to Titus for help, but he does nothing except nod me forward. This is where I speak, I suppose.

"People of Borealis," I begin in a loud, clear voice, "rise."

There seems to be some confusion, but slowly they follow my command until they are all on their feet again, looking up at me curiously. Maybe they didn't expect me to address them, or maybe they didn't expect me to release them from their deference so quickly. But I like that I've surprised them.

"I am truly humbled to stand before you as your future queen. I have spent my years away from this city fighting for our country and learning much. I now look forward to learning from you all the wonderful things I have missed in our city, and bringing peace and stability to it that all may enjoy."

Cheers of assent ring out in the hall, and Titus smiles approvingly at me. Somewhere in the back of the room, someone even starts a chant of "long live the Queen!" and it brings a smile so wide to my face that it makes my cheeks ache.

Another hurdle conquered. Now there is only the ritual sacrifice. Let's hope Nox doesn't find a way to completely ruin that for me.

When we exit the palace into the courtyard adjacent to the temple we are greeted by a throng of people. They are well behaved and well contained by guards, but still I feel Felix tense beside me at the sheer number of them. Merchants and commoners, children and beggars have all turned out to catch a glimpse of their future monarch. It is a rare opportunity to be sure, since these are the people who would never be permitted inside the palace, and I'm certain my father didn't make it a habit of wandering among his people.

I try to take in as many faces as possible as we pass through the crowd on our way to the temple stairs. Both surveying my people and looking for anyone suspicious. There are so many children reaching for me, and I long to go to them, but I settle for a smile and wave instead. Beyond that no one stands out to me.

With a squeeze of his arm I leave Felix behind at the base of the temple stairs and take Titus's offered arm instead. With my free hand I lift my skirts and then hope I make it to the top without falling.

"Is now a good time to ask what I'm supposed to do when we get to the top of these steps?" I mutter, making sure I keep a smile plastered on my face.

"Mostly just stand there," he replies in kind, a dazzling smile still on his handsome face. "The lamb has already been prepared. The High Priestess will say the blessing and then ask you to kneel.

She will then sprinkle you with the blood, and you'll rise consecrated."

I stumble, and Titus catches me before I can hit the ground.

"I can't."

Why? Why did I assume this would be easy?

"You said we were just attending the sacrifice. You didn't say anything about blood or consecration or…"

Titus actually laughs. "I didn't think you of all people would be bothered by a little blood. You can wash it off as soon as the ritual is over."

The blood is not what has my stomach in knots. It's the consecration to Caelus—a god who is a symbol for everything I stand against. The god to whom my mother was sacrificed, though not nearly as humanely as this poor little lamb whose blood they will sprinkle me with. Once again, I'm faced with the choice between what is right and what is easy. If Caelus isn't real then the ritual has no power, but even that isn't entirely true. It has power over my people and all who see me follow through. Including Nox and her Insurgos who I'm certain are watching. And if I go through with this sham, aren't I diminishing the power of the true God at least in the eyes of my people?

How am I going to get out of this one?

We reach the top of the stairs, and Titus releases my arm. For a wild moment I think about running. But where would I even go? Instead I raise a hand and offer another wave and a weak smile to the crowd below. Hopefully the distance is too great for them to see the trepidation on my face. But my eyes find Felix standing at the front of the crowd, and I know he truly sees me. The same way I know that I simply need to give him a sign and he'll ascend these stairs and carry me away without questions. That, at least, brings a measure of relief.

The High Priestess is a woman I recognize, not from my childhood, but from her appearance in Aurora to preside over the ceremony where Ronan made his oaths to Caelus and received the Imperial signet ring. She's an older woman with silver-white hair and a regal bearing. The top of her head comes just under my chin, and while she seems small, she is holding a ceremonial knife. I know better than to underestimate her. Besides, do I honestly think I can fight a priestess and live to tell about it? If she doesn't kill me the riots certainly would.

Without much of an acknowledgement of me or Titus, she begins to chant in the old language—the one used exclusively by the temple. If I focused I could probably understand her, but my mind is far from her words. My eyes dart left and right, scanning the crowd for their reactions. This isn't just any sacrifice. I suspect most of them aren't devout enough to care about religious ceremonies most days, but there's a sort of fervor about this that has them swaying in time with the rhythmic chant.

God, what do I do?

Heat blazes through me as the prayer comes unbidden from somewhere deep within me. Power swallows me up, not my own, but something far greater and stranger. I think of Felix's prayer I overheard.

"I ask great things of a great God."

For a moment I think my knees will buckle, but I keep standing. And I keep silently praying.

I cannot bow to this false god. I can't allow this blood to be applied to me. Show me a way out. Show your power to these people. Show them what a true God looks like.

Overhead the sky darkens. Several people look up, and the sound of distant thunder is enough to make even the priestess falter in her recitation for a moment. Where moments before the sky had been bright blue with just wisps of fine clouds, a storm has blown in seemingly from nowhere. Only I don't think it's from nowhere. My body hums with something that seems to echo in the first bolt of lightning that flashes directly over the temple.

This is real power.

Below us the crowd has lost focus. They no longer stare up at the priestess with rapt attention, but they look from the temple to the sky and to each other. With another crack of thunder, some at the back of the crowd begin to disperse. But not us. The sacrifice must go on.

"Highness," the priestess intones without so much as a glance at the sky. The sudden storm, it seems, doesn't bother her. "It is time."

I look away from the sky to find her gesturing for me kneel before the lamb, presumably so she may inflict another cut to the already dead animal so its blood will drip down on me. But I will not bow to this false god. Forget Nox and whatever display she had planned. My God is putting on a display all his own.

At that precise moment a blinding, deafening crash rings out so close to me that it shakes the entire portico. Screams echo from the crowd below, though it takes me a moment realize why.

Lightning has struck the column to the right of us leaving a thin crack in the marble that seems to grow by the second.

Titus grabs my arm to keep his balance, and I can see the terror in his eyes.

"We have to go. It's not safe here." My eyes dart from his face to the crack in the column.

"We must finish the ritual," the priestess insists from behind me. "Caelus wills it so."

I whirl on her. "Do you see this storm? This is true power, and the God controlling this storm clearly doesn't want this to continue."

The ground beneath us begins to tremble, and I know that's not from thunder. Either the portico is about to collapse or the earth itself is shaking. We have to move now.

I look around frantically for Felix, and suddenly he's there. Behind him are a handful of Titus's guards charging up the stairs shouting "to the king!" In a matter of seconds he is spirited away leaving Felix and I alone with the priestess.

Felix is breathing hard from his charge up the stairs, but his grip on me is almost painfully tight. There are all sorts of questions in his eyes, but there will be time for them later. Because right now the world seems to literally be falling apart around us.

"Come with us!" I shout to the priestess as the earth continues to shake. There's a terrible screeching sound as a crack opens up in the middle of the stairs. Above us small pieces of rock begin to fall.

"The sacrifice," she insists as she gestures to the lamb.

This is my first experience that there are those of the empire's religion that are just as loyal to their god as we Insurgos are to ours. It breaks my heart that she is willing to die for a god who, even if he were real, would care nothing about her.

I'm about to argue with her, to plead with her to come with us, when the arrows begin to fall. One hits the ground near the base of the altar, and by the time the next one lands on the portico, Felix has pulled me down several stairs at a near sprint.

I have no doubts Felix would keep going until I'm safe inside the palace, probably under lock and key in my room, but something in me needs to stop and look back. So I dig my heels in and pull him to a stop that nearly knocks us both the rest of the way down the stairs. He looks back at me wildly, and then something over my shoulder catches his eye. I turn just in time to see a flaming arrow land squarely in the middle of the altar and consume the sacrifice.

It's such a strange sight in the middle of all this chaos—lightning flashing, earth shaking, crowd screaming, arrows falling—a small flame that quickly grows into something that can't be stopped.

Tied to the fletching on the arrow is a scrap of paper waving wildly as the flames lick dangerously close. This is the message from Nox, I'm sure of it, and there are only moments to retrieve it before the fire consumes it.

I start back toward the altar, but Felix has anticipated my move and holds my arm with an iron grip.

"There's a note on the arrow," I insist, my voice raised over the thunder and the screams of the crowd below us.

Felix looks from me to the altar with the light of understanding dawning in his eyes. Even without knowing about Nox, he must know that whomever would destroy a temple sacrifice is a potential ally of ours, and we must attempt to preserve any communication. Still, he shakes his head.

"We can't. It's too unstable."

Though I can't see her from this vantage point, the High Priestess's screams cut through me like a dagger. A wail unlike anything I've ever heard, and I don't know if it's in mourning for the loss of the sacrifice or if she's physically injured, but even Felix can't ignore it. Despite his last words he glances back up at the portico and then to me.

"Wait for me at the bottom of the stairs."

He pushes past me and takes the stairs two at a time until he reaches the blazing altar. A sharp crack of thunder peals across the sky, and I turn and hurry down the remaining steps to find shelter in the masses. The arrows falling intermittently from the sky seemed to be aimed solely at the temple, so I feel safe from their reach here, but there are greater dangers to be dealt with.

Though the gathered crowd was already in a state of panic over the earthquake and lightning, the site of the arrows has nearly turned them into a full-fledged mob. No one seems to notice or care that they are not targets of the projectiles, but instead they lash out at anyone and everyone that gets in the way of their retreat as if they were the perpetrators of the attack. Punches are thrown, bodies tossed aside carelessly, and, to my horror, I see some of the guards—mine or Titus's, I'm not sure—drawing swords.

And then the cool calmness of battle falls over me. With the ground shaking, people screaming, and arrows falling like rain all around the temple portico, my body shifts into a series of well-practiced maneuvers without a second thought. I'm about to join the fray or at least make my way to a weapon so I might put an end to it before it gets any worse, but then I hear the small cries.

A group of children huddles on the bottom stair. It's only by some miracle they've yet to be trampled, but if they stay there much longer I'm afraid they won't continue to be so fortunate. My position on the stairs allows for some high ground from which to survey the chaos, but I don't see any adults that seem to belong to these children anywhere nearby. They must have been separated.

I make my decision without much more thought and jog down the few more stairs until I reach them. Behind me something rumbles, and I'm not sure if it's more thunder or the first signs of the collapsing temple. Either way, it's not safe here so getting these children away from the temple becomes my first priority.

"Shh. Don't cry." My attempt at soothing them is halfhearted at best, but there's little time for that. I take the hand of the nearest little girl and instruct her to take the hand of her friend. Soon we have formed a chain of half a dozen children and myself, and we begin to make our way carefully through the stampeding crowd.

Miraculously I spot Antony, head and shoulders above most of those around him, calling out to the other guards to sheath their weapons. I call out to him since I know I will never make it to him with the children in tow. It takes him a moment to catch my eye, but when he does he cuts through the crowd until he reaches me.

"Get these children to safety," I instruct as I place the little girl's hand in his. "Take them into the palace if you must, but keep them safe until we can find their parents."

I turn to leave, eager to put eyes on Felix, but Antony grabs my arm.

"You must come with us. He would never forgive me if I let something happen to you." I don't need to ask who he means.

"I'm going to find him," I shout back over the din. "I need to make certain he's okay."

Antony searches my face for little more than a second then nods his assent. As if he could have stopped me. I'm not sure anything could at this point. There's no wall I wouldn't tear down to get to Felix.

I let Antony and the children melt into the crowd behind me and fight the urge to look back. Maybe I should have done more, but I left them in capable hands. I have to trust that's enough.

God, keep them safe. Keep Felix safe.

The heat I felt earlier flares within me again, and maybe I imagine it, but I think the sky lightens a bit. Still, it's unusually dark when I run up the stairs toward the burning altar. The fire is glowing against the dark recesses of the portico, and I peripherally register that the steady fall of arrows seems to have ceased.

Priestesses rush past me down the stairs now, evacuating the temple and carrying books and objects I imagine they find precious. But where is Felix? He went back for the High Priestess, but if these other women haven't stopped to show any concern for her, does that mean she was beyond help? Does that mean he's in trouble? Why hasn't he come back to me yet?

I nearly knock two priestesses down as I push my way back onto the portico and closer to the altar. The heat is overwhelming as if the fire burns unnaturally hot. Still no sign of Felix.

I inch closer to the flames and put a hand over my mouth and nose to keep from breathing in the acrid scent. With my eyes closed for a moment, all I can see is that burned Insurgo village, the mother covering her baby in vain, and the scrap of blue fabric I've hidden in my room to remind me never to forget them.

A horrible sight greets me as I inch around the back of the altar. The High Priestess's bare feet hang off the table, just out of the reach of the flames. The rest of her is already a charred mess. She's thrown herself on the lamb, the sacrifice, and made herself one as well.

"Felix!" I scream as I look away from the burned remains. Yet another ashen imaged seared into my brain. Despite the heat, my blood is cold as I frantically look around for him. "Felix, please!"

"Emilia? Over here." The voice is weaker than I'd like and punctuated by a cough, but it also might be the most beautiful thing I've ever heard.

"Keep talking," I instruct as I make my way to the other side of the altar. The smoke is thicker over here, and I can't see very far in front of me. "Keep calling my name."

And he does until I literally stumble over him at the far edge of the portico. My foot catches his side, and he lets out a groan as he throws up a hand to catch me from falling down the stairs. It's then I realize he's lying on his side, half under the temple roof—which seems in danger of collapsing at any moment—and half on the stairs. And the site of him motionless in the midst of such chaos and danger is so incongruous that I almost don't notice the arrow sticking out of his leg.

"Look, you need to get out of here. I told you to wait for me at the bottom on the stairs." His words force their way out through gritted teeth, and his face, blackened by soot, is a mask of pain.

"You were going to keep me waiting a long time with this thing sticking out of your leg." It's a very lame attempt at a joke, but I get a breathy laugh from him in return.

"You've always been impatient."

A fresh wave of screams rises all around us as a low rumbling begins anew. Felix grabs my forearm hard, his eyes wide with fear.

"Run. It's not going to last much longer. You have to get away from here."

"Not without you." Tears sting my eyes, and I don't know if it's from the smoke or the impossible thought of leaving Felix to die in this wreckage. "You are coming with me if I have to drag you."

He sits up with much effort and reaches for my hands. I clasp his tightly and nod. With shaky breaths he uses my leverage to pull himself into a half standing position. Just when I think he might make it, he collapses back onto the stairs with a moan. Panic rises like bile within me.

"Just break it off," he groans, and for a wild moment I think he means his leg. Then I come to my senses and realize he must mean the arrow shaft. Any jostling of that would cause him tremendous amounts of pain, and if I can break it off close to the skin then it might be enough to allow us to get to safety. But doing so is going to put him through a whole lot more pain before it makes things better.

I don't ask if he's sure, because what other choice do we have? "Okay, okay. Keep as still as you can."

It's heartbreaking for me to hear him bite back a scream as my hands find their way around the arrow shaft and search for the best place to break it. I'm only going to get one good shot at this.

Why are the only prayers I know about making my hands ready for war? What about healing? Surely the Aletheia says something about God healing? But I don't know those words, so I make do with the ones I have as I prepare the snap the arrow.

God, I can't lose Felix. Please save him. He is your faithful servant and...I love him.

The arrow snaps, Felix howls, and I collapse back on the stairs, breathing heavy with both surprise and exertion. Did I really just...?

But there's no time to think about it because the rumbling grows louder and fine bits of powder that can only be masonry float down over us. With a strength I can't explain, I grab Felix's hands and pull him to his feet. He stands this time, just barely, and I support him under the shoulder on his injured side.

"Can you run?" It's a stupid question. Of course he can't. But he'll have to. He nods.

It takes a few steps before we move in sync, but we've just gotten the hang of our three-legged race when the dull rumble turns into a full-fledged roar, and Felix grabs me around the waist and practically hurls us both down the stairs. We hit hard, though I'm certain he takes the brunt of it, and then manage to roll the rest of the way down. It's painful to say the least, and I know if I survive this then every bone in my body is going to hurt tomorrow.

When we hit the packed earth at the bottom on the stairs, we stay that way for a few moments or maybe a few days. I have no concept of time because I'm waiting to be trampled by the mob of people or buried by rubble. Instead all I feel are the sting of a few cuts and Felix wrapped protectively over me. For a moment there is only silence and us.

Then the ringing in my ears subsides and they are filled with screams again. Felix and I both look up the staircase to see the portico we were under just seconds before has finally collapsed. The temple itself seems to still be standing, but all in front of it lies a crumpled mass of white marble and the smoldering remains of a priestess and her sacrifice.

"We have to move," I tell Felix as I push him off me. He rolls to his side, breathing hard, and then nods agreement.

It's harder to get him to his feet his time, but once he takes a look around, something in the scene seems to galvanize him. Wordlessly he and I descend into the madness in the square hand in hand.

The main gate is swamped with people looking to take cover from the storm as I suspected it would be. People are looking for their rulers to protect them now that they've calmed down slightly, which means it's even less safe for me to be seen out here. I have to assume Titus is already safely inside the palace, and I really hope to join him soon.

"We need another way in." Felix seems to read my mind. "What about the way you snuck in that first night we came here?"

He's referring to the small courtyard passageway between the temple and palace where inadvisably scaled a wall and was immediately captured by Titus's guards. Ironically because I was mistaken for this ruthless Insurgo leader—Nox.

"It won't be easy with your leg, but I don't see what other choice we have." So I lead Felix around to the side of the temple where I came my first night in the city.

"Over the wall," I say, nodding at the eight-foot stone wall in front of us. There are footholds that make for relatively easy climbing, but he can't really put any weight on his leg at all. "Do you think you can make it over?"

He's already gritted his teeth and found a foothold with his good leg as high up on the wall as he can comfortably reach. I can't help but admire his strength as he pushes himself up on that single leg until his hands grasp the top of the wall. With shaking arms he pulls himself up until he's up and over the wall. I hear him fall to the grass on the other side with a soft thud and a groan.

"Are you okay?"

I scrambled up and over the wall only to land beside him and find him laughing. It's a sound I've so rarely heard and certainly one I can't reconcile with our current situation. The grass is soft and cool under me as I kneel beside him to look him in the face. I can see now the laughter is mixed with tears, and sweat smudges the soot on his face. He's probably delirious.

"We have to keep moving," I insist, though in a much softer tone than I've been using. "Just a little further and then you can rest. Can you do that for me?"

The laughter dies away and he nods.

Somehow I manage to pull him to his feet again, and we enter the palace through the small, nearly hidden stone door adjacent to the temple.

I don't remember much about my last trip through this passage as I was being led by guards to my probable death. Clearly I've taken a wrong turn somewhere because I can't find the door the guards used to exit this passage into the main palace. Instead we continue along the passage, which seems to slope upward for miles, until I realize this is part of the maze of passages that I entered from my room. If I could just find my way back to that door.

But I've never come this way before, and I start to think this upward slope will never end when we finally come to a small wooden door. I have no idea where this leads, but as I'm practically carrying all of Felix's weight at this point, I don't much care. We just need to be somewhere safe, preferably where I can get him some help. So with a deep breath, I turn the door handle and pull it open before we step into dazzling light.

We both stumble to our knees a few steps into the room, but the pain from the impact barely even registers with me. Felix crawls a few paces forward and slumps against the cool tile at the edge of a pool at the center of the room. I collapse on my hands and knees, breathless both from exertion and from the astounding beauty of our surroundings.

I have a faint memory of this place as though from a dream. I may have only been here once or maybe never at all, but it's familiar all the same. All around us, stained glass rises to the ceiling in a kaleidoscope of colors interrupted only by the occasional white marble column. Unlike the ones we've just witnessed collapse at the temple, these are smooth and shiny, not weathered by time or sun or wind. It's completely impractical architecturally speaking, but the aesthetic is astounding.

At the center of the room is a marble pool with water flowing up from somewhere below. It moves about tranquilly, still peaceful enough to reflect the stained glass in a blur or a rainbow. And when the sun inexplicably pierces through the windows behind me, the room is awash in the most vivid hues of red, purple, blue, and gold I've ever seen.

The sun? Does that mean the storm is over? I try to tune my ears in the silence to hear any noise from outside, but nothing reaches me. Wherever this room is located in the palace it seems to be far enough removed from the square that it remains tranquil even in the midst of the chaos below.

"Emilia?" Felix's voice is soft as he lifts his head from the tile to look around for me. His eyes find me, and he starts to shift toward me, but I crawl to him before he can move much. I prop myself up next to him and look at his soot stained face.

"We need to get you some help." I glance down at his bloody mess of a leg and pray it's not as bad as it looks.

"In a minute. First..." He trails off as he reaches a shaking hand into his pocket and pulls out a scrap of paper. It takes a moment for me to realize what it is. The note attached to the arrow that set the altar on fire.

"You got it?" I ask in wonder.

"Of course. I couldn't save the Priestess though. I tried to pull her away before the fire got too high, but she pushed me away and jumped on the altar." He closes his eyes, and I don't want to imagine the scene he's remembering. It was awful enough when I stumbled upon the aftermath.

Felix hands me the paper, and I accept it with trembling hands. The edges are charred and threaten to crumble as I unfold it gingerly and hold it so we can both read the words written there. Words unfamiliar, yet I know with certainty they are from the Aletheia, and one look Felix's wide eyes confirms he knows it, too.

For our God is a consuming fire.

"So it was the Insurgos," he whispers. "I hoped, but I didn't think they would be able to pull off something like this. And that storm? How could they have known that was coming and the trouble it would cause."

"They couldn't," I say softly and look away from him. My own sort of storm is roiling inside me. Did I cause that? Are more innocent people dead because of me?

"I-I don't know how it happened exactly, but I was up there beside the Priestess, and she wanted me to kneel and be consecrated to Caelus. And I just couldn't do it. So I started to pray. It felt...different this time. I asked God to show the people what a true God looked like, and the storm began to roll in."

Though I can't bring myself to look at his face, I can feel his eyes on me. That keen, deep stare that sees so much even though the man it belongs to says so little. After a moment his fingers gently touch my chin and turn my face back to him. He's propped himself up on an elbow, making his face much closer to mine than I was prepared for.

He opens his mouth as if to speak, but no words come out. For a wild, impulsive moment I imagine what it would be like to kiss him again, but this is not the time for that. There may never be time for that again. But that only serves to remind me of the realization I came to as I prayed over him earlier. I have to steer us away from this moment before it makes things worse.

"What if the people think this was a sign from Caelus? A sign that I'm not worthy to be queen."

"They might." Felix removes his hand from my face and uses it to brace himself in a semi-upright position. "But I think they're just as likely to see it as a sign of power and favor with Caelus. These people know only what they're told about their gods. They don't experience them personally. We can control this narrative if we act swiftly."

He's right. With the High Priestess dead, only Titus and I know what happened on that platform. It will be easy, almost too easy, to convince the people that this was a show of favor from Caelus. Still, I don't like the deception.

"How is your pain?" I change the subject and let my hand drift down to his calf where a small bit of the arrow still protrudes from the skin.

"It's not so bad."

"Liar." But I smile at him and use the hem of my torn dress to wipe the soot from his face. It's only then I realize how pale he is. "We need to find a healer. I don't know exactly where we're at in the palace, but I can find someone and bring them back here."

"Not yet," he says. "I know it can't last, but can we have just a few more moments of just us?"

How can I deny him that? In answer I lie down beside him and rest my head on his chest. The soft rhythm of his heart is the most comforting sound I've ever heard. And I think how dangerous this is that I just want to stay like this forever when we both know we can't.

But I selfishly savor each moment, each breath, as the colors of the stained glass drape over us like a blanket. Cut off from the reality of all that's happened in the last few days I imagine I could be happy here. I will find a way to marry Felix and he will be my prince. And nothing will keep us apart. And I hold onto that foolish thought as long as I dare, until he is sleeping softly beside me.

13

The next two weeks pass in a flurry of activity. Titus and I agree on a story to spin to the people about the temple's partial destruction being Caelus's will and a show of favor toward me, and they seem to accept it.

Stormbringer. That's what they're calling me now. I'm not exactly sure why they think or know I'm the one who called the storm, but I don't know of anyone who isn't attributing it to me. Ironically, they haven't connected it to the Insurgo God. In fact many of them think I must have some special connection with Caelus or one of the lesser gods to control the weather. Either way, this display seems to have won me some favor despite the destruction it caused. The people think I'm powerful, and though it's not exactly how I envisioned it, I'm not complaining about their adoration.

Although adoration is not really what I need right now. What I need are some answers. Like how did that storm even happen? Did it actually have anything to do with my prayers? I have prayed fervently, before then and since, and haven't felt that surge of heat within me, and nothing has produced such dramatic results.

With possibly the exception of Felix. His wound wasn't as bad as I feared, still the healers were afraid of infection. They gave him something for the pain which caused him to sleep for almost three whole days, and when he woke the threat of infection was gone, and he was able to stand with little pain. Two weeks on and he's completely recovered save for a scar.

I still haven't told him about Nox. With everything that's happened and all I've had to deal with in the aftermath, we haven't had much time to speak about non-royal matters. There was a small ceremony where I presented him with a pendant of the Borealis seal and named him Lord Commander of the Queensguard with all the benefits that title entails. It was the least I could do as a reward for services to his future queen during the tragedy at the temple, or at least that's what I told the crowd gathered for the presentation. But my hope is that being promoted to Lord will make him a legitimate candidate as a suitor.

Of course he doesn't know this yet. I can't bring myself to actually have that conversation with him because I can still see so many ways it could go wrong. But if the Council can put forth suitors, why can't I put forth one of my own choosing?

Despite the devastation at the sacrifice, plans are moving ahead for my birthday ball. The only change seems to be that my suitors will not be arriving ahead of the ball as the Council originally hoped, but will instead attend the ball and then present themselves officially to me in court the following day. I'm hoping to speak with Felix after the ball and convince him that we could make this work. That he could stand among the suitors and we could be together.

Laborers are hard at work trying to repair the damage to the temple. The stairs have been nicely salvaged and patched, but the portico is beyond a simple repair. Instead the rubble has been cleared outside, and extensive cleaning and organizing is going on to set the inside back to how it was before.

This seems as good an excuse as any to follow Nox's instructions and visit the temple. I send word to the new High Priestess that I intend to visit and tour the temple to see the state of the clean up. I don't wait for her reply.

Felix and I show up in the temple's main hall without fanfare. I haven't exactly been forthcoming with him as to my true reasons for this visit, but he follows along without question.

I haven't been inside the temple since I was a child and attendance was mandatory. The grandeur of it all is just as I remember. Dark blue and bronze swirled tiles cover the expansive floor, and the glint of metallic flecks make it look like stars in the night sky. Altars and coffers accented in bronze and silver dot the circular main room. This is where services are held for the masses. Today Felix and I are the only outsiders.

A priestess gives us a cursory tour of the upper levels and seems hopeful that we'll leave, but I'm not finished.

"I'd like to view the lower levels," I insist as her face falls.

"I don't know if that's a good idea, Highness." Her voice trembles, and she won't look me in the eyes.

"Is it structurally safe?" Felix asks.

"Well, yes..."

"Then you will permit her down there." His tone leaves no room for argument. So while he makes conversation with the priestess, I sneak away down a stone staircase off the main hall.

As I descend the stairs the air around me cools and the hair on my arms stands up. I expect the chill to pass but it doesn't exactly. Instead it transforms me with each step into this small nearly forgotten room. Where the temple's main hall and altar is filled with rich colors and shiny gold metals that nearly assault the senses, this room is dim and drab. An otherworldliness seeps from between the ancient stones, and I'm grateful I've no need to speak. This is a place for silence. For reverence. For awe.

An excitement I can't begin to explain bubbles inside me, threatening to spill over if only I gave it cause or direction. Something just feels right here like it hasn't anywhere else I've been in my whole life. As if there was a small piece of myself I'd never known was missing until now. And I know in that moment I will fight to keep it.

Minutes pass or maybe hours before I hear the soft pad of feet on the stone stairs behind me. I don't need to turn to know it's Felix checking on me. His small intake of breath as he enters the room is confirmation enough for me. And it's beautiful because I know I haven't imagined the otherness of this room. He feels it too.

"The priestess says this room was discovered just after the attacks on the temple," he whispers, so close to me now that I can feel the heat of him behind me. "They gave it a cursory look and found nothing of interest to them."

"Of course not," I return in a whisper of my own.

"She says they plan to wall it back up. Something about it troubles the acolytes."

"It would, wouldn't it? Because they've spent years trying to convince themselves and everyone else that this," I gesture around the room as if that can possibly convey the awe we both feel, "isn't real. But it is."

In fact it's more real than anything else in my life at the moment or probably ever. If I close my eyes I can almost hear the echoes of something awe-inspiringly beautiful.

If for no other reason, this room lends validity to Nox's words about who she says she is and what she hopes to accomplish. As Felix has just reiterated, most people would find this room either troubling or simply empty. But it's so full of an otherness I can feel that I know she must have felt it too.

The broken altar stands against the wall opposite the stairs, a large crack splitting the stone in two. There were words etched into it at one time, but those portions of the stone are worn so smooth that I can only make out a few illegible indentations.

But I have other words to search for. I can feel Felix's eyes on me, though, and am unsure how I should go about finding the instructions Nox has told me are there. Perhaps I should "accidentally" find them after running my hands over every inch of the altar so I don't arouse his suspicions. I have my doubts about my ability to slip the note from its hiding place into my dress without notice from my keen-eyed companion. Besides, I promised I would not leave him behind. That means he must think we are on a level playing field with this issue or he will never go along with a crazy mission given to me by an equally crazy mysterious woman who insists on using my name.

I don't have to pretend to be drawn to this altar. There's a tug inside me pulling me closer. It's much the same feeling I felt my first night in the city, but now it's immeasurably stronger. I kneel before it, and Felix joins me.

I press my palms to the ground and bend forward until my forehead almost touches the cool stone. It's a position of prayer I saw my mother use many times, and I'm about to utter a prayer of my own when I see something underneath a crack in the altar. Curious, I push my hand forward until my fingers just brush something. With some effort I manage to trap it between my hand and the ground and drag it from beneath the stone.

"What is that?" Felix leans over to look at my discovery, which appears to be a stack of aged papers. So this is not a new letter Nox has placed here for me. It has been here for some time. "It has your name on it."

Startled, I look closer at the scrawled words and see my name peppered throughout the letter. Because that's what it is. A letter. Several of them in fact. Without looking at the signature I know who they are from.

My mother.

I don't realize I'm crying until the first tear splashes down onto the paper. To have something from her like this, words written directly to me, is something I never dreamed of. Bits of fabric and jewels from her old life can't compare to holding her words in my hands. I'm desperate to read them, but I know this isn't a safe place to do so.

"This is my mother's writing," I whisper to Felix as I gently caress the letters. "She must have hidden them because she knew they were coming for her."

"But how could she have known you'd find them here?"

"I don't know." There's no good explanation for it. This is not a room we visited together or even talked of. Had it not been for the pull inside me I wouldn't have known it existed. And Nox, of course. How did she know of the existence of these letters?

I hide the letters in my dress, and we ascend the stairs back to the main temple hall. We thank the priestess for her time and excuse ourselves back to the palace. More than once Felix has to reach for my arm to keep me from breaking into a run. But the letters I carry with me have given me both lightness and a terrible sense of fear of what I might find there.

Felix offers to stay with me while I read the letters but doesn't seem surprised when I turn him down. As much as I share with him, this is a moment between me and my mother. I spread the pages out of my bed but quickly gather them back up. Though Hannah and Cecily are busy doing other things and Felix has promised to leave me alone, I don't feel as if I have enough privacy here for what I'm about to read.

So I stuff the letters back into my dress and push the wardrobe aside to enter the passageway. I think I intend to read these letters in my father's tomb as an act of defiance, but my feet take me a different direction entirely. Before long I find myself in a surprisingly familiar passage. It takes a few wrong turns, but I finally find my way back to the rainbow room—the room Felix and I accidentally discovered the night of the temple destruction.

I don't know what it is about this place that brings me such peace, but I breathe a little easier almost as soon as I enter. I settle into a spot near the pool where the colors splash over the pages as I dip my toes in the water, and I begin to read.

My dearest Emilia,

I hope you know how loved you are, sweet girl. As I watch you sleep, my heart is so full. It is the joy of my life to be your mother.

One day I may not be here to remind you of my love, so I'm writing it here for you to know. Even more than that, I am writing to remind you of God's love for you. You are the child I prayed for, a gift from God. I pleaded with him to sanctify you for His service.

Your father will tell you that you have a more important service to your country and to the throne, but nothing matters so much as the plans God has for you.

Despite the years and tragedy that separates me from her, I can almost hear her voice if I close my eyes. As I do, tears roll down my cheeks. What I wouldn't give to have her by my side now. I shuffle the first page to the back and begin the next letter, smiling at her use of the nickname she used for me.

My darling Mia,

It isn't safe for me here anymore. I want to run, but I would be leaving too much behind. I could never leave you, but it isn't fair to make you a fugitive either.

There's still so much I want to explain to you. I wanted to introduce you to the man in the north tower. He is someone you should know even if your father has done everything he can to prevent it. I dare not even write his name, but perhaps one day you'll read this before it's too late, and he can explain to you what I could not.

I failed miserably as a queen, Mia, and I hope you will not make my mistakes. But this was never my calling. It was never my choice. I made the best of the life I was given, and then God gave me you. You are so much more than I could even think to pray for, and I hope in you I have atoned for some of my wrongs.

Be a good queen, my dearest. Be a woman who stands up to protect her people and metes out both justice and mercy from the same hand. Even now as a child you have a bravery and spirit like no other. God has gifted you this. Do not waste it. I hope I get to see the woman you become.

For hours I read and reread her letters. Some are instructive but all are full of love. Still, she knew her time was short. Why else would she write all this to me? I could not have understood these things as a child, but if she were here now, I can imagine her saying them to me. Maybe even as we sat beside this very pool with her stroking my hair. I would tell her all my problems, and she would guide me in the right direction.

When you are queen, you will be expected to marry. Do not take this decision lightly. Even with the duty and responsibility that will hang on you, you deserve to be loved for exactly who you are. Choose a man who can give you that. Crowns are overthrown all the time. Choose someone who will love you even if you lose it.

Most of all, be free, Mia. And give freely. Love and be loved and be happy. It is the prayer of my heart that you will see the truth at a young age and grow up in the light of the one true God. He will sustain you and keep you. He will uphold you with his righteous right hand.

If I am gone, find those who knew me and they will tell you the truth. They will tell you what I died for and what I lived for.

Felix wakes me some time later. My joints are stiff and my eyes are swollen from crying. He gives me space as I sit up and stretch.

"How did you know I was here?"

He shrugs. "I guessed. It's peaceful here, isn't it? I've wanted to come back since that night."

I don't reply right away. I like that he shares my sentiments about the room.

"Are you all right?" He nods towards the letters scattered all around me.

"It was good to hear her again. Sometimes I forget just how amazing she was."

Felix smiles. "I would have liked to have met her."

I think about one of her last letters and her advice to marry someone who will love for me for exactly who I am. She would have approved of Felix, I'm sure of it. "She would have adored you."

He seems surprised by this. "Adored me? Why?"

He's really going to make me say it. "If for no other reason than because you care so much for me." I can't bring myself to say 'love' because I realize I don't know if he does. If he can. "And because you serve the true God."

"Did she have anything to say about the Insurgos?"

"She did." I hesitate because I don't know how he's going to feel about this next part. "I need to visit one of the prisoners. He's locked away in the north tower. My mother seemed to think he could explain things to me. He could be the key to us understanding everything—the Gate, the Insurgos, this promised ruler..."

"I thought the cells in the tower were empty." Felix frowns. "Only the dungeons are in use now."

"Yes, but this man has been locked away for a long time, and apparently my father did what he could to keep that fact a secret. Which means he must know something of value."

Felix nods slowly. "And you want to go alone." It's not a question because he already knows the answer, and I can tell by the set of his jaw he doesn't like it.

"I think I have to. These letters were meant for me, and he might not talk to anyone but me."

"He might not talk to you, either."

"Perhaps, but I have to try, don't I?"

"Yes, I think you do."

14

The day before my birthday I wake before dawn and dress in a drab gray dress and cloak. I braid my hair and tuck it under the cloak's hood before meeting Felix in the hall outside our rooms. We don't speak as we walk with swift and determined steps toward an area of the palace I haven't visited before.

After the conversation about my mother's letters, Felix scouted out the best way for me to enter and leave the north tower without attracting attention. He has reluctantly agreed to stand guard at the bottom of the tower stairs while I speak to the prisoner. I'm not sure what he dislikes more—being unable to keep an eye on me or not being able to hear this information first hand. But I've promised to tell him everything, and tonight I intend to keep that promise.

The staircase to the top of the tower is narrow and winding, and I'm a little breathless by the time I reach the top. The stairs open onto a small landing which leads to three cells with iron bars. The first two are empty, but I see a shadow stirring in the far one.

"Hello?" I call, and my voice echoes slightly in the nearly empty space. At first I think he doesn't hear me, so I take a step toward the far cell.

"I waited for your mother to return." The voice that greets me is shaky with age, weak, and I move closer to get a better glimpse.

The old man is sitting cross-legged against the back wall of his cell. He wears tattered rags and smells horrible. Just how long has he been here? And what did he do to warrant such a sentence? I approach him with caution.

"She was sentenced to death—executed," I say, a little harsher than I mean to. "Surely you know that."

"I know many things, but very few of them matter."

"Who are you?"

"My name is Antioch. And you are Emilia the Stormbringer, are you not?"

"That is what they call me," I admit. But how does he know that? The only contact he supposedly has with the outside world is with the man who brings him food daily. Has the gossip spread this far? Or is there a higher source?

"What they call you but not who you claim to be." He nods slowly. "That is good. You know the power is not your own. You are so very like your mother. She has returned to me after all."

"My mother is dead," I say again as if my words can hurt him. But after years in this tower, I'm not sure much could hurt him.

"It is not the person I was waiting for but the spirit. And here you are." He looks up at me with startling blue eyes that hold a spark not dimmed by time.

I shake my head. "You are sadly mistaken. I am not my mother."

"A bit braver, certainly more reckless, but of course that's why you've been given your soldier to temper you."

But...he can't mean Felix? How can he possibly know about him? "I've been given very little in the last few years."

"Yet you have been given this opportunity to lead your people, our people. And perhaps you will soon have a husband to stand by your side while you do so."

Has he overheard something from the guards about the Council's marriage plans for me? Or has he, like most everyone else, assumed that as I woman, marriage is my life's aspiration? "I don't need a husband. I need information and someone seems to think you have it. I need to know my path."

"You need to know the next step. Were the entire path illuminated for you, you might think you could simply rush to the end. That is not the case. You must take the journey. Step by step."

I laugh harshly. "Until I fall off the cliff?"

"If that's where God leads, then yes." Silence fills the space between us. "God is not leading you to destruction, my daughter. He has a great work for you to do."

Despite my reservations I lower myself to the floor just outside his cell. The stone is cold and drafty, and I pull my cloak tighter around me. Surely this man must be freezing in his rags.

"Who are you really?" I ask again.

"I am a servant of the Most High God," he answers cryptically. "But if you mean who was I, then I was once an Augur of Caelus. I studied the omens to divine his will on matters important to the empire."

I heard stories of augurs when I was growing up. Titus and I learned about them in our lessons. In the past they interpreted signs from the gods to determine all sort of important decisions for the empire—from war to taxes and everything in between. They were revered as almost gods themselves and ranked even above the High Priestess. But the last of their kind were extinct before I was born...or so I thought.

"How long have you been here?" I gesture around to the drafty cell.

"Not nearly as long as I ought to have been."

Now that's surprising. I've never met a prisoner who thought he'd gotten what he deserved. Except maybe Levi.

"You seem surprised, Princess, but I have sinned greatly in my former life. Before I saw the truth I told people lies and led them astray from the True God. I sent men to war with assurances that a god who never existed would protect them. I made people forget the Most High God in favor of a fantasy."

"How did you learn the truth then?"

"Our God is merciful. When I was in the temple praying to Caelus, Our God spoke to me and struck me dumb. He revealed Himself to me and the truth of His glory. When I accepted Him for who He was I was permitted to speak again. Since that moment I have never stopped proclaiming Him."

"And that's why my father put you here." It's a punch to the gut. "Because you serve the Insurgo God."

"The only God," he confirms.

I recall the prisoners I visited one of my last nights in Aurora—the assassins Cyrus had paid to execute his own son. They were hungry for the truth of my God. I can only imagine what chaos a powerful man like Antioch would have caused by sharing that truth with a nation of starving people.

"If I become queen…"

"*When* you become queen," he corrects with a smile. "It is why God has brought you here."

That's the wrong things to say to me, and all the frustration I've been holding back bursts out. "Why does everyone seem to know what God wants except me? If I'm the one He's chosen to carry this out, why isn't He speaking to me?"

"Is that what you desire?"

"I don't know." I throw up my hands. "I guess so. I just want to know I'm on the right path. Does sitting on the Borealis throne help anyone? Or am I supposed to run after the remaining Insurgos? And what do I do if I find them?" The questions pour out of me like water spilling over a dam, and that's not even all of them. I'm not even sure why I think this man can answer any of them.

"And do you ask God these questions?"

"I pray," I say slowly, softly, because it feels like a secret even in this empty tower.

"The time for simple prayers has past, my daughter. You are a warrior of the High King. You must prepare for battle. Seek Him wholly."

"I can't instigate a battle against the Emperor. It would be playing right into his hands."

"The Emperor is not your greatest enemy. All around us rages a war we cannot see. We do not fight against flesh and blood. The enemy is not of this world and, therefore, neither must our weapons be."

"I don't understand."

"You have learned to fight with your sword and your hands. Now you must fight with your faith. In times past God has chosen few to work through to display His signs and wonders. These followers performed great works—healed sick, cast out evil forces, caused the earth to shake, called down fire… Even now I sense His work in you. He showed His work in you with that storm. But you must seek Him so His power can flow through you."

"I don't even know where to begin."

"It has already begun. The storm was no accident. You asked God for it and He provided."

"How can you possibly know all this?"

"God still speaks to me, too. Even alone in this little cell, we have conversations. He has told me about you, and I have prayed for you. His power flows in you. Let me show you."

He begins to sing, more of a chant really. It's in a language I don't know, perhaps the ancient ones of this country. And yet I find that some part of me understands it. His soft voice seems strong now as it echoes off the stone walls and surrounds me. It sounds like he's a whole choir by himself. He must have done this many times before.

The hair on my arms and neck prickles, and I feel almost lightheaded. As the music washes over me, my heart begins to thud with a feeling I've only had a taste of before. I close my eyes and picture the stars on that crystal clear night before we entered Borealis and remember how I marveled at God's creation of each one. He is the star breather.

The sheer magnitude of that revelation brings awed tears to my eyes. Because not only did this God breathe the stars into existence, He also created me and chose me. I am a daughter of the Highest King. Isn't that what Nox said? In this moment I feel the truth of that statement in a way I haven't before. How could I have taken for granted His presence? He is not only there when I want to pray, but He is all around me all the time.

By the time Antioch finishes the song and the last notes ring in the stone tower, a power courses through me like I've never known. It leaves me feeling both weak and powerful. Because it's not my power at all. I've tried to do things, to make decisions, based on the power I have because of my position as princess. But I see now that was all wrong. It was never my strength or sovereignty that mattered at all.

"But why me? Why didn't God choose you or Nox even? Why does all this rest on me?"

"It doesn't. It never has. You have the privilege of being chosen. It is your calling. But should you choose not to follow, God will raise up another. His plan will be accomplished one way or another. Only you get to decide if you will join Him in His work or stand against Him. I'm afraid you cannot be neutral."

"But how do I join if I don't know where to go? The Emperor wants access to this Narrow Gate—the Gate of Life. Do you know it?"

"Know it?" He laughs warmly. "Child, it is only the most holy place in all of creation."

"What can you tell me about it? Emperor Cyrus is willing to slaughter Insurgos for information about it, but I can't find anyone who knows the truth of it."

"It is a seat of power, where the Ancient One sits and none but those chosen can approach. It has been a source of both fear and desire for emperors for ages. They fear the one who sits on the seat, but they each want to enthrone themselves there for the power they think it brings."

My jaw drops. He shares this information as if it's common knowledge. "Are you saying it's a real place?"

"Of course it's real. When this land was young, legends abounded about the Gate and the Ancient One. So much so that the greatest lords of that day set out to find it. Seven of them travelled across the sea to seek the stuff of dreams. Only six returned. The seventh, Lord Caspian, was said to have been lost at sea, but many believe he simply chose to remain behind."

"But where?"

"Where indeed. The other six were dumb upon their return from the voyage and for months after only communicated very little in writing. They never spoke of Caspian or where exactly their journey had taken them. They only said it was a great and terrible place not to be revisited."

I sit in silence trying to take in the enormity of his words. The Gate is a real seat of power and that means it's a real threat that must be protected from Cyrus. But how if no one knows where it is other than somewhere across the sea?

"And this Princess That Is To Come that I keep hearing about?"

"Well, that's one translation of it. I don't believe the original text specified whether it would be a prince or princess, but of course with you being here it does seem rather obvious, doesn't it? There are those who thought your mother was the answer to that prophecy. I'm afraid that's why the Emperor insisted she be executed."

What?

But it makes so much sense. My mother was killed not just for believing in God, but because she was dangerous. At least in the eyes of an emperor who was terrified of losing his power.

"So you think *I'm* the fulfillment of some prophecy then? What am I supposed to do?"

"Oh no. As I've said, God's plan will be carried out whether you join Him or not. If you choose not to take the place He has ordained for you, He will call another. It is the work that is sacred, not the person."

Somehow that makes me feel slightly better. "But what is it this prince or princess is supposed to do?"

"I think you already know. They will lead the great battle against evil and defend throne of God our High King. And then they will be permitted to rule over a peaceful nation that worships God."

No problem. If that's all there is to it. But I'm tired of being put on a pedestal where I don't belong. I desperately want someone to know the truth of what I've done, maybe just so Antioch can tell me that I'm not qualified for this after all.

"I am not worthy of all that."

"None of us are worthy, child." He smiles sadly.

"You don't understand." Suddenly I'm on my knees, crawling closer to the bars of his cell. I press my face against the bars and feel the cool metal press into my hot cheeks which are covered with tears I didn't realize I was crying. "I killed a man. An innocent man who loved and served God. I should have found a way to save him, but I was too selfish to risk my own safety. I ran him through with a sword. The only man who's ever cared anything about me."

"Not the only man."

For some reason those words trigger a deluge of tears. Sobs pour from me uncontrollably as I close my eyes and press tighter against the bars. All I can see if Levi and the blood staining the ground around his lifeless body.

A gentle touch startles me, and I open my eyes to see through my tears that Antioch has moved closer to me. His gnarled hand pats my head tenderly through the bars.

"There is no sin so great that God's love is not greater still."

And I think of Felix.

"I ask great things of a great God."

"As soon as I am queen I will free you," I promise, my voice still shaking and thick with tears.

"I am already free." He pats my head one last time then leans away to give me space to sit up and wipe my face. "This is where our God has placed me. For such a time as this. You have been the answer to my unspoken prayer, Princess. That is more freedom than I could ask for."

"What was your prayer?"

"That God would give me a broken heart that yet carries home the water of grace."

With a fresh round of tears, I close my eyes and drink deeply of that water.

15

That evening Felix joins me in my room for dinner. Despite my insistence on keeping things simple, Hannah has gone out of her way to set up an ambiance that might even be called romantic. Bless her and her hopeful heart. Our table is set just inside the balcony where we can still look out and see the stars, and two candles sit on the table illuminating our meal.

If Felix has noticed these extra touches he doesn't show it. Then again, if you think something is so impossibly out of your reach, you're likely making every effort to ignore signs to the contrary. Still I have so much to tell him tonight, and suddenly asking him to consider being my suitor feels like the least important thing. I'm brimming with all the information Antioch shared and what that might mean for us.

"Tell me everything." Felix leans forward in his chair, eyes alight with curiosity. "Did he know as much as your mother thought he would?"

"More," I say as I mirror his posture. The words I've been dying to share with him all day bubble out of me without filter. I share everything Antioch said as well as I can remember it. God's plan, the otherness of the power that filled the room when Antioch sang, and of course the Gate.

"It's real," I whisper. "Somewhere across the sea, it's a real place."

His face falls. He quickly replaces it with a smile, but I saw the change in him. But why? This should make him happy, excited. But I know I didn't imagine the quick shadow that danced across his countenance.

"So what do you want to do about it?" His calculated words are at odds with the smile on his face, and my excitement recedes a bit. This isn't the response I expected.

"I have no idea," I admit. "It's not as if I can abandon everything here and just set sail for an unknown destination. I've never even been on a boat."

He laughs and takes a sip of his drink. "You've never been on a boat? First of all, I think that will be the least of your worries."

"Go ahead and laugh. It's not like you're an expert sailor." I raise an eyebrow and dare him to refute me. Surprisingly he does.

"I am actually."

I wait for him to continue but he doesn't.

"You're just full of surprises, aren't you? Tell me, where in your time in the landlocked capitol did you find the opportunity to become a sailor?"

"I never said I learned in Aurora."

I gulp my own drink and set it down on the table a little more forcibly than I mean to. "You know, for all that you know about me, I know very little about you. We always talk about me, but I have so many questions."

Felix's gaze turns inward as he looks away from me. "Another time perhaps. It hardly seems important with everything else that's going on. By tomorrow evening you'll be inundated with enough useless information about your new suitors that you'll forget all about your questions."

"No, I won't. Not when it comes to you."

"Emilia…" I don't like the reprimand in his tone. "My past is better left in the past. I don't want to burden you with it."

"What if I want you to? What if…" What if we can marry? What if I can spend the rest of my life hearing about his past and learning more about him? What if we can go on adventures like looking for the Gate together?

"Don't make promises you can't keep," he says softly. He knows. He knows what I want to ask him. "The Council would never approve."

"I can be very convincing."

"Then choose your battles wisely. You will need to use your influence over them for the Insurgos, for the Gate. You can't use it for me."

"I can if I want to."

He smiles sadly. "Your stubbornness is one of my favorite things about you. But you're smarter than that."

I am, and I'm angry because of it. He's right and I don't want him to be. I want to be selfish and naïve and in love with the man of my dreams. Except I never dreamed of loving a man. Not until I met Felix. No, first there was Ronan. And then Felix showed me what it really meant to love.

Then I realize he's simply being practical, and while he may be absolutely right, it doesn't mean he would say no to my proposal. It doesn't guarantee a yes, either. What it does is fan the small ember of hope inside of me that refuses to die. If only I knew what was behind those unreadable eyes. We've grown closer than I would have thought possible after Ronan put an invisible wall between us, but Felix hasn't exactly knocked the wall down either. It's maybe the last vestige of what holds us apart. To love me would be to betray Ronan, and no matter how much distance we've put there, it's the final step he seems unlikely to take. If only I knew how to give him a gentle shove.

"I should go." Felix places his napkin on the table and stands. "You have a big day tomorrow, and you should rest."

Once again he's right, but it's not what I want to hear.

"Of course," I agree a little stiffly. I remain seated in protest. "I will see you for the ball tomorrow evening."

His brows knit in confusion, and he opens his mouth as if to speak before changing his mind. Did he expect me to beg him to stay? Well, I won't. I won't beg for him to throw caution to the wind and take this leap with me.

I think back to Antioch's words—God's path is sometimes a lonely one. Tonight all I can do is stand on the step illuminated for me and pray the next one isn't my last.

The next morning is a flurry of activity and celebration. Hannah and Cecily take time out of their preparations of my wardrobe to share a special birthday breakfast with me. We laugh and talk for much too long before it's time to begin the actual preparations for the ball.

I am bathed and covered with thick lotion before Hannah sits down with a brush to tame my long, dark hair. Cecily disappears to retrieve some lunch for the three of us, and I eagerly relay to Hannah a bit about what I learned from Antioch.

"Across the sea," she muses, repeating my words as she works tangles out of my hair. "There were stories when I was a little girl, stories my grandmother would tell us about the King beyond the sea. I always thought they were fairytales."

"I wish I knew half of what you and Felix know," I lament as I fiddle with the hem of my robe. I have Felix's scribbled remembrances of the Aletheia, but it's not enough. "I'm so woefully ignorant of all this. Stories you were told, words from the Aletheia you memorized…I didn't have that."

"Well," she says slowly, "maybe that's why you have us."

Didn't Antioch say something similar? That I had been given Felix to temper my recklessness. But after last night I don't feel like I have him at all.

"You perhaps. As for the Commander…" I let the silence fill in all my unspoken feelings, and Hannah seems to understand.

"He cares for you. Anyone can see it."

"It's not enough." The tears come from nowhere, and I'm so sick of crying. It seems like everything moves me to tears nowadays.

Hannah drops the brush and pulls me to her in a hug. "Maybe he thinks he's protecting you because a match seems so unlikely. Or maybe he doesn't know how you feel."

But he must know. Especially after last night. And all my posturing and maneuvering to make it possible for him to stand up for me as a suitor was for naught. Because he won't do it.

I let Hannah stroke my hair until my tears dry. It feels strangely liberating to admit my feelings for Felix to someone else, though I'm certain she's known about them nearly as long as I have. Maybe even longer.

"You deserve a man who will love you completely, Emilia. Don't settle for less than that." She kisses the top of my head and reaches for the brush again.

By the time Cecily arrives with lunch, Hannah has woven my hair into a loose braid to keep the tangles at bay while I'm readying for the ball. The three of us enjoy a light meal before the real preparation begins in earnest.

My gown is one of Cecily's own design, and it takes both my ladies to lace me into it. It's a huge, hulking thing with jewels that glitter like the night sky against the dark blue fabric. I can't imagine how I'm going to move around the dance floor in this thing. Especially when I'm such a horrible dancer to begin with.

They keep my makeup simple, opting for kohl around my eyes and a light oil on my lips that makes them shine. The effect, however, is anything but simple. Especially when I try my mask on. The kohl around my eyes accentuates them as one of my better features, but the gold mask makes them shine.

"Beautiful," Cecily breathes reverently. She surveys me with an approving nod.

"Thank you." I clasp her hands and pull her to me in a quick hug. "For everything. The gown is more beautiful than I could have asked for."

"It's my pleasure." She bows her head in deference but smiles widely.

"Now go finish getting yourself ready," I instruct. "I can't have my ladies looking less than their best tonight."

Cecily starts for the door, but Hannah doesn't move from her kneeling position beside me. Her fingers are working furiously to repair a small tear in the hem of the gown from where I stepped on it earlier. Not a good sign for any of my dance partners tonight.

"You go ahead," she tells Cecily. "I'll be along in a minute."

Cecily nods and exits the room. The door hasn't even had time to shut behind her when I hear another voice.

"Emilia?"

I look up from smoothing the thick fabric of my gown to meet Felix's gaze in the full-length mirror. He's paused just inside my door and hesitation belies his usual confidence.

Hannah stands from putting the finishing touches on my hem and gives me a knowing smile. Without a word she excuses herself from the room while offering Felix a slight nod on her way out the door.

And then we are alone. I'm not sure why this realization causes a flush of heat in my midsection or why I have to steel myself to turn and face him. But there's something in his expression that tells me there is more to this visit than a simple escort to the ball.

"You look festive." I try for levity as I turn and take in his formal uniform. He does not wear the blue cloak of a Borealis officer, but a black one. Felix is an island. His loyalty lies not with a country or a monarch but with me and, more importantly, with our cause. The only thing that symbolizes the important role he has in my—Titus's—court is the gold and diamonds of the crown brooch that connects his cloak to his black shirt. The same one I gave him when I elevated his title to Lord Commander and pinned it along with all my hopes on him. For a moment I am dazzled by the sparkling of the diamonds against his all black ensemble until I realize how ill the gaudiness suits the man I know him to be.

"It's not every day your queen comes of age. I thought this called for a bit of extra effort with my wardrobe." As he speaks some of the uncertainty seems to ebb and is replaced by his warm smile.

"Cecily insisted, didn't she?"

"She did."

We both laugh. Leave it to my lady to make sure not only I show up to the ball in dazzling fashion, but my escort as well. With anyone else Felix might have refused for a more practical ensemble, but he has a soft spot for my ladies. He thought to rescue them from the imperial palace for me, after all.

"Well then I suppose we'll have to show up to this thing after all. I had hoped I could talk you into escorting me to the stables instead of the ballroom, but it would be a shame to let that outfit go to waste."

"The same could be said of you," he grins. "What a waste to get all dressed up for only a guard to see you."

"You're hardly just a guard, and nothing is ever wasted on you."

I'm not sorry I said it—it's more than true—but I wish I'd chosen a better time. Because suddenly all the light and levity between us settles into a nervousness thick with—dare I let myself believe?—hope.

Finally, after what feels like an eternity of looking into each other's eyes, Felix clears his throat and lets his gaze follow his hand to his pocket.

"I have something for you. For your birthday." There's an unusual nervous tinge to his voice, but his hands are steady as ever as he reaches toward me, offering a small wooden box. "I saw it in the market, and it made me think of you."

Curiosity propels me forward, and I take a few steps until I'm standing closer than necessary to Felix. Somehow it still isn't close enough. I take the box from him, letting my fingers linger in his palm as I wonder what it would be like to hold that hand or feel those fingers tangle in my hair. It's a feeling I will likely never know, and I'm bereft of something I've never even known nor—until recently—even imagined wanting. Because waiting for me in that ballroom are not only courtiers and guests to celebrate my birth and coming of age, but also suitors. One of which I must marry. And none of them are Felix.

He's watching me with those sharp eyes of his, and he doesn't immediately pull his hand away even when I have the small box firmly within my grasp.

"You didn't need to get me anything," I say, though I'm practically trembling with anticipation of seeing what he's chosen for me. My fingers find the small latch on the wooden box, and I flick it open with a shapely fingernail. The hinge is stiff as I raise the lid…and gasp. Because shining up at me, hanging at the end of a thin gold chain, is a gorgeous black stone.

At first glance I think it's solid black, polished and smooth, but then the light catches it, and I can't look away. It appears to almost glow from within, displaying an assortment of reds, golds, greens, and blues that dance as I move the necklace to examine it. Like fire sparking within an abyss. Like some embers of hope in darkness. Like the rainbow room where we held each other in a few moments of solitude. A room that is ours now.

And I know now why he thought of me upon seeing it, and that realization is both breathtaking and weighty. But when I look up from the stone to meet his eyes, I think I may have misjudged him. Certainly there is hope there but not the sort I was expecting. Or maybe it's just because it's mingled with something else, something so much deeper, that I know Felix did not just pick this stone for me because he has pinned the hopes of our cause on me.

"I know it's not a diamond or sapphire or anything grand," he says quickly. Probably because he's misreading the incredulous look on my face. "But when I saw it, it looked so simple and unassuming tucked away amid the other flashier stones. Even then

I thought it was something special. And when I picked it up and saw all those colors…”

“You saw me,” I finish for him. Tears sting my eyes as realization nearly knocks me over. I adore this man. A man who saw me, the black sheep of the imperial coterie of ladies and princess, as something dazzling and special. He believed in me when I didn’t believe in myself.

Words I have no business saying to him are on the tip of my tongue when I remember I have several potential husbands waiting for me in the ballroom. So rather than say what I ache to say, I raise my heels until I can press my lips to his slightly stubbled cheek. I let them linger a moment too long before I whisper against his skin. “I don’t deserve you.”

His breath hitches slightly, but enough for me to know the effect my words have on him. Felix’s hand comes to rest lightly on my waist as he searches my eyes. The placement of his hand is nothing more than what he might do as he guides me though a crowded room, but there’s something much more intimate about it when those deep brown eyes are so close to mine.

“You saw me,” he says. “You were the only one. I danced with so many girls, and they were all convinced I was a prince. But not you. I couldn’t fool you. And you *knew*. Not just that I was an imposter—which any of them should have known if they’d just bothered to look—but you knew it was *me*.”

It sounds like nonsense, but I remember the night he’s speaking of with clarity. My first masquerade ball at the imperial palace. Felix dressed as Ronan and dancing with the myriad of girls who were so desperate for that crown. The sense of relief and surprise I felt when I recognized the man beneath the mask.

A sharp rap on my door jars us both out of the moment, and he takes a deliberate step back from me though without looking away. It takes a moment before I can gather myself enough to acknowledge the knock at the door.

"Enter," I call to the unwanted visitor. What I wouldn't give for some uninterrupted time alone with Felix. Though given our circumstances it's for the best. Dare I hope that tonight, after the ball, I can speak to him freely and convince him to take the leap with me?

The door opens slowly to reveal both Antony and Hannah with subtle, knowing smiles on their faces. Though there's space between Felix and I, our friends seem to have realized that's a new development. I don't like what those smiles insinuate. As if there's some sort of hope of their wishes—my wish—coming true.

"What is it?" Felix asks, a little harsher than his usual tone. He's annoyed as well, but with the interruption or the smiles I'm not sure.

Antony snaps to attention and the smile leaves his face. "There's a security concern near the temple entrance to the palace. I have taken care of it, but I wanted to make you aware prior to you escorting the princess in case you wanted to make adjustments to security."

Felix looks to me and then lets his gaze dart to the box in my hand and back to my face. "Wait here until I return. Don't even think about going down without me."

"Of course," I say with a nod. The last thing I want to do is walk into that ballroom all alone.

Felix acknowledges my acquiescence with a nod of his own then crosses the room to join Antony.

"Happy birthday, Highness," Antony adds with a slight bow of his head before he leads Felix from the room.

Hannah watches them go down the hall before she steps into my room and closes the door behind her.

"Happy birthday, indeed," she adds as she joins me and looks at the necklace in the box I'm still holding.

"Hannah." I try for a note of warning in my voice, but it just comes out with a sigh. "It's gorgeous, isn't it?"

"Truly. Would you like me to put it on you?"

I look at myself in the mirror before answering. With all the adornments to my dark blue dress and the rope of jewels around my head I'm certainly decorated enough for the evening. But I find I want this jewel with me. This piece of Felix I can take with me into the fray of suitors. So I clear my throat and hand Hannah the box. "Yes, please."

With deft fingers she unlatches the small clasp and drapes the necklace over me before stepping behind me to fasten it again. The stone falls just beneath the bodice of my gown, and the chain is so thin it nearly disappears against the bare skin of my neck and collar bones.

"Oh the chain is too long," she notes, experimentally pulling it tighter so the stone raises above my dress and the stone sits just below the hollow of my throat. "I think I could make something work to shorten it for this evening."

"No, it's fine." I turn to face her and clasp her now empty hands. "I just want to know it's there. It's not for show." Much like my entire relationship with Felix.

Hannah looks me over with a knowing gaze that seems far beyond her years. I don't have to explain myself to her. "You are strong for doing this. But if there was any way you could…The way he looks at you…"

"I know," I say as I blink back the wetness in my eyes. "But the Insurgos need a monarch to stand for them, and this is the only way I can do that. It's a small price to pay—"

"There is nothing small about denying your heart what it wants," she corrects me. "There is nothing small about following God's will when it is anything but easy."

"I wish I had your faith."

"Oh Emilia, you are God's chosen. His hand is upon you, and He will guide your steps."

Still I wish I shared her surety. Even knowing what I should do—must do—an uncertainty simmers within me. I've lately attributed it to my selfish desires for Felix, but what if it's something more?

I stop myself right there, because no good can come of those thoughts. What did Antioch tell me? The entire path is rarely illuminated fully. Just the next step upon it. And this is the next step. This is what I must do, and I know Felix understands. Which only makes that part of the journey more difficult.

"What if I choose poorly?" I ask in a small voice. It's the first time I've voiced this concern aloud.

"You don't have to choose tonight," she reminds me as she clasps my hands in hers. "Simply enjoy yourself. Dance and laugh and eat cake. It's your birthday and there are hundreds of people down there who have come to celebrate you. So let them for once. There are no difficult decisions to be made tonight."

Hannah is right, of course. All I have to do is smile and eat cake. Oh and dance. Which will be miserable for everyone involved. Still I let myself smile. This is my first real chance to show myself to my people and let them know me a bit. And I don't want to present them with a sad, melancholy future queen. They deserve to know me at my best, or at least the best I can give them on this night.

Felix and Antony return a few moments later. Antony extends his arm to Hannah to escort her to the party. It took almost a week of begging for me to convince her that she could attend as a guest and not my lady. Her dress is simple but fine, and her plain golden mask shows off her long lashes and delicate nose.

I can't help but smile at the way Antony looks at her as they both offer Felix and I a wave and then exit the room. Hannah deserves that happiness.

"Where's your mask?" I ask as Felix offers his arm for me. I take it with as much nonchalance as I can muster.

"No mask for me tonight. I don't want anything obstructing my vision while I'm watching out for you."

"You know you could just be a guest at the party instead of a guard. You are the highest ranking member of the palace guard. No one expects you to be on duty tonight."

"But that's exactly why I should be." He frowns slightly. "Emilia, I'm not sure you understand how big the risks may be. There's already been a potential security breach, this is your official debut, and there are several high-ranking lords down there waiting to court you. The only way this could be any more dangerous is if Cyrus himself showed up."

I do understand all this, and I am glad that Felix will be the one guarding my back, but will he ever take a break? Or relinquish any control over my safety? Now is not the time for that argument. It's his choice how to spend his time at my party.

"Very well. I know I'll be safe with you there."

The compliment seems to relax him, and he even offers a smile. "Thank you for letting me do my job."

"Yes, well, you do it very well." And without bidding, Ronan's face flashes in my mind. Felix's desire to protect me may be driven by many admirable things, but I can't forget—neither can he, I'm sure—that chief among those reasons is that Ronan ordered it upon our flight from Aurora. Felix is protecting me for another man, another life, another crown.

"I won't hover," he assures me as we exit my rooms and make our way down the hall, descend the steps and move toward the ballroom. "I know you need…space…to spend time with your suitors. Antony and I will be watching though, so if you need something just tug on your ear and one of us will be there."

"Does that offer extend to rescuing me from boring conversations?" I tease as approach the ballroom doors.

"If they're boring, I'm sure you can accidentally arrange to step on their foot and make your escape."

"You're assuming my dancing has not improved."

"Am I wrong?"

I can only laugh because he most certainly is not.

We're at the doors now, and we pause in front of them. The two members of the palace garrison who are acting as doorkeepers look to me for instructions with their hands resting on the large door handles. With a sigh and a set of my shoulders, I nod and they throw open the doors.

Any remaining novelty held by masquerade balls has vanished for me since my time in Aurora. Yet here I am again, dressed in the most expensive gown I've ever worn with a rope of jewels resting heavily on my head and a glittering mask obscuring the upper half of my face. It's hardly necessary. Unlike the trick Ronan pulled on the night of the Emperor's masquerade ball so many months ago, there is no one here who looks enough to like me to pass as my double. So I'm stuck playing me, and tonight of all nights I do not enjoy the part.

Titus has outdone himself for my birthday celebration. It's everything a future monarch could want and then some. Lively music soars to the high ceilings of the ballroom, and nobles and commoners (at my insistence) alike fill the dance floor with intricate dances and laughter. I will be expected to dance, of course, with all of the distinguished suitors who have made their way here to make their bid for the king consort's crown. Not for a moment do I think any of them are actually here for me.

"Such a wonderful turnout, don't you think?" Titus takes the seat to the left of me and rearranges his royal robes—the blue of Borealis with silver stars embroidered on the cuffs.

"I didn't expect so many people," I say while smoothing my hands over my gown. I'm wearing a deep blue as well. All part of the plan to make me look as patriotic to my home country as possible. The jewels on my head are real diamonds and sapphires and the gathers in my skirt are accented with the same. It makes the whole thing impossibly heavy and cumbersome. Yet somehow it's the small black jewel hanging from my neck that feels the weightiest.

"The entire nation is excited to celebrate your homecoming and your coming of age."

Excited probably isn't the word I'd use. Curious is more like it. Skeptical is probably a better choice.

I've barely had time to acclimate myself to the room when a line forms in front of me. Chiefly composed of men who seem eager to make my acquaintance. Most wear bright colors and elaborate masks, but none of them catch my attention. Their pleasantries are just white noise on top of the music and laughter from my guests. But finally the inevitable happens and one of them—I didn't catch his name—asks me to dance.

Beside and slightly behind me, I hear Felix chuckle. I glare at him as I stand and attempt to corral my skirts. My lack of prowess on the dance floor is known to most, but especially him. He had the pleasure of having his foot stepped on by me the first time we danced when he was posing at the crown prince.

Despite my misgivings, I try to throw myself into the moment as my first partner attempts to twirl me around the room. A difficult task in the best of times and almost impossible with this heavy dress. I manage to stay away from his toes, but he seems disappointed that I maintain so much space between us.

I politely excuse myself after the song ends only to find myself faced with yet another partner. This one, Count Seneca from the southern part of our country, seems determined to make a lasting impression and claims the next three dances for himself.

Trying to conceal my panting in the most lady-like manner possible, I take my leave and try to get my bearings in the midst of the thick crowd. I just want to take my seat beside Titus, but it's not easy to see which direction I need to go. I've just made the decision to cut through the thinnest part of the crowd to the wall and then reevaluate my position when someone else grabs my arm.

"I'm so sorry, but I really must return—" I turn toward my would-be partner as I utter my apology, but as soon as I catch sight of his face, all words die in my throat.

That mask hides features I know all too well, but nothing could ever conceal the crystal clear blue of those eyes.

Ronan.

16

My lips part, but I can't decide between a scream or a laugh so no sound comes out. I can't stop staring for so many more reasons than I'm ready to admit. Heart pounding, face flush, I have the urge to run, but there's nowhere to go, and some foolish part of me wants to be right here.

"Majesty." Ronan bows his head and kisses my hand.

The small ember of memory bursts into a flame as I remember those lips on mine and then how they remained silent when his father would have killed me. Maybe he's here to finish the job. Why else—*how* else—would he be here at all and without fanfare?

"Perhaps we could go somewhere to talk?" He still hasn't let go of my hand, and I haven't decided if I want him to. If he's here to do me harm it's certainly better to keep him close than to lose him in the crowd.

"Felix," I say feebly because I feel certain the Commander did not know of this turn of events. He would have confided in me if he knew Ronan would be at the celebration. Wouldn't he? Then again, I did ask him to give me space while I courted my suitors.

"Will understand," Ronan finishes for me. "Besides, we have much to discuss."

That's an understatement.

"How do I know you don't mean me harm?"

"Emilia." There's hurt in those blue eyes, the depth of which surprises me. "Felix gave you my letter?"

That stupid letter. Does he have any idea how many times I wanted to rip it to shreds even though every word of it is burned into my memory? "He did."

"And you trust him?"

With my life, but I don't say that. I only nod.

"Then come with me, please."

So I do. I try to quiet the voice of dissent in my head as he leads me through the crowd. Because I do trust Felix, and Ronan is the reason for the enforced space between the Commander and me. Surely I owe it to myself and to Felix to hear what Ronan has to say.

As soon as we're free from the crowd he turns to me. "Where should we go?"

The reminder that he is in my territory now takes me aback. He is deferring to me. I am in control. And that power gives me a bit more boldness.

I lead him from the ballroom as discreetly as possible for a woman wearing more jewels than most people have seen in their lifetime. A few guests look our way, but they just give us a knowing smile and me a little bow. Let them think what they will. This is bigger than any romantic liaison they may be imagining. This the fate of my country and maybe our empire.

Other than my own quarters, which I'm not ready to give Ronan access to, there's only one place I deem worthy for the conversation that needs to happen.

I've been here exactly once in my life, but the circumstances around that visit have seared it in my mind. Memories of my mother's tight grip on my hand as we ran down this hall, the sounds of her maids protesting as they tried to delay the guards, and my own tears flood me as I navigate toward the tapestry on the third floor.

This hallway is deserted as I hoped it would be. Everything but the first floor is off limits to the party's guests, but the guards on the stairs let Ronan and I pass without much of a second look. Even with his mask now dangling from his hand, Ronan isn't recognizable as the Imperial Crown Prince by anyone other than those that came with me from Aurora. It's an interesting feeling to be the one in charge with him standing next to me.

With one last look to make sure we are alone, I pull back the tapestry and begin pressing various notches in the paneling. Finally I hit the right one and with a soft click a small door cracks open in the otherwise smooth wall.

Ronan and I have to duck to enter it, but once through the wall, the space opens into a small stone room with a high ceiling allowing us to stand. And though I expect it to be lit only with the moonlight streaming through the high narrow windows, I'm surprised to find a torch burning in the holder. The same sort of torches I've found along the hidden passageways leading from my room.

But all of this barely has time to register before Ronan pulls me around and presses his lips against mine.

The kiss is deep and almost desperate as he walks me backward until my back is pressed against the cold stone wall. And part of me wants exactly this—for Ronan to be here for me and nothing else with no one else to say how ill-advised this is. But it's Felix's face I see with my eyes closed, and I shove Ronan away with less gentility than I'd planned.

In the slivers of moonlight and torchlight his pale blue eyes practically glow and dance with fire. Though I've put distance between us, he's still close enough that I can feel the gasps of his warm breath against my skin. One of his hands rests on the wall behind me, just beside my head, and for a moment all I can do is stare at him and try to remember why I pushed him away.

And I remember Felix…and my father…and his father. Anger bubbles up from so deep in me it frightens me. "How dare you," I hiss.

"How dare I?" Ronan takes a step back and rakes a hand through his dark hair. "Emilia, what happened to you? We were going to be married."

"Before your father decided to unburden me of my head and you sat there and watched." I stalk past him but the room is too small to allow much pacing. I'm not much further away from him than when he had me pressed against the wall. "And you never acknowledged your feelings for me in front of anyone. It's all secrets with you. Just like now."

"Would you rather I had kissed you in front of your entire court? Got down on my knee and asked for your hand? Or maybe you would rather I had asked my father to spare you so we both could have died together. How romantic."

How could I have forgotten about this Ronan? The one who is not used to being challenged or having anyone question his motives. It's the thing that always held us a bit apart.

"I never wanted you to die for me. But maybe if you'd believed me about your father then neither of us would have been in that position."

"And why exactly do you think I'm here? At my father's request?"

"Aren't you?" I scoff. As if Ronan could just escape the imperial court without notice especially now that the empire has been thrown into chaos by the attacks on the kings.

"You know, you were never forthcoming with your feelings either." Hands on hips, he turns away from me, though in the dim light his expression would have been unreadable anyway. When he turns back to me, he might as well be wearing his mask again for the lack of vulnerability he shows. "When I said I would choose you I meant it. You never said you would choose me."

No, I didn't. But I'm not sure if that's because I wouldn't or because I wanted to be assured of his affection first. I'm afraid it's the former. Ronan is never just Ronan. I remember thinking that the last time he asked for some indication of how I truly felt about him. But now I am not just me. I am a princess, a warrior, and the future queen of a people who desperately need me. I have plans and they did not include Ronan riding into my city to sweep me off my feet like I need to be saved.

And yet...

"I didn't think I would ever see you again."

He seems to relax a little at my words. "I promised you I would come to you when I could. I know the promises of a king mean little to you, Emilia, but I don't want to be that sort of ruler anymore. You made me want to be better."

"Does your father know you're here?"

"He does," Ronan replies with a grave nod. "I…persuaded him."

He looks away from me as he says it, and I know there's something darker behind those words. Pain runs deep in this prince. Why did I not see it before?

"Doesn't he still want me dead?" I can't imagine Cyrus was willing to just forget the whole execution idea.

"He wants too many things much more." Ronan takes a step toward me and reaches out a hand. After a long moment, I take it. "I won't pretend my father has come to love you, but I think he can see that I could. Perhaps on some level he actually wants his son to be happy. Perhaps not. But what he does want is to not fight a war on several fronts. He knows your death, especially now, would certainly lead to rebellion from Borealis and the surrounding lands. The empire is crumbling in light of the…executions."

It's his use of that word more than anything that convinces me to hear him out. Though Emperor Cyrus insists the kings of the realm were assassinated by Insurgo rebels, those deaths were nothing more than imperially decreed executions. Much like my mother's.

"He will let me live to keep peace?" I should sound more grateful than I do, but Ronan doesn't challenge me on that.

"More than that. He offers me to you in marriage. To unite our kingdoms and secure the empire."

I drop his hand and raise my own to my mouth. Believing Ronan was here on his own rogue mission or simply an ill-advised trip to see me or Felix was one thing. Comprehending this offer from the Emperor is much more difficult.

"Emilia, this is what we wanted. It's what was meant to happen. Just because he's willing to support it now doesn't mean we should be less happy."

He's right I suppose. But I don't know if I was ever truly happy about it to begin with. And I certainly don't know if I can be happy with it now that I know the tender kiss of a man I can never have and the power the Insurgos wield.

"You're right. Of course you're right." It's what I'm expected to say. It makes sense. If I'm to take my place as queen I will have to marry someone. If it can't be Felix, why not Ronan? My smile wavers, but I reach for his hand again. "We should announce our engagement as soon as negotiations are finalized. Do you have letters from your father?"

"I do. A royal proclamation listing the terms of our marriage and the dispensation of power between Borealis and Aurora. It only awaits your signature and those who sit on your Council."

How romantic. "Very well. The presentation of the suitors is tomorrow. Will you officially present yourself at court tomorrow evening? Then I will have Titus call a Council meeting for the day after tomorrow."

"As you wish." He raises my hand and kisses it before grinning. "I'll make a grand entrance befitting the lucky man who is to be your prince."

I have no doubt he will.

"Where are you staying tonight? Do you and your party need rooms in the palace?" I don't want to think about how I will make that happen while still keeping his presence a secret, but thankfully he shakes his head.

"No, we have taken rooms in fine inn near the wall. I didn't want to call attention to myself until I'd had a chance to talk to you. That way if you rejected the offer..."

He doesn't finish. I'm surprised it even crossed his mind that I might not agree to marry him. Here is a man used to getting his way. Could he ever actually be subject to me as his queen?

"We'll begin the negotiations at the Council meeting." I try to soften my words with a warmer smile, and it seems to work because Ronan smiles right back.

"I dreamed of this moment, you know?" He tentatively raises a hand to tuck my hair behind my ear.

"You dreamed of standing in a dark panic room with me while everyone eats my birthday cake downstairs?" My small laugh dies in my throat as he leans in until his lips are only a breath from mine. One tilt of my head would change everything.

"No. Of this."

And he's kissing me again, and I allow it. More than that, I welcome it. Because I want it to be this simple. I want it to be this sure. I want to love this man who seems so determined to love me back and forget about the one who can't.

Ronan is assertive and confident and my resistance melts away in his arms. It's a weakness I've never felt that seeps into my bones.

Ronan and I part ways outside of the ballroom rather than be seen reentering together. He gives my hand a last squeeze before exiting the palace, presumably to return to his inn for the night. I give myself a moment to rest against the wall, mostly hidden behind a cascade of decorative greenery.

How can I make my entrance inconspicuous? I'd rather no one—especially Felix—realize how long I've been absent from the celebration. But since I'm the guest of honor I'm sure my absence has already been keenly felt.

With a resigned sigh I step out from behind the greenery and run straight into myself.

The girl in front of me wears a dark blue gown, not as fine as mine, but similar enough in style that it could certainly pass for the same dress unless we were side by side as we are now. Her dark hair is styled similarly to mine and her simple mask emphasizes large brown eyes. The jewels on her head and dress look cheap and fake this closely, but I have no doubt they could fool many at any distance.

"Miss me, Princess?" Her lips curl into a wicked smile that's about as unlike me as it could be. But the effect is chilling. Because I know that voice.

Nox.

"Your cake was delicious, by the way. Shame you missed it."

"What makes you think you can show your face in here?"

"I didn't show *my* face. I showed *your* face."

She's quick, I'll give her that. And with the mask she does look too much like me. Since my birth I've looked different than everyone around me with the exception of my mother. But this girl has the same glossy black hair and honeyed skin I see when I look in the mirror. Felix is the only person I've seen with skin darker than what is considered normal in the empire, but even he is lighter than the two of us.

"Why are you here?" I try a softer approach in hopes she'll give me some answers. It's a slim chance considering she didn't even allow me to see her face when she held me captive.

"I thought you might need a little help with the wedding plans."

"How do you even know about my marriage?"

"Ever since your dear cousin made your presence known in the kingdom it's all anyone can talk about. And I have to say, after making my rounds in there, you have some less than impressive options to choose from. But that prince you disappeared with...well, he is something special."

"How could you possibly...?"

"I have my ways," she smirks. "You royals have a swagger about you. It's bred into you. That prince has it in spades."

"Whatever you want with me, leave him out of it." I don't know what I'm protecting Ronan from, but I do not trust the woman in front of me, and I certainly do not trust the idea of the two of them together.

The ballroom doors fly open, and several boisterous guests stumble into the hall. I grab Nox and pull her against the wall with me, hoping the greenery will hide us enough to not raise any alarms.

"Enjoy your party, Princess. We will speak again soon."

I look away for the briefest of moments when a guest knocks over a brass flower stand and it clangs loudly on the marble floor. When I look back, she is gone.

Both envy and annoyance snake their way inside of me at her abrupt departure. Mostly envy, because I would love to disappear as well. Instead I throw back my shoulders and smooth my skirts. She has taken my name and the little bit of enjoyment I might have had at this party and left me with the responsibility.

I brush past the guests who have spilled into the hallway and push open the doors to reenter my party. The music is livelier than when I left and the remaining attendees seem to have abandoned the stuffy sense of decorum they'd been wearing like a badge of honor. Instead everyone is laughing, the music is light, and the dance floor is full of couples and groups whirling in bright colors and jewels.

My eyes finally look past all of this to find the empty thrones on the dais. Felix stands solemnly beside the one I occupied earlier, but Titus's is empty. Either he is somewhere amidst this throng, or he has retired early. I suspect it's the former. He always enjoyed these things when we were children.

It takes a long time to weave my way through the crowd back to the dais. Suitors and courtiers alike keep pulling me into dances before I have a chance to refuse. It seems Nox has managed to convince everyone that I was a willing partner, and the annoyance I felt with her earlier fans into full blown loathing. When I finally sink into my chair with less grace than I'd hoped for, my hair is beginning to fall from its pins and my feet ache.

Felix says nothing but raises a dark brow. I know that look. There will be a conversation later, one I probably don't want to have.

He keeps his silence until it's time to escort me back to my room. Now that we're alone, I know I can't avoid what's coming.

"You seemed to enjoy yourself tonight." Felix's tone is neutral but there's still an undercurrent that indicates his displeasure. If only he knew it wasn't even me. But I don't dare tell him, at least not until I know what Nox wants.

"It was…interesting," I admit as we turn down the hallway to our quarters. When I'm queen I'll be expected to move into the royal wing and Felix will be expected to take up his post with the rest of my newly named Queensguard. Maybe then the frisson of tension that buzzes between us will dissipate.

He hesitates before asking, "Did any of the suitors show any promise?"

"Well, they're all better dancers than me. So there's that."

"That's a low bar. With those qualifications even I would make the cut."

I ignore this comment as best I can. Why can't he stop sending me mixed signals? "It's a formality anyways. I don't need a king to rule, but the Council won't admit it. I simply have to choose the one I won't want to kill after a few weeks so I can do what has to be done."

"And what about an heir?"

I stop walking. "What?"

"You'll be expected to produce an heir eventually. Otherwise won't Borealis be open to civil war? Or worse, Cyrus will appoint your successor."

My face grows hot with the thought of it. I hadn't thought that far ahead. And now that I know Ronan's offer is on the table, that thought is very very real.

"My apologies if I spoke out of turn." He takes my silence as a reprimand.

"No, I just…I didn't want to think that far ahead."

"You should. You know how Cyrus is. A good soldier needs to anticipate their opponent's next move."

But I don't want to be a soldier anymore. And I don't want to be a queen. I just want to be Emilia for once. It's something I've never been.

"Emilia?" There's a warmth and concern in his tone that wasn't there seconds before, and it takes a moment before I realize it's likely due to the tears that have pooled in my eyes. I wipe fiercely at them, but it's useless. "Come here."

I don't fight him as he wraps calloused fingers around my upper arms and pulls me to him. Not close enough to press against him but near enough that I have to lift my chin to look into those dark eyes.

"I believe in you. You're smart, intuitive, brave, and just the right amount of reckless—"

"Can I remind you of that next time you worry about me?" I smile and blink away the tears I'm determined not to let fall.

"You can try." The half lilt of his mouth melts my heart.

We don't look away from each other, and it feels like the first time in a long time that we've been so vulnerable with one another. All without a word. There's something different here, even different than those few moments we shared in my quarters as he gifted me the necklace.

The faintest brush of his lips against my forehead makes me feel beautiful, fragile. No. Not fragile. That's not quite right. Precious.

My kisses with Ronan earlier tonight made me feel many things, but this… Felix makes me feel precious. And without taking away any of my strength. And I will certainly need it all for the days ahead.

17.

It's all I can do to sit still as, one by one, my would-be suitors present themselves to me at court the next evening.

The gathering is small, mostly comprised of the Council members and a few of their guests as well as a small party each of the suitors brought with them. None of Ronan's people are here though. At least no one I recognize. Felix doesn't seem on edge, so I assume he doesn't recognize anyone from Aurora either.

I barely listen as each one of four men presents himself to me and offers a brief proposal. Each one has something to say about my beauty and how they could offer me something of value, but none of them hold my attention. Because where is Ronan? It's all I can think about.

Did he have seconds thoughts after last night? I thought we parted on good terms. Or was it all some sort of twisted game he and his father are playing? Maybe he doesn't intend to show himself at all. That thought is so depressing that I slouch in my throne with a sigh, and the suitor before me stumbles in his prepared speech.

Titus and Felix both give me a questioning look before I straighten and bestow a gracious smile upon the poor man standing in front of me. He finishes his speech and then takes his seat with three men who came before him.

That's it. Time is up, and Ronan hasn't shown.

"Thank you all," Titus says as he stands and straightens his crown. "We are honored to have you as guests in our fair city. We will now adjourn to—"

"There is one last suitor, Highness." The guard who dares to speak up and interrupt Titus's speech looks terrified.

Titus pauses, mid grand gesture, and looks to me. I shrug slightly. I'm not about to give away who I think—hope even—is on the other side of that door.

We don't have to wait to find out. The door swings wide, booming as it hits the wall behind it, and in strides Ronan. His gait is measured and purposeful, and he looks every bit the prince. Behind me, Felix audibly gasps.

He's not the only one taken aback by the prince's entrance. The small group of my suitors has lost their rigid composure and are now shifting in their seats, some whispering to others as they all eye the man making his way down the aisle. Though most in the realm have no idea what the crown prince looks like, the symbols of the Aurora sun gleam against his black cloak, and he has the unmistakable swagger of someone who is used to being in charge. It seems to be enough for everyone to put the pieces together.

Ronan stops directly in front of our thrones and bows to me with a sideways smile. To Titus he simply nods his head. "I am

Ronan, Crown Prince of the Atlas Empire and Defender of the Realm. And I have come to ask for the hand of Princess Emilia Aurelius."

Titus sighs. "Does everyone from Aurora think they can barge into this throne room without the proper clearance? Or does the princess just have that effect on all men?"

He's thinking of Felix bursting into the room in a much fiercer fashion on our first night back in Borealis. It's a thought that makes me smile. Perhaps Ronan is made of similar stuff after all.

"Having gotten to know her, I would say it's the latter." Ronan's smile broadens as he looks me over. "She is truly unforgettable."

"So she is." Titus sinks back into his chair. "As you wish then. Do you have a proposal for the princess, or is your name status enough?"

"I think that will be for her to decide."

"It is," I say, rising from my throne. I'm done letting men speak for me. "Prince Ronan, I am honored to accept you as a suitor for my husband and my king consort. No proposal is needed. I am privileged that you have travelled all this way to join our court no matter how long or short the time."

"Thank you, Highness. I only wish I had arrived in time to attend your birthday celebration last night. It's all anyone can talk about."

I could throttle him for making light of such a thing when all I want is to keep our clandestine meeting from the night before a secret from Felix and from the other suitors. But this is the Ronan

I remember—brash and bold and not caring what others may think.

"Yes, well, perhaps you will be here to attend the one next year."

"I intend to be."

"Please join the others in having a seat over there. Members of our royal council will escort you to dinner momentarily."

Ronan gives me another bow and then a wink before joining the group of four other men.

"Shall we, cousin?" I look back to Titus, hoping he's as eager to exit this uncomfortable situation as I am.

"Yes," he agrees. He stands to join me, and together we step down from the thrones.

Felix and two other guards take their positions in front of us to escort us from the room. I can feel the tension radiating off the Commander. He doesn't look at me or Ronan as we walk the length of the room to exit. It seems I succeeded in keeping Ronan's visit last night a secret after all. Though I never expected the coldness of this reaction from Felix. I thought he would be pleased to see the prince.

We all file into the dining room, the same one where I had dinner with the Council before that disastrous night at the temple. I cross my fingers this night won't be equally as destructive.

Tendrils of savory warmth curl up from the long table, and my mouth involuntarily waters. But there's a sourness in the pit of my stomach that doesn't mix well with hunger and rich food. It could be nerves perhaps, but it feels like something more. I can feel every pair of eyes in the room on me as I take my seat...all except one. Even without turning to find him, I know Felix is watching everyone else. It's his duty, I know, to size up any potential threats among the guests, but I miss the comfort his presence usually brings. He feels a million miles away.

As soon as I'm seated, Titus takes his seat at the head of the table and gestures for everyone else to be seated as well. Ronan doesn't hesitate as he claims the seat on my left hand for his own, and that significance doesn't seem to go unnoticed by anyone in the room. It's the consort's place, to the left of the monarch, and by choosing my left side over the right, Ronan has indicated that at least for tonight, he thinks himself subservient to me. A low murmur filters through the other guests as they take their own seats.

Amid the bustle of suitors, Council members, and other assorted parties taking their chairs, I finally look over my shoulder in search of Felix. As I would have expected, he his standing watch a few feet back from the table.

"Commander," I say without raising my voice. I'm very much hoping we can have a quick conversation while everyone else is distracted with the seating arrangements. From my periphery I see Ronan perk up at the mention of Felix.

Felix approaches the table on my right side, careful to avoid Ronan, though I'm not sure why. Have I misjudged everything between the two of them?

"Highness?" he asks in a perfectly emotionless voice.

"Sit with us. With me," I correct quickly when I see his dark eyes flicker to Ronan. "You are my right hand. Please take your place at the table."

"My place is with the guards, not at the royal table."

If we were alone I would roll my eyes or sigh, but I can't in front of all these people. Then again, if we were alone we could discuss what's really bothering him and none of this posturing would be necessary.

"Your place is with me," I say calmly but firmly. He's being ridiculous, and there's no need for it.

"Is that an order?"

His words feel like a slap. I hate his gift of reminding both of us he will do anything I say if I only command it. It feels impossible to know what he really wants. Does he ever do anything because he desires it? Or simply because he thinks it's what I want? Maybe I have misjudged so much about him.

"Of course not," I reply, my voice thickening with emotion. "You can do as you wish."

"Then I will stand with my guards." He gives me a small bow and returns to his place behind me.

Stunned, I turn back to the table to find most of my guests in various conversations with each other. Only Ronan sits silently. Maybe I imagine the flicker of hurt in his eyes, but I don't think so. I'm sure he heard every word Felix and I exchanged. He must be hurt, too, that his old friend doesn't seem happier to see him.

Beneath the table, Ronan's fingers slide through mine, and he gives my hand a gentle squeeze much as he did in his father's court what feels like ages ago. It feels too similar now. The two of us against everyone else. He gives me a tight smile and leans in to whisper in my ear.

"He is afraid."

That's maybe the last thing I expected him to say. "Felix?"

"Yes. He's afraid we don't need him anymore."

My instinct is to immediately refute the accusation, but all protests die in my throat. Because it makes a bit of sense, doesn't it?

There's no time to ponder it now because the servants have arrived at the table with the last bit of food. They busy themselves serving this impressive gathering of people with an equally impressive selection of food.

I do my best to enjoy the evening and Ronan's company. Though everyone present seems a bit overawed at his presence, he only has eyes for me. He is charming and deferential at all the right times, and everyone seated around the table seems to genuinely like him. Even my other suitors can't seem to resist engaging him in conversation.

So when dinner ends and it's time to retire for the night, I'm surprised to find I haven't had an entirely terrible time. This could be my life now. My future with Ronan.

"Tomorrow is the Council meeting, correct?" Ronan asks as he offers his arm to me upon our exit from the dining room. I take it without hesitation. I may be confused about many things where he is concerned, but this much feels natural.

"It is. Though I'm sure it's merely a formality. You certainly charmed them this evening."

"Well, I'm glad at least a few people in the room were happy to see me."

I don't need to ask to know he's referring to Felix. We pause at the top of the stairs and I turn to face him head on. I want to see his face for this conversation. "You said he was afraid we didn't need him anymore. What do you mean by that?"

"Just that. From the time he met you, he served as our go-between. He sang your praises to me as soon as he returned to the palace from fetching you. With as much confidence as I've heard him say almost anything, he told me you were the one—my future queen. Felix watched over you on my orders, spent time with you when I couldn't, and spoke of you to me in such tender words that I couldn't help fall for you. But now I'm here with my father's blessing, and there's no need for clandestine operations or secrecy. We can be together freely, and he feels as if there's no need for him anymore."

I have to give Ronan credit. It seems an accurate description of our current situation. "I would have thought he would have at least been happy to see you, though."

"So would I." He hangs his head just for a moment. "But it was fairly obvious, at least to anyone who knows you and I, that we arranged today. Felix doesn't like being kept in the dark as you well know. Your impulsiveness was a continuing source of frustration for him."

"It still is." I smile weakly, but there's so much to unpack in Ronan's statement. Was that frustration borne out of concern for me or Ronan's order to keep me safe? Maybe we'll never know.

"Felix has always been incredibly loyal since the moment we met. He lives to protect those he loves. And he does love fiercely, probably more than anyone I've ever met. It's a quiet fire, for sure, but that doesn't mean it doesn't burn hotter than most."

"So he sees our arrangement without his knowledge as a slight against his love for you?"

"For us," Ronan corrects. "He would die to protect us both. I truly believe that, Emilia. That we planned this huge thing without at least giving him a warning so he could plan for all possible outcomes must seem like a punch to the gut."

"So why didn't you tell him you were here?" Why didn't *I* tell him? It's as much of a valid question as the one I asked, but I don't want to explore the answer to it yet.

Ronan sighs heavily, and his shoulders sag a bit. He's silent for a moment, and I'm afraid he isn't going to answer. "I was afraid."

It's not what I expected at all. Between last night and today, Ronan has looked anything but afraid. As always, he's exuded a confidence that seems as natural to him as breathing. "Of what? Of me rejecting you?"

"Well yes, but that's not what I mean. I thought he would tell me—and rightly so—that I don't deserve you. That he would tell me not to come here because you were happier without me."

I take a moment to let those words sink in. Except there doesn't seem to be any space for them to sink in to, so they hang there while I try to understand them. Ronan thinks he doesn't deserve me?

"Felix was loyal to you always. From the time we left Aurora until now. Nothing's changed." And what a heart-crushing loyalty it was. For the briefest of moments I recall how Felix tore himself away from that kiss only to hand me a letter written by the prince standing in front of me now. Felix loved Ronan and saw the good in him even when I couldn't and didn't want to try.

"Everything's changed. He found someone more deserving of his loyalty in you, and I don't blame him at all. I see it in his eyes. He would do anything to protect you...even from me."

I have no immediate answer for that. There's no way to refute his assumption that doesn't involve me telling him about those kisses Felix and I shared. And that's something I'm not about to do. It would kill Ronan to hear it and Felix would lose his confidence in my discretion.

"Felix is too good for both of us," I finally say. That's the truth of it.

"It wasn't even my idea to save you." Ronan's laugh is tinged with bitterness. "It was his. The whole situation terrified me, paralyzed me, but not Felix. He came to me the night before and said he was going to get you out at all costs. He came to say goodbye."

"He trusted you not to stop him." It's not much, but I can offer him that much. Basically Felix trusted Ronan not to act...just as he always did.

"It's not much trust, is it? Especially when I told you in that letter that I made him promise to save you. I didn't have to make him promise at all. He swore it to me without prompting. I told him I would come to you when I could, but after seeing his reaction tonight, I don't think he believed me."

I think about Felix's insistence that he was serving Ronan even as he pushed me away and handed me that letter. As I read it, I had thought Ronan's lack of action was a calculated move, the likes of which would make him a great king someday. But even then Felix had known it for what it truly was and still he let Ronan play the hero.

"Who knows, though." Ronan shrugs. "This is what he wanted though. The three of us together. Maybe once he gets over the initial shock, he'll be happy about it."

We continue down the hall in silence, but all I can think about is Ronan's last words. Despite what he imagines, I don't think either of us has any notion of what Felix wants.

18

It's such a rare thing that I can observe Felix without him knowing. The only times I can actually recall it occurring he was unconscious. That's definitely not the case now, and my eyes hungrily follow every move of his body.

Having grown up in a military camp I'm used to men in various states of undress. My fellow soldiers had paid me such little mind that they often forgot I was a girl. Until I became a woman and a few of them began to notice.

Even seeing Felix shirtless as he nursed an injury on our way out of Aurora didn't affect me like this. Seeing the way he moves now, shadow boxing with a dagger in each hand and sweat running down his tanned back... How often is he parading around shirtless that his back is so tanned? I'm suddenly very jealous of anyone who's happened upon him this way.

Purely as an objective spectator his skill is something to behold. While my movements on the battlefield have never transferred well to the dance floor, he displays the same grace I know him to have when he's swinging me around a ballroom. Each strike against an imaginary opponent is lightning quick and powerful. Any of those blows landed on a foe could incapacitate them, I'm certain of it.

Felix is full of power, speed, deadly skill, and ultimately a lot of contradictions. Those same hands gripping the daggers are the ones that have stroked my hair with such gentleness. That mouth, now gritted in pain and exhaustion, so soft against mine. That warrior spirit so kindred to my own, cloaked in kindness and loyalty. What more could a man be?

"I could train nonstop and never be as good as him."

Ronan's voice jolts me from my staring. Heat blazes in my cheeks as I look up to find he's joined me by leaning against the stone wall. Was I really so preoccupied with Felix that I didn't hear the prince approaching?

"He was always a natural fighter. Surpassed me after a couple months of training together, but I certainly enjoyed those few weeks when I could beat him." His smile is wide and genuine, and he looks very much like a boy who has just been gifted his favorite toy. "You can beat him, though."

"Mmmm." I don't know what to say to that. "I think maybe he takes it easy on me despite my insistence otherwise."

"Yes, well, in the past I may have threatened him with his least favorite form of guard duty if he harmed you in any way."

"What was his least favorite form of guard duty?"

"Waiting on those simpering girls from Zephyros. Truth be told, he couldn't stand any of the girls but you. But then he did see you first, and you did have the fighting thing in common."

I start to protest at the way Ronan has trivialized my bond with Felix when I realize that he doesn't know the extent of it. Nor would it be very smart to draw attention to just how close I am with the Lord Commander.

"I made him a Lord, you know," I say casually as if this is a thing one does every day. "Lord Commander Felix Fidelis of Borealis... holdings to be determined at his leisure."

"Yes, I did hear that." Ronan rubs the back of his neck. "I wish I'd done that for him when he came of age. He's very deserving of the honor. But I wouldn't hold your breath about him choosing his holdings."

"Oh? Why is that?"

"Because he's never going to leave us long enough to see whatever holdings you grant him. Besides, Felix has always been a man without a land. Even after all the years he spent with me in Aurora I don't think he ever considered it his home."

I'm formulating a list of questions to ask Ronan about Felix and his background when Ronan shouts down to Felix and causes the Commander to pause his movements.

"You're putting on quite the show for my lady up here," Ronan yells down with a laugh. "A lesser man might be jealous."

Felix puts a hand to his forehead to block out the glaring sun. I know the exact moment when he sees me standing with Ronan because his daggers fall to the dust, and he reaches for the shirt he discarded on a nearby post. I'm sure I'm blushing fiercely as his muscles disappear beneath the fabric.

A few moments later Felix joins us on the mezzanine overlooking the training grounds. I can't look him in the eyes since I've been caught spying, but I don't think he's too keen to look directly at me either. Instead we both turn our attention to Ronan who called this impromptu meeting.

"Very nice work down there," Ronan says with only a hint of teasing. "I thought maybe Emilia was making you soft here."

He's trying so hard to break the tension between the three of us, but the dynamic is so different than the last time we all interacted freely. Ronan is the outsider now, or he would be if he hadn't just driven a huge wedge between me and Felix. Now I think maybe the three of us are our own islands, and it's lonely despite the company. I chance a glance at Felix and see him bristle at Ronan's words.

"I told you I would protect her. I take that charge very seriously." There's a definite coolness to his tone that Ronan seems determined to ignore.

"Well, you've done an admirable job as usual," the prince commends. "She is just as perfect as I remember her."

Felix looks away as Ronan wraps his arms around me and kisses my cheek. I'd like to just disappear from this situation completely. Is Ronan really that oblivious, or does he simply think he can will things to be as they were between the three of us?

"Oh come now." Ronan releases me and places a hand on Felix's arm instead. "I'm sorry I didn't tell you I was coming, but I'm here now. I'm fine. Emilia is fine. What do you have to be upset about?"

How can he be so cavalier when he and I had such an insightful and vulnerable conversation about this very thing last night? Ronan knows exactly why Felix is upset.

Felix clenches his hands into fists and his nostrils flare. "You were reckless, both of you." His eyes dart to me then back to Ronan. "You ask me to protect you and then you go out of your way to make my job more difficult. Do you have any idea how hard I work to make sure neither of you have to worry about things?"

Even Ronan is speechless at this outburst. For a moment I think he might yell at Felix or try to reprimand him, but his frown turns into a slow smile. He claps Felix on the shoulder and pulls him into a quick one arm hug.

"You've always taken excellent care of me, and I've never made it easy for you. I entrusted you with something precious to me, and you risked everything to save her life and bring her here. You know I'll never be able to repay you for that."

I watch the iciness melt from Felix as if he's stepped too close to the fire that is Ronan. Without an actual apology, Ronan has managed to smooth over the situation. At least for now.

This Council meeting has been much less lively than the last one I attended. I'm jealous Titus was able to sit this one out. Since the holy number of six must be maintained, he volunteered to abdicate his position, at least for this meeting, so that it would include the five Council members and me.

So far this meeting has been a halfhearted interrogation of four of my suitors about what they would bring to a marriage alliance with me. It's a formality at best, and we all know it. Everyone is simply waiting for Ronan.

When the fourth suitor is escorted from the room, the mood shifts from gloomy to enthused. The men sit up straighter in their chairs and adjust their clothing until they seem satisfied they look as presentable as possible for an imperial prince.

By the time Ronan is shown into the council room, I'm pinching myself just to stay awake. Each of the four previous suitors answered the same questions from the Council in nearly the same way. There have been few surprises. It's for the best, I suppose, as I've already made up my mind that I will choose Ronan. Still there is much to be discussed, and I want to make sure I'm alert to hear how he answers the questions the Council poses.

Unlike with the other suitors, the Councilmen stand to greet the prince as the guard—one I'm unfamiliar with—shuts the door behind him. They each offer a bow as he passes them to take the seat next to me. I remain staunchly seated. These men don't even stand when I walk in the room. I don't like that they're showing more respect to Ronan just because he's a man.

"Your majesty," Lord Orrin begins as the other members reseat themselves.

"Ronan is fine for this meeting," the crown prince says with a warm smile.

"Very well, Ronan." Lord Orrin seems a bit flustered at this invitation to familiarity. Probably because I've never allowed it for myself. "We are honored to have you here. We never expected such a distinguished suitor…"

"That was your first mistake. Your princess is a priceless jewel. You should always expect the best from her and for her."

I bite the inside of my lip to keep from grinning at him, but he goes to no great lengths to hide his own smile. The Councilmen, however, are clearing their throats and shifting in their seats as if they've just been reprimanded.

"Are we to understand that you are here with your father's blessing?" Orrin asks.

Ronan reaches inside his vest and produces a rolled scroll sealed with the bright gold sun of the Emperor. "He sends his blessings and his greetings to the great country of Borealis. He also sends this letter in his own hand as his official offer of marriage between myself and Princess Emilia."

Ah, so Cyrus is framing Ronan as a gift he is offering. That makes me bristle as Ronan passes the scroll to Lord Bryn to read aloud.

"From His Imminence Emperor Cyrus Dominus to the royal court of the late King Alector Aurelius of Borealis."

I clench a fist under the table as Ronan reaches for my hand. Even now Cyrus is asserting his dominance. He sends his son to marry me but refuses to acknowledge this as my court or my country.

Lord Bryn continues. "I was deeply saddened at the death of my dear friend King Alector in the terrible Insurgo rebellion. The realm lost many noble men that day, but I will miss none as much as your good king.

"With uncertainty and the threat of war consuming the Atlas Empire, it is of paramount importance that we all band together in order to maintain the peace. As a token of goodwill and with the hope it will give us a happy celebration to lift our spirits, I have decided to offer my son, Crown Prince Ronan Dominus, to your princess in marriage. Your princess is the servant of the gods and my son is the servant of the empire. May their marriage be a picture of our commitment to Caelus's will and may he bless our empire with prosperity and peace.

"I will leave the marital negotiations to my son, but send him to you with the full authority of the Imperial Crown. May Caelus be blessed."

There is silence around the table for at least a full minute as the weight of those words settles on us. I'm not sure what I expected but it wasn't that. If anything I'm even more confused. Does Cyrus really think so little of both Ronan and I that he will use our marriage to unite an unsettled empire? Or is there some larger plan? I wouldn't put it past him to use either of us to pacify the masses.

Were we to wed, it would certainly draw members from all the royal houses to attend. The wedding of the century they would call it. But if that's all he wants, Cyrus certainly could have found a way to accomplish it that didn't involve giving up his heir. Then again, he did try to have Ronan killed the night his assassins killed the kings of Atlas. There isn't much I wouldn't believe of him.

"Well, I believe you come very highly recommended." Orrin finally breaks the silence with a weak laugh which the other Council members join in on. Ronan and I don't.

In fact, Ronan's smile looks a little tight and his grip on my hand under the table is firmer. He had no idea what was in that letter either.

"While I am honored at your presence, Prince Ronan, I don't think I understand how this alliance would work," Lord Bryn says. "Are you willing to give up your claim to the imperial throne in order to marry our princess? Or do you intend to steal her away to Aurora when that throne becomes yours?"

As if Bryn is even slightly concerned about me being stolen away. But the other men nod in agreement with his questions.

"Oh I don't expect that throne will ever be mine," Ronan says casually. "My father's planning on living forever."

Everyone around the table laughs except for me. My blood has gone cold. Does Ronan know what he's saying? Because I fear that is exactly what Cyrus is planning. If he truly thinks the Gate brings immortality then Ronan's words are not the joke he thinks they are.

"Long live His Imminence," Lord Orrin agrees with a chuckle. "But I do have to ask how you foresee this marriage working. You see, we have to maintain the autonomy of our nation, and while an alliance with Emperor Cyrus is attractive for many reasons, we don't want arrangement that will put us more under the control of Aurora. We are our own nation."

Begrudgingly I have to admit I'm impressed Orrin is taking this stance. They're all so eager to fawn over Ronan that I truly expected them to hand him the kingdom as soon as he walked in the door.

"You are your own nation, and Emilia is her own person. She is the sort of ruler any country would be fortunate to have. When we are married my loyalty will be to her. I believe I can be a great asset to her. I have experience ruling, and I can show her how to govern—"

I kick him under the table.

"I would, of course, only be a guiding hand. It is her country to lead as she sees fit."

The Council seems more than satisfied by his answer, but I'm conflicted. How can I feel like I want to both kiss and punch him? Something about all of this still has me feeling uneasy. I really wish I could talk it over with Felix, but that doesn't seem like a possibility any more.

"Well, I have no objections. Shall we take a vote?" Orrin looks around to the other Councilmen. They nod in agreement. "Prince Ronan, would you please wait in the hall?"

As if there's any need for that. We all know how this vote is going to go. Still Ronan acquiesces and steps outside the door to wait on their decision.

"Well, Princess, is this your choice for your King Consort?" Bryn surprises me by asking.

No.

"Yes," I say instead. Because Ronan is my choice, albeit my second one. The first one still isn't speaking to me.

"Then are there any objections?" Silence follows Orrin's question. "Then we'll put it to a vote."

For such a monumental decision, it's over in a few seconds. Ronan is the Council's unanimous choice for King Consort. While

I should be happy, part of me feels as if a door has just been slammed in my face.

<h1 style="text-align:center">19</h1>

The entire palace is alight with excitement after the Council meeting. Word has travelled fast through the ranks of the servants that I am to marry the Crown Prince of Aurora, and another grand celebration will be given where I am to announce our engagement.

I'm somewhat surprised everyone seems so cheerful given that my last official appearance left a portion of the temple in ruins. But their joy seems to be less about me and more about Ronan. Titus has happily excused himself from most royal appearances in favor of letting Ronan and I take up the mantle. He was all too eager to step aside once Ronan arrived.

Ronan's taken up rooms in an area of the palace reserved for visiting royalty and seems to have wasted no time in charming everyone he comes in contact with. They all seem genuinely happy to have him here.

Well, all except one.

Felix seems to be going out of his way to avoid both Ronan and myself. I see him in passing as the prince and I take our daily strolls through the gardens or when we both happen to step out on our balconies at the same time. He is cordial to me but offers nothing more. I've never known him to hold such a grudge, but it seems he's got a death grip on this one.

As if the silence weren't enough, he seems to be injured nearly every time I see him. Nothing serious, but there's always a new bandaged cut or he's walking with a limp. What could he possibly be doing to cause so much damage? I can't get close enough to ask him. One night, after I've been on my balcony and heard him praying from his rooms, I pluck up the courage to knock on his door, but he refuses to answer.

My concern grows enough that I resort to confiding in Ronan on one of our evening walks through the gardens.

"He won't speak to me, Emilia. He's avoiding me as much as you." Ronan does little to disguise his hurt. "I've been down to watch him train the new soldiers. We used to bond over that, you know."

No, I don't know. In fact, it feels like all I do know is how little I know about Felix and Ronan and their friendship.

"He leaves directly after training ends, and he never answers his door. I think maybe he's sleeping in the barracks now with the rest of the soldiers."

That would explain why I haven't heard him moving around his room since the night I knocked on his door. Does he really need to be that far away from me? "We need to fix this. Felix is the best of us, and I can't stand to have him mad at me."

"Why on earth would he be mad at you? You haven't done anything wrong."

If only that were true. More like I haven't done anything right. Or at least it's felt that way lately. No matter how noble my intentions, someone always gets hurt.

I want to fight it when Ronan wraps his arms around me and kisses the top of my head. It's a very Felix-like gesture, but it feels different, and I don't *dislike* it. Since this is my new reality, I allow myself to relax a bit in his arms. Strange how only a few weeks ago this is what I thought I wanted. Now it just seems like an imitation of the real thing, but one I'll have to live with.

"I am sorry, Emilia, for how things have played out. It's not what I wanted for you. Maybe if you and I had met under different circumstances..."

Can he tell then that my feelings toward him have changed, cooled?

"...then there wouldn't be the shadow of my father looming over us, and we could just be together without all the pressure. And Felix would never have had to be the middle man, and I wouldn't be so jealous of the time he's spent with you these past months."

"We were both born into the wrong families to ever hope for that." I smile weakly. Ronan is a good man. He may even be a great one someday. But if he knew the half of what's transpired between Felix and I there would be fireworks. And I'm not sure what it says about me that, while Felix may feel guilty about it, I certainly don't.

"Yes, I guess we were. Regardless, I'm glad I've found you now."

❖

On the eve of my engagement celebration I decide I can't take any more of the silence. Perhaps it's because I don't want to think about the lifechanging announcement I am to make tomorrow, but I can't think of anything but Felix. Even with Ronan and my ladies, it's been lonely without his companionship these past two weeks.

I dress in the split skirt and top I commissioned the seamstress to make for me and decide to visit the training arena once more. It's the one place of Felix's I haven't invaded since he put up this barricade between us, but it's time for drastic measures. According to Ronan, it's where Felix spends most of his time these days, and I'm starting to think that's the reason for his myriad of injuries.

My confidence falters the closer I get to the arena, but I push forward anyway. I forgo the mezzanine in favor of marching right up to the wall encircling the arena where Hannah, Cecily, and I watched a few weeks ago.

Unlike then, everyone knows who I am now, and one by one they stop with their training as eyes turn to me. It's like a wave of stillness falls over everyone, save Felix. He's got his back to me and seems both confused and angry at whatever has distracted his men.

"Did I say stop?" he asks a pair of young fighters.

"Apologies, Commander, but the Queen…"

Felix whirls around to face me with no warmth in his eyes. Perhaps this was a big mistake.

"Your Highness." He gives me a great sweeping bow. "To what do we owe this pleasure?"

"I...I just wanted to." I stop, take a deep breath and restart. "I needed some fresh air, and I miss...training. So I thought I'd visit."

"You miss training?"

Well, I couldn't exactly tell him that I miss him. Not in front of all these men. What else could I say?

"Yes, it's been too long since I held a sword or a staff."

"Perhaps her Highness would like to take a turn?" Antony steps up beside Felix and bows his head to me.

"Word of your prowess with a sword has not been exaggerated." He turns to Felix and claps him on the shoulder. "Perhaps a demonstration for the men?"

I don't know what he's playing at, but I'm eager to participate. I *do* miss training and sparring, and though that was not my intention when I came down here, I will happily join in if it means Felix actually has to look at me.

The men cheer in assent at Antony's suggestion, and Felix's shoulders slump a bit. He has no good choice but to acquiesce.

"Will you fight her then?" he asks Antony through gritted teeth.

"I'm no match for her, sir," Antony insists. "It has to be you."

His intention is blatantly obvious to me, and I'd love to hug him for his determination to get Felix and I speaking again. How much has Hannah told him about our predicament? Maybe nothing. He is one of Felix's closest companions, and anyone can see the Commander has not been himself since Ronan arrived. It doesn't take much to put it all together.

"Fine," Felix growls. "Clear out of the ring and give us space."

The guards eagerly exit the ring and line up around the wall. Antony helps me over the wall, and I set my feet down in the dust of the arena.

The last time Felix and I fought it was not for show, and the stage was much bigger than this. I recall with painful clarity how we bloodied and bruised each other until Emperor Cyrus called a halt to it all. And I remember with even more pain the way Felix came to my rooms after and checked my injuries with his gentle touch. I'd like to hope that today might produce similar results, but somehow I don't think so.

Felix removes his sword belt and tosses me a staff from a rack of weapons. Surprised, I catch it just before it can hit me.

"No swords then?" I ask as I take a few experimental swings with the staff. It's nicely balanced and light in my hands.

"Too dangerous," Felix answers as he picks up his own staff.

Antony approaches us to see if we're ready to begin. I feel the familiar sing of adrenaline in my veins, and I nod in response. Felix responds in kind. Antony gives the word, and the sparring commences.

Felix begins with halfhearted swings in my general direction, close enough to appear competent but not nearly close enough to convince me he's giving me any sort of effort. I tilt my head and raise my brows in question, but he only responds with a light smack of the staff on my legs.

This will not do. I didn't come down here to easily defeat the Commander of my guards in hand to hand combat, and I didn't come down here to be ignored while we're sparring. I will make him pay attention to me.

It takes only a couple swings of my staff to realize I am mad at Felix. More than just him, probably, but he's the target of my anger now. Still I'm surprised to feel it. I've felt many things for him in the time we've known each other, but this is new.

My movements are sluggish after weeks of palace life and no training, but my muscles remember this dance. I swing and parry, and Felix is easy prey when he's not even trying. But I see his eyes widen as I advance on him in a flurry of attacks. He still has his pride, and I know he does not want to be defeated in front of his soldiers.

But I show no mercy when I spin kick his feet out from under him and pin him with my staff across his chest. My knee rests on his stomach, and I can feel him seething under me. Good.

Good natured jeers ring out from the circle of soldiers, but I barely pay them any mind. Felix is looking up at me with blazing eyes and flaring nostrils, and I know I'm about to pay for what I've just done.

Perhaps he's angry at me too, because he wastes no time in throwing me off and landing a blow across my back that nearly sends me crashing to my knees. In times past I've had to beg him not to take it easy on me, but he needs no such instruction now.

The crowd grows louder with cheers for each of us. Again I try to ignore them because it's taking everything I have to dodge the blows Felix throws at me. Even when I thought we were both giving it our all in the past, I can see now he's been holding back on me. He's absolutely terrifying to watch, and it requires every bit of skill I have to avoid being dismantled by his staff. If we'd chosen swords I might be carved into tiny pieces by now.

I let this go on a little longer until I'm panting for air and there seems to be no end in sight. I feel I put on a good show for the guards who have gathered to watch. At least they will know their queen is not weak. So I don't feel guilty at all when I finally concede by throwing down my staff at Felix's feet. He seems surprised—disappointed?—and throws his own staff down.

There is no smile of victory on his face, but I do recognize the frustration there. Beating each other up won't dissipate it though. It's not as if it's even my fault. I gave him the chance to choose me, and he didn't. He had to be noble and loyal and all the things that made me love him in the first place. How cruel they should keep us apart now.

I start to turn away, but his shout stops me.

"We're not finished."

The rowdy soldiers go still and silent. This, it seems, is more interesting even than the sparring match.

"You win," I shout back, my voice breaking. "I'm spent. I don't have anything else."

He doesn't speak for a moment, considering my words, then turns to the soldiers. "Leave us," he commands. "Be back in fifteen minutes."

They do.

Once we are alone, he storms toward me and pins me against the training ring wall without actually touching me. But he's close, so close, and I can see the veins pounding in his neck.

"I'm not finished with you," he says.

"You have a funny way of showing it."

He is so close, and I can't stop staring at his mouth. I want to channel all this adrenaline coursing through me into kissing him. Hard. Thoroughly. Like I've yet to be permitted to do.

I have just reached for his face, prepared to pull it down to meet mine, when he steps back as if I've slapped him instead.

"What are you doing?"

Incredulous tears prick my eyes no matter how hard I try to blink them back. Did I really read this so wrong? But I don't think I did, because I can see he's had to crush his hands into fists to keep them from shaking.

"What are we doing to each other?" My voice trembles as I look pleadingly at him.

"Nothing," he says flatly. "We can't."

"Felix, I—"

"Not here." It's so infuriating how in control he is. "Whatever you feel you need to say to me can wait. I have a job to do."

He turns his back on me and picks up both our staffs from the dirt. I wait for him to look back, but he doesn't.

"Lord Commander," I call in the most authoritative voice I can muster. He freezes and, through the thin fabric of his shirt, I can see his muscles tense. "We will continue this conversation later."

Felix turns and gives me a halfhearted bow. "As you wish."

I leave the sparring arena more hollowed out and bereft than when I arrived.

20

After another formal dinner where I sit back and watch Ronan charm the members of my council, I decide to seek Felix out to finish our conversation. Once again, he isn't answering his door, and a quick visit to the barracks confirms he's not there. I'm about to issue an official summons for him to be found and brought to me when I run into Hannah and Antony exiting her room.

They're hand in hand and smiling brightly, and despite the clouds in my own life, I can't help but be happy for them. When they see me they pause, exchange knowing smiles, and then give me a slight bow.

"Good evening, Highness," Antony greets with a knowing grin. "Your showing in the arena today was impressive."

I don't have time for pleasantries. "Where is he?"

The smile on Antony's face falters, and Hannah looks anxiously between the two of us.

"I don't know if I should…"

"Antony," I warn as I narrow my eyes. "I am not playing games. It's urgent I speak with him."

"He's been in a foul mood lately and doesn't want company. I think he usually goes to the rooftop terrace garden to be alone in the evenings. Or sometimes I see him going back to the training ground. He's been training, pushing, too hard. I'm concerned for him."

No wonder he's been injured. He's trying to work off the frustration we both feel.

"Thank you."

"He asked me not to tell you." Antony bows his head, and I know what it must have cost him to betray that confidence. But he's concerned for Felix, too.

"I won't let on that I heard it from you," I promise. Before he can say anything else, I turn and head for the rooftop garden.

It's not a place I've visited since I've returned to Borealis. Honestly, I forgot it was even there. It used to be a favorite location for tea or dinner parties in the warm months, but as there's still a chill in the air, I've had no reason to visit it recently. Still, something tells me I'll find Felix here.

Sure enough, as I top the stairs to greet the inky black sky, I see him leaning against the railing that encircles the entire terrace. He doesn't look up when I arrive, but I know he can sense my presence.

"You should go inside," I say as I wrap my arms around myself to fight off the sharp bite of the cool wind. "You'll freeze up here."

"I'm fine."

He doesn't make eye contact with me, and we both know it's a silly notion anyway. Felix is tough and rugged, and the thought that he would freeze on the roof of a Borealis palace when he survived weeks in the snow-covered mountains is almost laughable. But it's the only thing I can think to say that won't open a discussion I'm not sure I'm ready to have.

Felix looks across my kingdom as words continue to fail me. I rehearsed this conversation as I climbed the stairs and paced outside the rooftop terrace door, but with him in front of me now, I can't think of anything else to say. So I join him, arms crossed and leaning on the iron railing.

It's been far too long since I've allowed myself to feel at home anywhere. But even now, something about my city tugs at my heart. These are my people by birth. Now I must make them so by choice. That's as much a part of this deal as anything else. My people deserve to know my truth. They deserve to be free.

I jump when something warm and solid touches my hand, and I scold myself for not being more aware.

"Your hands are like ice." Felix is much closer than I remember him being. He takes my hands and presses them against his chest, rubbing them vigorously in an effort to warm me up. This is not what I expected from him.

The steady rhythm of his heart teases my palm and produces a definite heat inside me. I can't control a sigh as the warmth from the friction spreads up my arms, and his face twitches in what might be a smile.

"How are you so warm?" I ask. He's wearing only the thin tunic I saw him in earlier—no cape or cloak to brace against the wind—yet heat seems to radiate from him.

"Adrenaline." His voice is flat as he releases my hands. He starts to move again, but, against all reason, I throw myself against him and press my face to his chest. My heart knows what it wants even if it defies all logic and practicality.

Felix doesn't move for what feels like ages. Then, slowly, his arms find his way around me until he holds me in place. Finally, his hands begin rubbing gentle circles on my back. I close my eyes, and the tension and knots begin to dissipate from between my shoulders as his fingers concentrate there.

His hands slow after a few moments, but he makes no immediate move to release me. Will there ever come a time when his hands on me don't make me feel as if I'll burst into flames? He can rip me apart, expose the darkness, and stitch me back together with the barest press of his touch.

"Are you okay?" My words are muffled because I don't want to lift my head from his chest. As if I move at all, this will all vanish.

"I am now."

I might have thought his answer implied something about my presence if he hadn't chosen that moment to gently push me away. The ebb and flow of emotion between us leaves me barer each time.

"You have to stop training so hard. It's not good for your health. I need you in one piece."

"Well it's a bit too late for that."

"What exactly do you mean by that?"

"You know what I mean. You're smart, Emilia. I don't have to spell it out for you." The ice in his voice is colder than the wind whipping my hair from its braid.

"Felix, you know it has to be done."

"That doesn't mean I have to like it."

Anger flares in me again. "I thought this was what you wanted. Ronan is your brother, your friend. He's the reason you pushed me away, right? Because I belonged to him?"

"I hoped in time you would see you didn't belong to anyone."

We stare each other down in a fierce silence. Unlike our other disagreements, this feels dangerous. As if one wrong word will tip us from our precariously perched position. This is not about the Insurgos or political policy or my impulsiveness. It's about us.

"I can't do this without you."

It's exactly the wrong thing to say. Felix turns from me and throws his hands in the air. Then he spins back with a terrible coldness in his eyes.

"Just stop it. You are not a spoiled child. You can't make this decision and expect there to be no consequences, no fallout. I'm not made of stone, Emilia. I'm allowed to feel something about all this. Through it all I've stood by you, I've protected you, and I've—"

My heart hangs on the word he chooses not to say. Despite everything, I want him to love me. Maybe he's right. Maybe royal privilege is innate to every princess rather than a learned behavior. And by wanting to secure my alliance with Ronan—a man I once cared deeply for—and have the blessing of the man I would do anything not to lose, I am no better than the girls I looked down upon in the imperial court.

"You've always known this was who I am. Even when I didn't know it about myself. From the beginning you saw better than most that royals don't have the luxury of love. I can't sacrifice the lives and well-being of a nation or of the Insurgos for my own happiness. There's a weight on my shoulders you can't understand."

"Playing the victim doesn't look good on you. But you're right. Perhaps you and Ronan deserve each other."

As much as I'd like to believe he doesn't mean that, Felix has never been careless with words. He speaks rarely and when he does his words carry weight. These are simply too heavy to bear.

Tears overflow my eyes, and I turn my back on him and his stunned expression. There's nothing else to say. The responsibilities of royalty are not something I can make him understand, and I certainly can't make him accept them. He deserves more—someone who can love him openly and give him all he deserves. As much as I want to be that woman, I am not her. I am a queen.

And so I walk away carrying a weight much heavier than my crown.

21

I've become quite adept at putting on a smile when I feel anything but happy. My engagement celebration is just another such occasion. The official announcement of my engagement to Ronan was met with raucous cheers from the nobles gathered in court, and a lively party has ensued.

As expected of me, I've danced with Ronan, laughed at ridiculous jokes from courtiers, and smiled until my face hurts. None of it is real. Not when I've got an irreparable crack in my heart from my conversation with Felix last night.

In an interesting turn of events, it's the Commander who has tried to get my attention tonight, but I'm doing my best to ignore him. I don't know what else there could possibly be to say. He said everything I feared on the rooftop last night, and I can't stand to hear any more disapproval from him.

In order to avoid Felix, I stay on the dance floor even after Ronan starts to accept dances from other ladies. Felix stands watch next to my empty throne so I don't dare return to it even though my feet ache and I just want to separate myself from all the mindless chatter of court. Instead I take a glass of juice from a passing servant and busy myself making conversation with members of my court.

It brings back memories of that ridiculous party in Aurora where I was expected to charm and flatter the guests in order to keep my place by Ronan's side. I hated it then and I hate it now. I'm seriously considering feigning illness to retire early when a chorus of giggles draws my attention.

Near one of the columns, partially concealed from the masses, Ronan is holding court with half a dozen ladies who are hanging on his every word. His face is a bit flushed and his smile is wide and genuine.

Now I do feel sick. When he casually touches one of the ladies' arms and leans forward to whisper in her ear, rage nearly blinds me. I did not give up Felix to be treated like this.

With a calmness I do not feel, I join Ronan and his harem with a wide smile of my own.

"Apologies, ladies, but I need to steal my fiancé."

They sober slightly and offer me deep curtsies. Ronan makes his apologies and follows me across the room, still laughing at some unknown joke. I lead him through a side door to the alcove Felix and I sought shelter in after Titus made the announcement I was to be queen. As soon as the door closes and we are alone I whirl on him.

"This has to stop."

"What?" His dark brows raise in surprise.

"This. You. It's like I'm right back in some sort of competition for your hand even in my own palace. You can't act that way with those other girls."

He visibly relaxes and puts on an easy smile. "I have a persona to uphold, Emilia, that's all."

"Maybe in Aurora, but here people only know you as the crown prince and my betrothed. And how weak does that make me look if I can't even win the love of my future husband?"

Ronan's smile melts into a frown. "You know how I feel about you. How I've felt about you for a while now."

"Then act like it. I will not be your secret sin. All I ask is that you be honest with me and yourself. If I'm not worth the truth of your feelings no matter who's in the room then—"

"You are not my sin." He tangles his fingers in his black hair, tugging as he turns his back on me and then turns back to face me. "You are my hope. One I'm terrified to hold too tightly."

"Hope doesn't expect the worst. You act like I'm a weakness, and you combat that by pretending you don't care at all."

"The prince in me has to be prepared for anything. And I *was* prepared for everything, except to feel this way about anyone. Especially you."

I roll my eyes. "Well, thanks. I—"

"No, listen. I tried to kill everything in me that made me weak. Just like my father would have wanted. I poisoned loved. I strangled affection…. But hope is the last to die. It still lives. Every time I look at you."

They are nice words, but I'm so tired of trying to be everyone's hope. My position is an accident of birth just as Ronan's is, and he of all people should know that doesn't mean we're made of stronger or better stuff than those below us. I can't help but think of Felix. Of Nox even. They may be worthy of the hope of a nation. I'm not sure I'm worthy of a single heart. It won't stop Ronan from pinning it on me though.

"But your father supports our marriage. He wants this to happen. Why would you think that means you can't feel anything real for me?"

"My father wants peace. He wants immortality. If he can use me to obtain that he will. If he knew what I really felt for you, that it's you whose orders I will follow, he brings me home at best and kills me at worse."

I know all too well what it feels like to be a pawn in a father's game. And if what he's saying is true, the danger from Cyrus is very real. Does Ronan actually love me or just the idea of freedom from his father? Freedom can make men do crazy things. But so can love, or so I've heard. Can I really believe Ronan is deceiving his father and not me?

"That ballroom is full of my people. They're your people too. And they need to believe that my marrying the imperial prince is not signing the kingdom over to heavier control from your father. They value their independence too much to let me do that to them, and I value mine as well. They already think I'm weak because I'm a woman. I will not have it appear as if you're manipulating me as well."

His demeanor softens, and I'm amazed at just how much it changes his appearance. Ronan is every inch a prince, but in this moment he looks like a boy who just desperately wants someone to truly love him.

"I'm sorry," he says. "I want to help you, truly, Emilia, but I don't know how best to do so."

"Could you just do your best to pretend as if you adore me?" It sounds so shallow, but in absence of a better plan, I need Ronan to get me my crown, and I need my people to believe it is I who will be ruling and not the Emperor by proxy. And I won't ask him to love me, because it's a word he himself has not used. It's such a small word, but its absence is huge.

"I don't have to pretend, Em. You are amazing, exquisite. I am lucky to have you."

"You don't have me yet. We still have lots of hoops to jump through."

"I don't mean publicly. I mean in these moments where it's just us. You're mine and I'm yours."

I am no one's.

Those words I keep for myself because it would only hurt him. It's a game he and I have played before when our courtship *was* just a game. He professes his affection for me with none of the words I really want to hear, and I offer him just enough to keep things moving forward but never the affirmation he desires. Someday soon he will realize he's been assuming too much about my feelings unless I can somehow make myself truly love him instead of only harboring a fondness for him. Maybe time will fix that.

I leave Ronan to return to the party and make my apologies. I can't even stand the thought of returning to that room. All I can think of is my bed and hopefully falling into a dreamless sleep.

That's not to be, however. I'm barely inside my room when I'm shoved roughly against the wall and I feel the sharp point of a knife in my back.

All I can do is sigh. I simply don't have the energy for these dramatics tonight.

"What do you want, Nox?" Even without seeing her I know who my assailant is. The hand that encircles my wrist is too small to be a man's, and I have been halfway expecting something like this from her since the night of my masquerade ball.

"Don't you know how to follow instructions?" she hisses in my ear. "If you had just listened to me and left me a sign on that altar like I asked then we wouldn't have to meet like this."

"Since you've presumably been watching me, you'll know I've been a little busy trying to run a country," I huff as I try experimentally to pull my wrists from her grasp. She tightens her grip and digs the knife a little deeper into the voluminous fabric of my dress. "Also, there's no need for the knife. I'll talk to you without it."

I could disarm her. I just need a little bit of space from the wall to have room to maneuver. Possibilities are racing through my mind when the door to my room swings open.

Nox jerks me back against her and pulls me across the room away from the door. She moves the knife from my back to my throat, and I go still as we both stare at the person standing in the doorway.

Felix is as still as a statue as his hand rests on his sword pommel and he takes in the situation before him.

"A-Alara?"

It's Felix's tone, laced with an uncertainly I can't reconcile with my steady commander, rather than his word that shock me. Behind me a blade clatters to the tile floor.

"Felix?"

A hesitant familiarity hangs between my would-be captor and my rescuer, and I'm uncomfortably trapped in the middle. They know each other?

Along with confusion and so many questions, jealousy creeps into my gut. How does Felix—*my* Felix—know this vigilante who clearly has no scruples with holding a knife to my throat?

Quicker than I imagined possible, Alara brushes past me and throws herself at Felix. Instead of bracing himself for an attack he opens his arms and welcomes her fierce hug with wide incredulous eyes. I've never seen that expression on his face for anyone...including me.

"Ahem." I clear my throat with some force after what feels like too long, and they break apart without the least look of embarrassment at their outburst. "Would one of you care to fill me in on what's going on here?"

"We're old friends," Alara responds with a smile that does little to make her look less lethal. "Separated by tragedy and reunited in the palace. Quite a story, don't you think?"

No, I don't think. Because it's a story I don't know, but I don't like the implications in her tone.

"We knew each other as children," Felix supplies dutifully. His eyes are still full of incredulity. "But we haven't seen each other since…"

"Since you hopped aboard a ship and left us all behind."

Oh I definitely want to hear more about this, but preferably without my would-be evil twin in the room. I'm not sure how much of the truth I'd get from her and how much Felix would be willing to say with her there. Though he initially looked shocked and happy to see her, now he just appears uneasy as if he knows of a good reason why Nox—no, Alara—shouldn't be here and doesn't want to voice it.

"Well, as happy as this reunion is, can we get back to the reason you were holding a knife to my back?"

My question seems to jolt Felix back to reality, and he steps between me and Alara. "Yes, what are you doing here? How did you get in?"

Alara looks past Felix to me. "Yes, Princess, tell him how I got in."

I cringe. Because the last thing I need is for Felix to know I've kept more secrets from him. So I ignore that part of his question. "She's here because she's Insurgo. Apparently the leader of the rebel group that's been terrorizing the city."

"Not the entire city," she insists as she retrieves her knife from the floor. She's entirely too comfortable in this situation. "Just those affiliated with the heretic religion."

"So it was you with the arrows?" Felix asks. "*You* shot me?"

"Well, I'll admit my aim was thrown off a bit by the massive storm that rolled in." Alara turns an accusatory glare in my direction. "How did you do that?"

"I don't know," I admit. "I prayed and then things started happening. It's not like it was under my control."

She considers this for a moment then turns to Felix. "You should have known better than to run under a hail of arrows. Serves you right you got shot. Trying to be a hero, I presume. You always were the type."

I take a step toward her, ready to wring her neck when Felix steps between us.

"So you're with the Insurgos," he says carefully. "But that doesn't explain why you're in the palace."

"She's here because of the prisoner in the north tower—Antioch. She came for information." I keep my eyes on Alara's knife rather than Felix. I don't trust her enough to look away.

"But stayed for the touching reunion," she quips. "Does he know how we met?"

"And when exactly would I have had time to make that connection for him? You had a knife at my back when he walked in if you remember."

"Yes, you keep saying that. I'm sure it's not the first time that's happened to you. You really should be more careful."

"Careful, Alara." Felix takes a step toward her with a hand raised. "If you provoke her you'll have to deal with me."

It takes a moment for the coy smile on her lips to fade, but it does, leaving a sort of wistful admiration in its wake.

"I heard the stories of the princess and her guard, but seeing the two of you together—knowing the two of you—it really is something altogether different, isn't it?"

Is she jealous? She's been so good at pretending to be me that maybe she's upset she doesn't have her own Felix. Or does she? They have a history, and he hasn't ripped her limb from limb for holding me at knifepoint. That counts for something, right?

"The Gate is real," I say to direct the conversation back to the reason for her visit. "That's what you wanted to know, isn't it? Somewhere across the sea. There's nothing more than that."

"Oh I think there's a great deal more than that." Alara narrows her eyes at me. "So what do you intend to do about it?"

"Do? I plan to take my throne, and try to talk some sense into you so I can make this a safe place for Insurgos to live," I snap. "But I can't exactly do that if you're out there causing chaos. You are exactly the sort of Insurgo they're all afraid of."

"These people need to see action. They need to see the consequences of their choices."

"They need to see the truth."

"And they will." Felix once again tries to break the tension between us. "Emilia will make a good queen, and there are plans to make peace with the Insurgos in Borealis."

"And what about the rest of them?" Alara asks pointedly. "What about those the Emperor wants to slaughter for information on his way to greater power. Who will defend them?"

I don't have an answer for her. Because it will take everything I have to make Borealis a safe haven. I don't know how to protect thousands of people who are too afraid to even show their faces.

"The nations don't support Cyrus's war," Felix supplies. "He can't get far without support, and he certainly doesn't have that here."

Alara laughs coldly. "Maybe the two of you should talk to your little princeling then. He seems to have a very different idea of loyalty if his letters are to be believed. You need to bring him into the fold or things are going to get much worse."

For the first time since he entered the room, Felix and I really look at each other. Forgotten is the rooftop fight and all else between us. What has Ronan been doing right under our noses? Have we truly been so preoccupied with each other that we've missed something this huge?

"I can see you two have much to discuss." Alara sheaths her knife in her boot and offers me a mocking curtsy. "Until next time, Highness. You can leave any messages for me in that room behind the tapestry on the third floor."

So that's how she got in the night of my birthday party. No wonder there was already a torch burning when Ronan and I entered.

Without waiting for a response, Alara slips across the room, behind the wardrobe, and disappears from sight.

22

As soon as she is gone, Felix and I both speak at once.

"You *know* her?"

"Why didn't you tell me there was a secret passage in here?"

I pause, collect myself, and try again. I might as well preemptively answer his questions. "I met Alara several weeks ago when she…arranged a meeting between the two of us. She was going by Nox then."

I wait for the realization to dawn on him, but then I remember he never knew me by that name.

"It was the name I used for myself when I was in the military. She was apparently quite adept at passing herself off as me because she managed to fool everyone at my birthday masquerade." His eyes widen, and I know he understands. "Ronan was there that night, and when he and I left to talk she must have seized her chance to play the role of a lifetime."

"I knew it wasn't you," he practically whispers.

"She's the one who told me about the room under the temple where I found my mother's letters. She wanted the information

Antioch had about the Gate. Beyond that, I'm not sure what she wants."

"She wants to burn the world down for what she believes is right. Alara has been that way since we were children." Felix's eyes are somewhat vacant as if he's remembering another time and another life.

There are so many questions I want to ask about that, but I don't dare. I can't forget Felix and I aren't on great terms, and there are so many more important things that need to be discussed.

"What made you come to my room tonight? Did you know something was wrong?"

"Not in that sense. I was worried when you disappeared from the celebration. Ronan told me the two of you had an argument, and I wanted to see if you were all right."

"He hasn't seen an argument with me yet if what Alara said is true." I clench my fists until my fingernails dig into my palms. "We can't have been that wrong about him, can we?"

"Ronan is complicated at best. Every time I think I can predict what he will or won't do, he surprises me by doing something like showing up here unannounced. He might be sympathetic to the cause because of you, but I don't think he's loyal to it."

"You honestly think he's been writing letters to his father about the Insurgos here?" What about all the pretty things he said to me earlier? But didn't he also say that if his father could use him to obtain what he really wanted he wouldn't hesitate to do so?

Felix looks broken at the thought. "I don't know."

"Well, I know how we can find out."

Ronan's rooms are empty as I knew they would be. He is, no doubt, still at the party and still charming all my guests while making apologies for my absence. No guards try to stop me as I enter. Now that Ronan and I are publicly engaged, it's not abnormal for me to be sneaking into his rooms, although it's not a romantic liaison I have on my mind.

I left Felix behind in our wing of the palace. This is my mission, and I'm not emotionally stable enough to handle his company anyway. We were civil to each other, but I'm not sure how it can be more than that at the moment even if we are united in our hope that Ronan is innocent of what Alara accused him of.

The prince's room is neat but lived in. It hasn't taken long for him to make himself at home. The rooms are finer than mine and much larger, so it takes me a moment to locate a writing desk in an alcove off the bedroom. There papers are strewn across the desk. Some bear the Imperial seal, and others look half finished.

With a shaking hand I pick up a partially rolled scroll and begin to read. My eyes widen with every word. A letter from Cyrus to his son, commending him for being so thoroughly accepted in Borealis court. Asking for information on the Insurgo rebellion in the city. Insisting Ronan tell him more about the unrest among the citizens.

I set the letter down and take a deep breath. It's fine. I could expect nothing more from Cyrus. Just because he's asked for information doesn't mean Ronan gave it. But a sinking feeling in my gut leaves me anxious as I pick up the partially finished letter in Ronan's own hand.

Father,

You were right to say the true rebellion is in Borealis. Though I haven't seen any actual violence since I've arrived, the marks of it are all over the city. Portions of the temple are still in ruin, and the people here are on edge. It seems they want peace with the Insurgos and are willing to put Emilia on the throne if that means she can negotiate. Without that bargaining chip, I'm not sure they would accept her as monarch. Many on the Council fear she is too much like her mother, but my presence seems to have tempered those concerns for now.

I am concerned if news of the Borealis rebellion gets out that more of the Insurgos will take up arms. They are having some success here and that may prove dangerous to your empire. However I am taking measures to quell the rebellion before it can...

"Emilia?"

Ronan stands in the doorway, watching me as I read his words. When I look up at him, I crumple the letter in my fist and hold it up for him to see.

"How could you?" My tone is so sharp it feels as if I'm spitting daggers.

"Em, don't." Ronan holds his hands up to stop me from coming any closer. "Don't reprimand me for something you don't understand."

"What is there to understand?" Tears sting my eyes as my vision blurs. I'm such a fool. How could I actually believe he was here for me when all he wants—all he's ever wanted—was to make his father proud. "You traded everything for him. You traded me."

Ronan opens his mouth, but I cut him off before he can speak.

"Don't pretend you didn't, because I read it all. You're going to bring order to Borealis, quell the Insurgos in the city. You're going to make him proud?"

"It's the only way. You don't know what it's like—"

"To be blinded by love for a traitor? I think you underestimate just how much I do know about that."

He steps back, eyes glazed and stunned as if I've slapped him. I still might. I don't know if my insinuation of his traitorous actions or my near admission of love shocks him most.

"How can I ever trust you enough to marry you? I will always have to wonder if you're spying on me for him. Well, let me save you the time. When I am queen I plan to allow the Insurgos to worship freely here. In fact, I hope my country will become a safe haven for all Insurgos where we can protect them from the likes of your father. He won't kill another soul if I have my say. If you can't get on board with that then you should leave now."

"Emilia, I'm truly sorry. I told you earlier I had a part to play, and this is it. If I don't give him something then he'll remove me from the equation, and there will be no buffer between you and him."

"I don't need your protection," I snap. I want to believe him more than anything, but this is not something I will allow him to charm his way out of.

"I know you don't." His voice breaks and so does my heart. "You don't really need anything from me. Do you know how that makes me feel? I am completely useless next to you, and when I try to do something to help it just blows up in my face."

Help? He honestly thinks he was helping me?

"This will kill Felix. Regardless of what you pretended to feel for me, I know you care about him."

"This isn't about him, or you for that matter. It's about me and my father."

Silence. What can I say to that? It's exactly as I feared.

"He's not wrong, you know," Ronan continues in a cautious tone. "To want to bring order to this chaos. To give the realm peace and security and show them that rebellion will not be tolerated."

"This isn't about the realm!" I throw my hands up and begin pacing the small room. "If you are to be my consort you have to give up your allegiance to Aurora and pledge it to Borealis. If you can't do that then you should leave now. There's no point in a wedding if things have not changed since I left Aurora."

"Look, all I ultimately want is peace, and I think my father does as well. The only reason he did all those awful things to the Insurgos was because he wanted their information on that stupid Gate. And he only wants the Gate because he thinks the added power it gives is necessary to guard the kingdoms against the Insurgo rebellions...which I might have been convinced didn't exist until I saw what they've done here. You have a true rebel group right under your nose, and it will destroy your city if you let it. But if there were peace, well, then my father would certainly give up this search for the Gate and leave the Insurgos alone. There would be no need to hunt them down."

I laugh bitterly. "There is no chance. Your father was willing to kill me for even the slightest Insurgo inclination. You think he's going to be willing to talk peace?"

"You don't know the whole story. There's so much history there you just don't understand."

I can't hear anymore. No more excuses and no more masks. For at least the second time I have been fooled into thinking Ronan could love the Insurgos as I do. That he might truly want to make the realm a place where they could live in peace worshipping their God—my God. The pain is a deep ache in my chest.

"Well, what I do understand is that you're not the man I thought you were. I will not marry a tyrant nor be subject to one. You're no better than him."

His blue eyes narrow, but his voice is soft and broken when he speaks. "I warned you."

"At least you were right about one thing."

Three days after my confrontation with Ronan I receive my own letter sealed and stamped with the Imperial seal. Felix shows up at my door, carrying it with a frown on his face. I haven't spoken to him about my fight with Ronan, but I know he knows. I hope Ronan managed the courage to tell him himself. Honestly, I've gone out of my way to avoid both of them since that night.

But now I can't ignore Felix standing here with such an important document. The timing seems suspicious. What has Ronan written to his father to set this in motion?

"May I come in?" Felix asks, and I realize I've been staring at the letter in his hand without speaking.

"Yes," I say as I take the letter from him. No matter what is or isn't between us, I value his counsel tremendously.

He steps just inside the door and shuts it behind him. I can feel his eyes on me as my trembling fingers break the wax seal. A quick glance at the signature on the letter confirms what I already knew—it's from the Emperor.

I pace the room as I read and reread the words, hardly believing them. I'm on my fourth read of the letter when Felix speaks up.

"Emilia? Is it that bad?"

"No." My voice is shaky as I speak. So many emotions course through me that I'm not quite sure which one to latch on to. "It-it seems too good to be true."

I hand Felix the letter and let him read as I continue to pace the room.

Ronan was right. Cyrus himself is offering me peace. Not only between me and him, but between himself and the Insurgos. All I have to do is marry Ronan and agree to moderate peace talks between Insurgos leaders and the rest of the empire. He wants Ronan and I to model the harmony that can exist between the empire and the Insurgos.

"He did it," Felix says softly as he finishes reading. "I didn't think he could, but he actually did it."

"What are you talking about?"

"Ronan. He told me he was going to stand up to his father, to insist on peace. To insist on you." Felix swallows hard. "I didn't think it was possible, but here's the proof."

What I wouldn't give to have heard that conversation between the two of them. I was so harsh on Ronan, but Felix, it seems believed in his motives even if he didn't believe in his ability.

"So you think it's real?" I want to believe it more than I've wanted to believe almost anything. But it means I've been so very wrong about Ronan.

"I do."

I can't read the emotion on Felix's face. Pride maybe? Relief? I'm sure he never wanted to imagine the worst of Ronan. He's been his blind spot for years.

"It means I can begin inviting Insurgo leaders to court…if I can convince them to come." I hesitate. "It means Alara will be at court."

He doesn't react. I'm sure he can sense me fishing for information, and he seems determined not to give me any.

"It means you can marry Ronan."

And there it is. But I'm not having that discussion right now. I'm not sure there's anything left to say on the matter. At least not to Felix. Ronan on the other hand…

"Will you take a note to him for me?" I ask as I rummage around for a scrap of paper. It's time I either embrace this for what it is or abandon it completely. I want to look Ronan in the eye when I make that decision.

"Of course." Felix takes my hastily scribbled note and tucks it away. "I'll deliver it at once."

He doesn't leave time for me to say anything else before he's gone.

Since there is no court today and no formal dinner to attend, I don't see Ronan at all. I hope my note was well received, but part of me would not be surprised if he fails to show in my room this evening. Still I make an effort to make him feel welcome should he come. There's a large fire in my fireplace, and I pull a large thick blanket from my bed to spread out in front of it.

We had a conversation once in front of a fireplace in Aurora that looked much like this. Perhaps I'm hoping to recreate the vulnerability of that night with much better results. Either way, I intend to end the evening with a decision made.

I'm still pondering what I will say when Ronan arrives when I hear the soft slide of the wardrobe over the marble floor. I look away from the fire, and Alara stands in my rooms once again.

The last time she was here I didn't get a great look at her. With all the confusion of Felix entering and the weight of our conversation, studying her was the last thing on my mind. But now I survey her with a critical eye.

Without the mask she looks quite different from me. We are about the same height with similar builds, but her features are sharper, more elegant than mine. Her mouth is pressed into a thin line as she holds a rumpled piece of paper in her hand and narrows her eyes at me.

"He knows," she seethes. Alara stalks toward me and shoves the paper into my hands. "A letter from the Emperor. Delivered directly to me."

"But how...?"

"That's what I'd like to know," she snaps. "He knows exactly where we are despite all the precautions we've taken."

I scan the letter and find it contains much the same sentiment as the one I received earlier today. Peace. Cyrus has written directly to the Insurgo leader of Borealis to ask for peace and for her to attend my wedding to his son. Does that mean this is for real?

"It's a wedding invitation," I say slowly.

"It's a threat." She rakes a hand through her unbound dark hair and sighs. "He could wipe us out any time he wishes. Today it was a letter. Tomorrow it could be an army."

I'd like to think she's overreacting, but I know where she's coming from. As good as all this sounds, I don't trust Cyrus. I'm not even sure I trust Ronan.

"I can put you up in the palace," I offer. "All of you."

Alara laughs. "Under the same roof as your prince? For what? So he can give his father more information about us?"

"Ronan is the one who lobbied for peace." I don't know why I'm defending him when I haven't even made up my mind yet. "It is because of him that we even have this chance to bring the Insurgos into the conversation. To the palace. You could come to court and represent, and after the wedding is over, we'll talk terms of peace."

"I know Cyrus's kind of peace," she practically spits. "It ends in ashes. But not this time. I have plans. I won't go quietly, and neither will you if you're truly our queen. Felix will side with me. I'll raze this city to the ground if—"

The door behind us creaks, and we both turn to see a wide-eyed Ronan in the doorway.

Oh no. He could not have worse timing.

"Ronan, wait," I try. But he's already turned on his heels and disappeared from sight.

"Stay here," I instruct Alara, leaving no room in my voice for argument. For the first time tonight she looks amused.

"Fine, go after your prince. I'll be waiting."

23

Ronan's raised voice reaches my ears long before I reach Felix's door and I slow from a run to a walk. Should I just barge in? My presence will likely only make things worse as I have spent several days ignoring Ronan anyway. But I need to know what he overheard. I need him to know that Alara doesn't speak for me.

"No more lies! I won't have it." Ronan yells as I approach the partially open door.

I peek through the crack and watch Ronan pace back and forth across the room while Felix stands still as a statue.

"No one's lying," Felix says. His voice is as calming and confident as ever.

"Someone is. Because I just walked in on Emilia and some girl talking about attacks on the city and they mentioned you. Imagine my surprise to find my friend and my betrothed are planning a rebellion against my father with no scruples about who will die in the process. And she had the nerve to accuse me of treachery."

"Look, what you overheard—" But Felix doesn't get to finish.

"You knew what she was planning, and you didn't tell me?" Ronan's voice breaks slightly. He clearly hoped Felix would plead ignorance of the whole thing, but Felix is much too honest to do that. "We don't keep secrets, Felix. Not from each other."

It still shocks me to hear Ronan address Felix as a friend rather than a servant. For not the first time I wonder what events led to the strange bond between them, but both of them are a closed book where that's concerned.

"Only from Emilia, right?" The coldness in Felix's tone snaps my focus back to the present. "You really want the truth? You realize she was nothing more than a pawn in a game, and your father wanted to capitalize on that. But he's lost control now."

"This isn't about him," Ronan snaps as he steps closer to Felix and pokes a finger in his chest. "This is about why you didn't tell me she was planning on organizing a rebellion, an attack, on my subjects. I have a duty to protect them—"

Felix smacks the prince's hand away from his chest, and I have to shove my fist against my mouth to keep from audibly gasping. "Then start by protecting them from your father."

Ronan shoves Felix with enough force that the Commander staggers a few steps backward. I know from experience that's not an easy feat.

"Take that back," Ronan insists, but the fight is bleeding out of his voice, replaced by resignation and exhaustion.

Felix looks down at his shirt, slightly rumpled where Ronan grabbed him, and then looks back at the prince. "Is that all? You've been waiting for years to do this. It'd be a shame to hold back now."

"I don't want to hit you."

A wise choice because I'm sure all three of us know Felix could easily overpower Ronan. But it's like watching Ronan transform into a different person before my eyes. His posture, moments ago so rigid and regal, is slumped now.

"Don't you?" Felix asks, and I hear the weight of history in his words.

"No." Ronan sounds utterly defeated and collapses onto the bed with a groan.

"I assure you Emilia is not planning a rebellion. I did what I thought best. To protect both of you." Felix doesn't sit, but he approaches Ronan cautiously. I'm in awe at his composure and self-control, and I wonder if this isn't the first time the two have had an argument. Felix seems to know exactly how to handle him. "Haven't you always trusted my judgment?"

"It's usually better than mine," Ronan agrees with a sigh. "Besides, I understand why."

For the first time, Felix's composure falters and his eyebrows raise. "You do?"

Ronan looks up with the sort of tragic beauty you only see in paintings. How is he even real? "You thought I might be like him."

A silence follows those words that's so loud I want to clamp my hands over my ears. But it makes sense now. The way Felix lashed out at me on the rooftop as if marrying Ronan was the worst thing I could do. Even he had doubts, it seems, about the prince.

"I don't blame you for thinking it. I'd be lying if I said there weren't some things I admired about him. After all, he's the one who made me strong."

"He made you hard," Felix replies in a much gentler tone than he used a few minutes before, and I know he will forgive Ronan of everything. "I have seen you with him, seen the scars he's given you both inside and out. You are nothing like him."

"Am I not?" Ronan's laugh is mirthless. "It's not for want of trying though. I have to believe it is you who kept me from what my father always wanted me to be, and I'm am grateful for it. For whatever reason I found grace in your eyes. You always believed I could be more than what I am. So did Emilia, I think."

"She still does."

He's right in a way. Ronan is so much more than I thought he would be, and yet that does not equal love. I agreed to marry him because it is what is right for my kingdom, for the Insurgos, but he is not the one my heart would have chosen if I had been born common. Still, I see the brokenness in him, and it speaks to something deep within me.

"I wrote to my father after Emilia and I had our…disagreement the other night. I told him after having seen the Insurgos firsthand, I believed much of the strife between our people is due to miscommunication and misunderstanding. My proposal was a gesture of goodwill to open conversation. I asked him to send word that all Insurgos were welcome at our wedding and afterward for a peace conference."

Felix seems stunned by this news. For a mere instant hope and apprehension both share his face before being replaced with something far more neutral.

"And what did he have to say to your suggestion?"

"He agreed." Ronan huffs an incredulous laugh. "I never really expected him to, but he's already begun sending word by messengers to all the villages between here and Aurora. His royal proclamation just arrived here this evening, and I had planned on sharing it with Emilia tonight as an early wedding gift. So imagine my surprise when I stumble upon her making plans for more Insurgo violence. I've finally convinced my father to consider peace and now I've got to have that fight with her as well?"

"Emilia is smart. She doesn't want the violence to continue. She's done what she can to pacify any sort of rebellion since she's been here."

No, Emilia has done what she can just to survive. Any success on that account must be attributed to God or Felix's good sense. Still, I appreciate him championing my weak attempts.

"Why do she and I always seem to think the worst of each other?" Ronan asks with his head in his hands. "But you understand her."

"I trust her," Felix corrects. "I don't always agree with how or when she chooses to act, but I trust her judgment. She is chosen of God."

There's a moment of heavy silence and then, "so you truly believe in this God as well?"

"Yes," Felix answers without hesitation. "I have worshipped Him since childhood. For the past eleven years I have done so secretly at the risk of death should your father find out."

As much as I want to hear more of this, I take that as my cue to leave. Felix may share that story with me some day, but I want to hear it because he wants to share it, not because I was eavesdropping.

I return to my room to find Alara sitting on the blanket in front of the fire. She stares intently at the flames, and doesn't even look away when I join her on the blanket.

"This has to stop," I say softly. "You have to give me a chance to make this work, and I can't do that with you threatening violence."

"That's what Felix said, too."

"You've been talking to him?" I study her profile for any trace of emotion but find none.

"A bit. We have a lot to catch up on, but he seems to mostly want to discuss you."

Heat that has nothing to do with the fire flushes my face. "Then trust him even if you don't trust me. You should move into the palace and begin attending court. If you are to represent the Insurgos in the peace talks it would be good if my court got used to seeing you now."

"So I am to barter for peace on behalf of all the Insurgo people? I thought that was your job."

"It's a duty that we'll share. And if you will, I'd like for you to send riders to as many Insurgo encampments that you know of and invite them to come to my wedding in two weeks' time. Tell them about the peace talks and tell them it will be my husband who will be speaking on the Emperor's behalf."

Husband. It sounds so strange to say, and I have much work still to do to make sure it actually happens. But for tonight there is nothing to do but trust Felix to talk Ronan off the ledge so he can find his way back to me.

24

Early the next morning I approach Ronan's door with as much courage as I can muster. I had hoped he'd come back to my room after he finished with Felix last night, but I waited for a knock that never came. So I've decided to swallow my pride and pay him a visit instead.

He answers the door in an untucked shirt, pants, and his dark hair mussed in all directions. I must have woken him. There's a moment of hesitation and then a sleepy smile crawls over his face. He opens his arms and I walk into them.

For a few fleeting moments I relish the warmth of them. There are moments like this where things seem so simple, and then there's reality.

"Can we talk?" I gesture toward the inside of his room, and he steps aside to allow me in. As soon as he shuts the door I begin. "I'm sorry. I'm sorry for thinking the worst of you, and I'm sorry for what you heard last night. You should know Alara doesn't speak for me."

"No one speaks for you, Emilia. Not even me. I'm just sorry it took me so long to realize that." Ronan slides his hand in mine and pulls me toward a small couch set up in front of the fireplace. The fire is burning low, but it's still cozy when I curl up next to him.

"We are both difficult people, aren't we?" I ask.

"That we are. It's amazing Felix has put up with both of us for this long."

"I told you he was the best of us."

Ronan sighs. "The first time I met Felix, when I stumbled upon him as a stowaway on our ship, I felt like my feet were finally on solid ground. Like even at seven years old, I had found where I belonged. With him by my side I had the courage to do anything. He makes me a better man."

I don't want to talk about Felix right now despite the enticing bits of history Ronan has just let slip. Because if I allow myself to think of the Commander, all I'm trying to accomplish will fall apart before I've even had the chance to put it back together.

"I know he thinks of you as a dear friend."

"I didn't know until last night that he was Insurgo," Ronan admits. "I mean, I knew he had to know about you and accept it, but I didn't know he believed as well. And it hurt to hear that he's been keeping something that big from me for the entire time I've known him. It's almost like I don't know him at all."

Add that to the list of things Ronan and I have in common. "Felix is an entire ocean of secrets. But honestly, Ronan, I didn't come here to talk about him. We need to discuss us...if there still is such a thing."

He looks me over with those deep blue eyes. "I don't want any more secrets between us. I realize I've been at fault for much of that, but I truly do care for you Emilia, and I want this to work. We need it to work for the good of the empire and Borealis. But I'd be lying if I said I didn't have my own selfish reasons for wanting you by my side."

"No more secrets," I say slowly. Can I really agree to that? I feel like my entire life has been a secret, and the thought of not having to hide who I am anymore fills me with relief. "But can you really pledge your loyalty to Borealis and to me?"

"You mean because of what I know about the Insurgos?" He musses his hair further. "I won't pretend I understand it all, but I do trust Felix…and I'm learning to trust you. My father's methods are…less than ideal. I've been on the receiving end of them myself, so I'm not as ignorant as you may think."

"It's still not an easy truth to acknowledge," I concede. What exactly has Cyrus done to Ronan in the past? Felix mentioned scars last night, but I can't bring those up without letting on that I overheard a conversation I was never meant to hear.

"No. No one wants to think their father is a monster. But the things he's done, Emilia…You were right when you said he was the one who hired those men. I don't know if they would have actually killed me or just made a valiant attempt, but what kind of father does that to his son just to further his own agenda?"

"The same sort of father that murders his wife and makes his daughter watch," I whisper. "I know what it's like to be the child of a monster."

He looks at me curiously. "I forget that you do. You are better placed to understand me than almost anyone else."

"Then can we be honest with each other about our motives from this point forward?" I wish I wouldn't have jumped to such conclusions about his motives, but I was taken off guard by his actions. I expected him to be like his father because it was the ultimate excuse not to give my heart to him. But now what choice do I have?

"Yes," he agrees. "I want what you want concerning the Insurgos, Emilia. Maybe in time I will understand completely why you want it. But in the meantime I will trust you."

It's more than I expected though not as much as I'd hoped. Still, I give his hand a squeeze.

"We have a lifetime to learn each other, and I'm sure there'll be many more fights. But there's no one I'd rather fight with than you." He smiles then kisses me gently.

Things run smoothly in the days leading up to my wedding. Alara has reluctantly taken her place in the court, and though I'm too busy to show her around, Felix takes that duty upon himself. I shove any insecurity I feel about this deep down, because what can I say when I'm preparing to marry someone else?

Less than a week before the wedding something wonderful happens. Small groups of Insurgo travelers begin to arrive just outside the city. They set up tents and camps just outside the wall in preparation for the festivities that are to come. I long to be able to go to them, to speak to them all, but royal business and gown fittings keep me occupied from sun up to sun down.

Felix and Alara take it upon themselves to be my ambassadors. They visit the camps and bring food with them every day, sometimes more than once. Though I've had little time to speak to Felix alone, I can see a change in him, a spring in his step that I've never seen before. He loves this work, and that only makes me love him more.

Which is probably why I never see it coming when he steps into my room two days before my wedding and delivers the news.

"I've come to tender my resignation."

The words, so clearly and emotionlessly stated, jolt me to my feet. "Y-your what?"

Felix stands with his feet apart and hands behind his back in the "at ease" posture of a soldier. But his eyes indicate he is anything but at ease. "Effective after the wedding and the peace talks, I'd like to resign as the Captain of the Queensguard."

Though we've never discussed it, I thought we had moved past that conversation on the rooftop. Made peace with it. But I never expected this. With all the changes in my life, Felix was the one person I counted on to be my rock. He is a soldier, the most devoted and loyal I've ever known. The glittering starburst pendant on his cloak mocks me. What will he do with it when he leaves me? Cast it aside like it was nothing more than a symbol of his servitude to me?

"But where will you go? What will you do? You've been a soldier your whole life."

"*Nearly* my whole life. I'd like to join Alara and her band in riding for the coast to spread the news of peace There's much to be done and I'm needed there."

I try to imagine him as something other than a soldier and fail. It's part of him and who I know him to be. Though I've wondered from time to time, I've never given serious thought to who he was before he took up sword to defend Ronan and his father. He can't leave before I've had a chance to really know this part of him at all. And with Alara of all people.

My heart squeezes at the mention of her name. She is everything Felix hoped I would become. A rebel passionate about her cause and unencumbered by the crown. It makes sense he would want to follow her. Above all, he is loyal to the Insurgo cause, and I've disappointed him.

"You're needed here."

He smiles a bit sadly and breaks his military posture. With a few steps he closes the distance between us and looks down on me with those warm brown eyes I have come to adore.

"We both know that's not true. You have Ronan, you have your crown, and you will be a good queen for your people. I have no place here anymore."

"Felix..."

He shakes his head. "Some people are born to shine and others are born for the shadows. You are radiant as the sun, Emilia, but where does that leave me?"

I want to tell him that stars cannot shine without darkness. That night is necessary to love the dawn. But that's not what he's asking. He doesn't want to be necessary. Felix wants to know if I can love the darkness, the shadows. Can we ever coexist or will we be forever cursed to come impossibly close and never touch?

"Is this truly what you want?"

"It's what I need to do. I need to go home."

Home. He doesn't mean Aurora and the Emperor's court.

"And where is home?"

He hesitates so long I think he won't answer me. When he finally meets my eyes again, I see true fear in his for maybe the first time. "Solitarius."

The word hangs in the small space between us as I try to wrap my mind around the implication. Solitarius is the deserted island. The kingdom in name only so the Atlas empire could achieve the holy number of six kingdoms subservient to the seat at Aurora. So how could an empty island be home?

A sharp knock at my door wrenches both of us from the unspoken questions flooding the room. I jump back as if I've been burned, but Felix takes a calm step away from me to a position more proper for his station.

"Emilia?" It's Ronan's voice on the other side of the door. "May I come in? You're not trying on your gown, are you?"

The humor in his voice and his concern seem so childish compared to what I've just heard from Felix.

"Come in," I call as I glance at Felix who has resumed his rigid military posture. He masks his pain well, but I know him better than that.

Ronan steps through the door with a beaming smile on his handsome face. In most other circumstances that grin would be enough to put a smile on my own face. But not now. I'm not sure I'll ever smile again.

Felix excuses himself but pauses to look at me one last time before he exits the room. It takes everything in me not to run after him.

25

The day of my wedding arrives with a bright clear sky and the promise of good things to come. Unfortunately I'm having trouble remembering what any of those good things are. I had another dream last night like I haven't had in weeks. The same one I had when we were camped outside of Borealis. When I close my eyes I can still see Felix's blood-stained body sprawled lifelessly on the ground before me as the ocean air whips away my screams before they can even leave me.

Because of the circles under my eyes and my tear-streaked face, it takes Hannah and Cecily longer than usual to apply the makeup I'll wear for my walk down the aisle. They work in silence as if sensing I'm not in the mood to celebrate no matter what the expectation is.

A brand new tiara is placed upon my head once my hair is twisted up into an elegant style. The crown is heavy despite its delicate design, but I must admit it's beautiful. Still, my favorite jewel I wear is the necklace Felix gave me on my birthday. I have opted to wear it on a shorter chain so it is clearly visible above the neckline of my white dress. The prism of colors emanating from within the black stone reminds me vividly of the conversation he and I had in this very room that night.

When I start to tear up at the memory, Cecily dries my eyes with a tissue and retouches my makeup. When she has done her best to make me look my best, I dismiss her to take her place in the throne room.

Hannah stands alone with me in front of the mirror. Her busy hands finally still as she takes my hands in hers. I tear my eyes away from myself in the mirror to look at her. She smiles, a bit sadly, and squeezes my hands.

"You look beautiful."

"Thank you," I say as I look down at the floor. I don't want her to see the sadness in my eyes. But Hannah knows me too well, and she has brushed my hair while I cried over the love that could never be.

"It's not too late to choose differently."

"He doesn't want me," I say, though the words have to fight through my tightening throat to make themselves heard. "He's leaving after the wedding celebration."

"Perhaps that only means he wants you more than he thinks he should," she offers. Forever my optimistic Hannah. I'm grateful for her hope when I don't dare to hope for myself.

"I wish he wasn't so honorable." It's a stupid thing to wish because Felix's honor is one of the things that made me love him. "Or that he wasn't so loyal to Ronan."

"If he wasn't those things then he would not be the Commander." Hannah smiles again. "And if you were not putting the needs of your people above your own, you would not be you."

She's right, of course, but it's of little comfort now. I look around my nearly empty room and then back to her.

"By tonight we will be in the royal quarters. You'll have a room at least this large all to yourself. At least that's something, right?" Somehow my attempt at optimism isn't as effective as hers.

"And you will be a queen."

A queen. Of course. That's what all this is for. So I can be a queen who makes the right decisions for her people, who offers the Insurgos sanctuary in the city, and who openly worships the God of my choosing. And I will have a king consort by my side who supports my decision to do so even if he doesn't exactly understand it. A year ago this was more than I could have dreamed.

A sharp knock at my door startles both of us, and Hannah drops my hands to cross the room and answer it. She looks back at me with her hand on the doorknob. Both of us know who stands on the other side of this door, and somehow I can't breathe when I think about actually seeing him. But I nod at Hannah, and she pulls open the door with a bow to Felix.

For possibly the first time, he completely ignores her, and his composure fails. His dark eyes find me immediately, and his mouth falls open. In a too brief moment I see the vulnerability in his features like I never have before.

"E...Emilia." He mumbles my name as if it's a struggle to utter anything, and it comes out sounding more like "Mia". Intentional or not, that name reminds me of my mother and her letters. How I wish she were here for all of this.

"Hannah, you may take your place with the wedding party now." She accepts my dismissal with a knowing nod and disappears past Felix and out the door.

Alone with him, all the emotions I've been trying to corral suddenly feel like too much. I feel too much when he's near, and this of all days is not the time.

Felix slowly and deliberately crosses the room to me until he stands closer than he usually dares. But he can't take his eyes off me, his mouth still parted in wonder.

"You are the most beautiful thing I have ever seen," he whispers as he finally lifts his eyes from my dress and jewelry to meet my eyes. There's such a wistfulness in his gaze that I have to look away. I remind myself there is no future here even if I weren't marrying Ronan. Felix is leaving me. "You're wearing the necklace I gave you."

"I wanted to keep a piece of you near me always."

A heavy silence fills the space between us with each of us wrapped in our own tangle of thoughts. This is so much harder with him standing in front of me. I know what I must do, but with him so near it's easy to forget why I must do it.

"Are you ready?"

His question seems so simple, and it deserves a simple answer, but I can't give him one. I don't trust my words to cooperate, so I just nod instead.

He wordlessly offers me his arm. Felix is clad in new armor with shining silver accents. His cloak is the deep blue of Borealis and the star pendant I gave him fastens it to his chest plate. Despite all that, he doesn't look like a soldier. He looks royal, and for the first time I can actually see him as a prince.

But there is a real prince waiting for me at the end of an aisle. So I take Felix's offered arm, only letting my hand rest against his forearm with the lightest touch.

We navigate the empty hallways from my room toward the throne room without interruption. Though I'm quite certain there are guards strategically placed throughout the palace, they are not visible here. The bulk of their presence will be felt in the throne room itself, where both Borealis and a few Imperial guards will stand watch over the ceremony.

Too soon we reach the atrium outside the throne room. The small area seems bigger due to the high walls culminating in a ceiling made entirely of windows. Then I look at Felix, and it feels like the smallest space I've ever been in. My heart thuds against my tight gown. This is my last chance.

"You don't have to leave," I say. It's not exactly what I had planned, but Felix doesn't look surprised. "There will always be a place here for you."

"I do have to go. There is so much you don't know."

"Then tell me. Is this what you really want?"

"What do *you* want?" His voice is barely a whisper. "Tell me."

It wouldn't matter. There is no use in voicing my feelings when he's made it clear he is going to leave me. I shouldn't love him. It should be Ronan, only Ronan.

"Emilia."

I open my eyes to find his face only inches from me. We are alone in the atrium with hundreds of guests on the other side of these doors waiting for this man to walk me down an aisle and give my hand to another man—a man I care for, but not like this. Nothing has ever felt like this. There's a spark of something in Felix's eyes. Something I haven't seen for far too many days.

"Please." The word sounds odd in his voice, though he's said it to me before. But not this way. Never this way.

"It doesn't matter. You said—"

"Forget what I said. It *does* matter. You are the only thing holding me here, the only reason I have not to return to Solitarius. From the moment I saw you in that military camp everything else ceased to matter. You stirred something in me I thought was dead. So this, what you want, is the only thing that matters to me."

My heart breaks in two. I owe him the truth of it all.

"You," I whisper, not trusting my voice. "I want you."

I expect a response from him—a kiss, a sigh, a smile—anything except the step back he takes. In a rare moment of vulnerability, Felix presses his back to the wall and sinks to the floor.

I want to go to him, but I don't make a move. Instead I'm replaying our conversation. I said I wanted him. He said I mattered. It's hardly the same, and in a terrifying moment I know I've shown him everything only to be left empty-handed.

"Felix?" It's much more than a question. It's a plea for him to speak, to make this right, but as soon as he does I wish he would take it back.

"But?"

Such a small word but it pierces me just the same. "But what?"

He isn't looking at me. The light streaming in the window catches his face, and I see thin lines of scars on his face and hands. Many of which he took for me.

"You want me, but you still have to walk through those doors and give Ronan your hand."

"I don't. I—"

"You do. The same way I have to leave. It's our duty. We are soldiers. We don't neglect our duty."

His eyes dart up to meet mine then, a glint of pride fracturing the pain I see there. This is a man I do not deserve, but I want to. I lower myself to the floor beside him, not an easy feat in these layers of fabric. We are close, so very close, and I want to make the space between us nonexistent.

With a trembling hand I touch his face, and he leans into my palm as my fingers brush the loose curls of his hair. In the too few moments of intimacy we've shared I've never initiated the contact like this, and now I wonder why. Because it's more than I could have imagined, watching a part of his stoicism crumble at my touch. One of his hands slides to my waist, and though I want to look down to make sure this is real, I can't look away from him.

"I could step down."

"No." His answer is quick and insistent. "If you step down they will say you fell."

And he's right. But does it matter? I know I should care, but if it means I could walk away from these expectations and do what my heart is begging me to do, I would give almost anything.

Almost.

I was born for this, and as much as I despise it at times, to give away my crown would be to give away part of myself. Felix would not love that version of me any more than I could.

His eyes look only at me now, his arms loose around my waist as if he expects me to vanish as a cruel joke at any moment. But I ache to be held tighter, so I press my cheek to his, the feel of his usual stubble secondary to the wetness pressed between us.

Am I crying? My eyelashes feel heavy with drops of liquid. Felix pulls away just far enough to wipe the tears from under my eyes with the pad of his thumb. And I see it. Drops of liquid tumbling past his lips, dripping from his jaw and landing on my hand.

And when I kiss him, his gasp against my mouth tastes like salty tears and heat.

This is what I want. Each press of his lips against mine is like a deep breath of air after drowning. Why is fate so cruel? Why do I love Felix when another man waits for me at the end of an aisle? I had thought to have him even for a short time would be enough, but I see now that it never could be. I want him forever or not at all, and this kiss is just a cruel reminder that it has to be the latter.

Behind us the hall doors crash open, and though our kiss ends abruptly at the noise, I jump into Felix's arms rather than away from him.

A stream of guards pours from the hall without a second glance my way. They charge down the corridor, presumably to the front entrance of the palace, and in their wake, they've left a panicked people in the hall. My wedding guests.

Faintly I hear other soldiers shouting orders for the crowd to remain calm and in place, but two people who have ignored those orders now stand in the doorway, looking directly at Felix and me.

Ronan and Alara.

Could things get any worse?

Alara smirks with a hint of knowing in her dark brown eyes as she looks between the two of us. Ronan, on the other hand, looks confused. I'm certain he's running through a list of explanations for the position he's found us in, but none of them are an appropriate reason for delaying my walk down the aisle to him.

"What's going on?" I ask as I stretch out a hand and allow Ronan to help me to my feet.

"Some disturbance at the wall," Alara replies. "We were all waiting not so patiently for you to make an appearance when a guard rushed in from that back passage and made the others follow him to the wall."

She shouldn't even know about those passageways, but I've long since given up telling Alara what she should and shouldn't know.

Felix clears his throat as he stands. "I should go check on things."

"They will be fine. You have a wedding to attend to if you haven't forgotten." Ronan's tone is cool and curious, not angry exactly but clearly still trying to puzzle out what he's walked in on. Then he turns those clear blue eyes to me. "Your people are waiting for you."

"Well, they can wait a bit longer. If there's a threat at the wall that requires that many soldiers, I need to know what's going on. Felix, keep the guests in the hall—"

"No."

His single word hangs heavy in the air. It's the first time I can remember him refusing me anything.

"No," he repeats. "I'm going with you."

I want to argue that his authority will be of more use here, but there isn't time for this discussion. All I need to do is make sure the guards have whatever this disturbance is under control and then I can resume this wedding.

"Fine. Ronan, please keep the people calm as best you can."

He shakes his head. "I'm coming too."

I throw my hands up and sigh. "Fine. Everyone do whatever you want. I'm going to the wall for anyone who wants to follow."

And they do. All three of them. I can hear their footsteps echoing off the tile floor behind me. Even Alara seems to have made this her mission for the moment. Or perhaps she caused whatever this disturbance is and she only wants to admire her handiwork. That's entirely too probable for my liking.

The four of us exit the palace to a mixture of cheers and murmurs from the crowd gathered in the courtyard. No one seems quite sure what to make of my sudden appearance or my entourage that follows—a prince, a soldier, and a rebel leader. But I don't take the time to do much more than acknowledge them with a look.

Instead my gaze drifts upward to see soldiers falling into position along the wall's parapet. I expect to see them draw bows or prepare some other sort of defense, but they just stand there, staring at something in the distance. Their inaction is enough to chill me.

Forgetting propriety, I lift my skirts and rush toward the stone stairs that lead to the top of wall. By the time I reach the top I'm panting from exertion, but Felix, Ronan, and Alara are right behind me. I'm about to ask the nearest soldier why they aren't doing anything when something just beyond the wall catches my eye.

Smoke.

26

Desolation. Pure devastation. The tents as far as the eye can see are nothing more than ash. Bodies litter the ground, some burned, some with arrows piercing flesh. All dead at Cyrus's command. There is no one else as cruel or so devious as to lure Insurgos here under the guise of peace only to burn them all alive. It's a message for me, I think, and one I'm done ignoring.

As soon as I saw the smoke from atop the wall, I rushed back down to exit the city through the nearest gate. I must have looked terrifying because no one tried to stop me. Once outside the city, I didn't stop running until I was so close I had no choice but to believe what I saw.

Ronan slides to an abrupt halt beside me, a terrible gasp issuing from him. I know how he feels. He hasn't seen the damage his father can do to the Insurgos firsthand like I have, and I know he's torn between wanting to believe someone else is responsible and the horror right in front of him.

On my other side, Felix approaches with a quiet dignity and stands tall. He doesn't so much as look at Ronan who is now doubled over, heaving breaths and gagging on bile. We must look like quite the trio—Ronan and I in our wedding best and Felix in his finest armor—standing in the middle of this wasteland with ashes falling like snow. Alara disappeared somewhere after we left the wall, and I have no doubt she is making plans of her own.

"You have a ship scheduled to meet you at the coast?" I ask Felix without looking at him. His steady presence beside me is all I need. If he and Alara were planning to ride for the coast after the wedding, I have no doubt he will have made provisions for a ship as well.

"Yes," he replies. "It leaves at first light."

Neither of us feel the need to bring up that he is only hours away from leaving me. Perhaps because we both know that isn't going to happen now. There will be no peace talks. There will be no peace.

"Get the horses ready, Athena, too. I'll have Hannah gather my things, and I'll meet you at the stables. Find Alara, too. We'll ride for the coast."

"You're leaving?" Ronan looks up at me, still bent over with his hands on his knees. "You can't run away."

"I'm not running away. I'm preparing to fight. You can pass the message on to your father if you like when you return to Aurora."

He straightens and wipes his mouth with the back of his hand. "I'm not going back. Don't leave me here with this. Take me with you."

I look at Felix, and he nods gravely. There is no time to explain everything to Ronan or even be considerate of the turmoil I'm sure he's facing right now.

"Very well. Go with Felix. I'll bring your clothes from your quarters."

"I should stay with you." Ronan's tone doesn't match the bravery of his words. I don't need his protection anyway.

"Don't argue with her." Felix's reply is cool and emotionless, but I know what it costs him.

Ronan's eyes widen, and he looks from Felix to me. This is certainly a new position for him, and Felix has just made it very clear that I am in charge and will be calling the shots. Something that looks like relief flickers across Ronan's face before it is replaced by shock once again. For all his bravado, Ronan does not know how to make the hard choices.

The two men walk wordlessly away from me and toward my city wall. They don't speak, at least not that I can hear, but I imagine when they are alone and our plans are settled, there will be many words pass between the two of them.

But I don't have time to worry about them now. There is much that still needs to be done—people to inform, arrangements to make, bags to pack—and I don't have the luxury of concerning myself with my feelings or anyone else's.

I kick ashes from my shoes and notice the ashes have stained the white hem of my wedding dress a dingy brown-gray. A long tear in the gown leaves the gossamer like fabric trailing behind me in the slight breeze. My hair has fallen from its perfectly coiffed style to tangled strands that brush my shoulders. I no longer look the part of a bride or a queen, but that's fine, because those are two things I am not meant to be.

With trembling fingers I reach for the crown so heavily perched on my head. It's not the one I would have been given had I made it to my coronation, but it's nicer than anything I've ever had, and that's exactly why I don't want it.

Tears flood my eyes as I yank and pull until the crown comes free of my head, taking a few strands of hair with it. Whatever they polished it with seems to help repel the ash as only a few specks have stuck to it. The crown is the only thing that looks nearly pristine here, and it doesn't belong.

It tumbles from my hands and lands amid the ashes with a soft thud.

I walk away, leaving a crown and a kingdom behind me as well as a trail of ashes from the ruined fabric of my wedding dress.

Next time, I will bring my own fire.

ABOUT THE AUTHOR

Amory Cannon is an author of Young Adult and Romantic Suspense novels. Her favorite things include autumn (anything pumpkin spice), Harry Potter (proud Ravenclaw), and Sherlock Holmes. She published her first book under the name Amryn Cross while working as a forensic scientist. Her non-writing time is filled with running, crafting, and snuggling her two dogs—Luna and Argo. She currently resides in Tennessee.

Visit her at her website amorycannon.com or on Instagram @amory.cannon